Praise for The Fir

Magical... never fails to evoke tl ... o-
is as compelling as the next... *Through the Uncrossable Boundary* strikes the perfect balance between magic and reality... A read that amazes and inspires.
Danielle McDowall, Dani Reads on *Through the Uncrossable Boundary*

An exciting re-enactment of the age-old conflict between good and evil... Like all the best stories, it can be read on different levels... at times there are echoes of C.S. Lewis. Young people and adults alike will be taken up by the tension of what will happen to the Apprentice Adventurers... A thoroughly absorbing read.
Rt Revd John Packer, on *Rise of the Shadow Stealers*

This fantasy adventure is aimed at middle grade readers to young teens, but I would say that adults would get as much enjoyment from the story too. The writing is rich with atmosphere and the quirky characters come alive with the wealth of descriptions and unusual names given to the inhabitants of the World of Mortales... I was gripped... when I got to the last page I was left bereft as I wanted to read on... Fans of the Narnia books or Inkheart will love this read.
Debbie Coupe, The State of the Arts on *The Nemesis Charm*

Take the first book's magic, the second book's adventure, and multiply them by 100... you've got a book that's bigger, bolder and even harder to put down than the last!
Charlotte Clark, Wonderfully Bookish on *Through the Uncrossable Boundary*

This rollicking adventure...is reminiscent in tone of the Harry

Potter series and Jeanette Winterson's *Tanglewreck*. Packed with literary references and cleverness, it focuses on the age-old conflict between light and dark, good and evil, and on the power of story. An engaging read for 9- to 14-year-olds.

Lucy Pearce, Juno Magazine on *Rise of the Shadow Stealers*

5/5 STARS I loved the book, the plot was captivating and engaging. I was hooked… from the beginning and it was a one sit read for me. The characters were well developed and the prose beautiful. The book was wonderful and I would recommend it to everyone.

Rubina Bashir, Booklove blog on *The Nemesis Charm*

Through the Uncrossable Boundary is the sweeping conclusion to the adventure that introduced us to Scoop and Fletcher and their story-centric world. It's a true adventure story that will become an instant classic… No matter how old you are, you will want to revisit over and over again.

Emily, That Weird Girl Life blog on *Through the Uncrossable Boundary*

A well-paced, absorbing read that will appeal to many adults as much as it does to children… Both the premise and the writing are reminiscent of other fantasy authors such as Terry Pratchett and in particular, Jasper Fforde, although this is certainly unique and interesting enough to stand firmly on its own two feet. Confident pre-teen readers will enjoy it as an intriguing adventure story, while older readers will enjoy reading between the lines for a more philosophical experience.

Isobel Jokl, Dig Yorkshire on *Rise of the Shadow Stealers*

I love the world created for this story… The writing reminded me of that in a great picture book – the words flow, smooth and easy to read. They are nearly lyrical. The writing is some of the

best I have read since becoming a book reviewer...
Suzanne Morris, Kids Lit Reviews on *Rise of the Shadow Stealers*

I absolutely loved this book...not since Harry Potter have I enjoyed a series this much... There's magic and danger.... A wonderful story the reader can get completely lost in.
Judith Taylor, NetGalley on *The Nemesis Charm*

This thrilling quest is a wonderful read for all fantasy junkies...
Zyllah, Miss Literati on *Rise of the Shadow Stealers*

I loved this book! The world created by Ingram-Brown is so creative and whimsical... In all honesty, I haven't wanted to enter another world so much since I first read Harry Potter... Fletcher and Scoop are really likeable characters... The plot is thoroughly engaging... Would I recommend *The Nemesis Charm* to a teen? Most definitely... Would I recommend it to an adult? Without a doubt. My rating: 5 stars.
Jo, My Little Library in the Attic on *The Nemesis Charm*

After both my children had devoured the book, I finally got to see what all the fuss was about, and I was instantly hooked. Fast-paced and gripping, my son compares this to his favourite, Artemis Fowl, whilst my daughter declares it 'a book you can lose yourself in.'
Platform Harrogate Magazine on *Rise of the Shadow Stealers*

The Firebird Chronicles:
Through The Uncrossable Boundary

The Firebird Chronicles:
Through The Uncrossable Boundary

Daniel Ingram-Brown

Recipient of the Taner Baybars award (2016) for original fiction in the field of Science Fiction, Fantasy and Magical Realism, awarded by the Society of Authors Authors' Foundation.

OUR STREET
BOOKS

Winchester, UK
Washington, USA

First published by Our Street Books, 2018
Our Street Books is an imprint of John Hunt Publishing Ltd., No. 3 East St., Alresford,
Hampshire SO24 9EE, UK
office1@jhpbooks.net
www.johnhuntpublishing.com
www.ourstreet-books.com

For distributor details and how to order please visit the 'Ordering' section on our website.

Text copyright: Daniel Ingram-Brown 2017
Map illustration copyright: Si Smith

ISBN: 978 1 78535 900 2
978 1 78535 901 9 (ebook)
Library of Congress Control Number: 2017960371

A CIP catalogue record for this book is available from the British Library.

Design: Stuart Davies

Printed and bound by CPI Group (UK) Ltd, Croydon, CR0 4YY, UK

We operate a distinctive and ethical publishing philosophy in
all areas of our business, from our global network of authors to
production and worldwide distribution.

Other Books in the Firebird Chronicles Series

Rise of the Shadow Stealers (2013, ISBN: 978-1-78099-694-3)

The Nemesis Charm (2016, ISBN: 978-1-78535-285-0)

Short stories (visit www.danielingrambrown.co.uk for details):

The Gell (2016)

The Imp's Possibility Bird (2016)

Contents

If you'd like to recap the **story so far,** or haven't read the first two books and would like to catch up (and don't mind a few spoilers) visit www.danielingrambrown.co.uk/story-so-far/ and enter the password F1r3b1rd

PART ONE

PART TWO

For Mum, Dad, Vanessa and Kenny

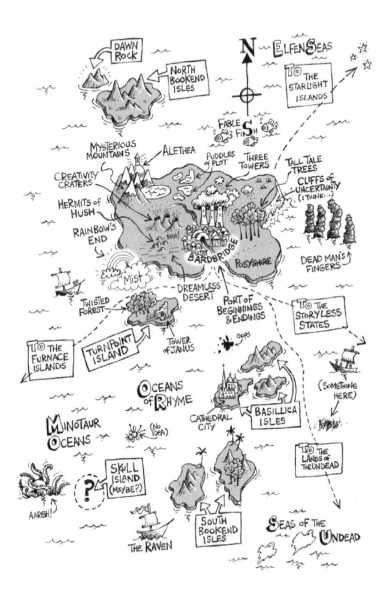

PART ONE

Chapter 1

The Black Horizon

'Dead Man's Fingers!' the Dark Pirate cried. 'Hard to port!'

The outline of a flinty column emerged from the mist. It looked scaly, like the decaying claw of a fallen sea monster waiting to snare ships. The Boatswain swung the wheel hard to the side, sweat pouring from his bristly beard. The ship lurched, making the crew stumble. Knot, already unsteady on his feet due to his considerable bulk, grabbed a rope as the vessel tilted. He watched, wide-eyed, as the ship curved away from the wrecking rocks, sending a cloud of sea spray into the night.

* * *

At the prow of the ship, two young Apprentices, Alfa and Sparks, fought the buffeting wind. Their waterproof hoods were pulled tight, frizzy hair whipping their faces, as they pressed into the storm. Sea lanterns swung from their hands, the beams trying to pierce the night. But the mist twisted the torchlight into ghostly shapes and rain formed a curtain of jewelled light in front of them.

'I can't see a thing!' Sparks called, her voice shrill above the waves.

'Me neither,' Alfa replied, 'but we have to try. Dead Man's Fingers are notorious wrecking rocks. A little light could make all the difference.'

Sparks's hands were trembling. 'Do you think they'll come after us?' She glanced to her side, looking for the flicker of lights in the ocean. Moments ago, the crew of the Black Horizon had been captive, surrounded by an army of Red Hawk soldiers. But then, as their leader, Falk, had met his end, the soldiers

2

had retreated. Sparks had barely had time to take in what had happened.

'I don't know,' Alfa replied. 'They'll probably regroup and come after us. Red Hawks aren't known for their mercy. That's why we must get out of here now, even though it's dangerous to sail these waters at night. I heard the Boatswain say we had to make it past Turnpoint Island by dawn.'

'We better had,' Sparks said, 'because you know who else is out there.'

Alfa knew exactly whom Sparks was talking about – Grizelda. The old woman was their deadliest enemy.

'She's not going to leave us alone, is she?'

Alfa shook her head. The old woman would probably be even more dangerous now Falk had been defeated.

'Watch out!' Spark shouted. 'Look!'

Alfa swung her lantern to reveal a second jagged needle puncturing the sea.

'Hard starboard!' the Dark Pirate called. Sparks felt the ship adjust its course. She gripped her lantern tightly, holding her breath as they narrowly cleared the rock.

* * *

At the other end of the galleon, Mr Snooze watched the coastline of Fullstop Island disappear into the darkness. The skin of his face was paper thin, his silver hair pale in the night. Tears stung his cheeks. He closed his eyes for a moment and imagined the calming candlelight of his little Bedtime Story Slumber Shop in the village of Bardbridge. This was the first time Mr Snooze had been away from home and he was scared. It felt as though a chasm had already opened between him and everything he was familiar with.

I wonder when I'll see my home again, he thought. *If I'll ever see it again.*

He opened his eyes and blinked back a tear.

You mustn't think in that way, he told himself. *Stay strong.*

Mr Snooze squinted, trying to make out the cliffs, but he couldn't see them anymore. There was nothing but inky blackness, smudged by cloud.

His home was in terrible danger.

That's why I'm here, he reminded himself. *That's why we must leave.*

Fullstop Island was under the curse of a strange sickness – a living death that had swallowed many of his friends. He pictured them: Mr Bumbler, the Quill sisters and Isaiah Scriven. Mr Snooze took a sharp intake of breath and wiped his eyes.

Be strong, he told himself again. *Be strong for them.*

* * *

Above Mr Snooze, Fletcher looked down at the ship from the topmast. From there he could see the whole crew: the Dark Pirate on the quarterdeck, his black cape flying out behind him; the Boatswain pressed against the ship's wheel; and Alfa and Sparks on the forecastle, the beams of their lanterns crisscrossing the ocean. His friend Nib was battening down the hatches. Fletcher watched as Rufina passed. She stumbled. With lightning speed, Nib reached out to break her fall. He always seemed to have peripheral vision where his girlfriend was concerned. Fletcher watched Rufina grin, her hair fiery under the ship's lanterns. Then she crossed the deck to join Knot, who was straining to tighten the mainsail. These were Fletcher's friends. They were like family to him. Fletcher felt sick to his stomach. He believed it was his fault their lives were now in such deadly peril. And he believed it was his job to keep them safe.

He scanned the ship looking for his Academy partner, Scoop. She wasn't on deck.

She must be below, he thought.

4

Ever since he'd discovered Scoop was his sister, he'd felt protective of her, although he wouldn't have admitted it to anyone. The little things she did – how she brushed her thick, black hair from her eyes, or tried to straighten her spectacles – had become as familiar to him as his own sharp features. It was they, Fletcher and Scoop, Apprentice Adventurers from the Department of Quests, who'd been given the task that had led to this flight from Fullstop Island. They had been charged to bring an end to the sickness that now plagued their world.

Fletcher felt small as he clung to the mast. The task was huge. He knew the odds of success were tiny. For a moment, he was acutely aware of his thin, awkward frame. He stared into the swirling cloud that obscured his vision, and replayed the task they had been set: to sail to the island with a cliff shaped like a skull and to enter the cave they found there. They had been told it was a doorway between worlds, a Threshold leading beyond the Uncrossable Boundary. He recalled the words he and Scoop had heard before accepting the quest:

Once such a doorway is crossed, there is no going back. There is no returning from a Threshold. It is like entering the mouth of death itself.

Fletcher shivered.

He looked down to where the crew of the Black Horizon scurried and scuttled, working with all their might to master the vessel and bring it safely to open waters. He was glad to have his friends with him, but he still couldn't shake the guilt. It was his fault they were in this situation. His quest had plunged them into this chaos. He carried the responsibility for putting their lives at risk.

* * *

Below deck, in the captain's cabin, Scoop knelt across a narrow bunk. She pulled the final strap across the body in the bed and fixed it in place.

Now, that should keep you safe, she thought, as the ship tossed and plunged. She watched the body rock with the motion, but the straps held it firm. Two other bodies had also been secured to their bunks. Scoop studied them. They looked so still, almost peaceful as the ship creaked with the rhythm of the petulant sea.

This is wrong, so wrong. You're the ones who should be looking after me. You're my rocks, my lights.

She stared at the three bodies. They lay unconscious, victims of the sleeping sickness. How was it the most powerful people in her world had been reduced to this? She, Fletcher and the crew of the Black Horizon might have rescued them, bringing them to the ship, but they hadn't saved them. She looked at each of their faces in turn, trying to recall moments she and Fletcher had shared with each of them, remembering how safe she felt in their presence. She looked at the Storyteller's face. It was pale. He looked like a statue on a tomb. Scoop remembered him showing her and Fletcher around his castle, Alethea. His eyes had sparkled as he'd revealed the mysteries of the castle. She remembered how proud she'd felt that she and Fletcher were able to call him father. Next to him, her mother lay – the Storyteller's Princess. Scoop studied her fingers, so long, so elegant. She remembered her mother holding the Golden Feather, teaching her how to use it as a quill to reveal the truth. Her mother's fingers were now limp and lifeless.

She turned to the third body.

'Yarnbard,' she whispered. She struggled to see the old man so frail. His grey beard was barely rising and falling as he breathed. How she loved him. How she hated seeing him like this. The Yarnbard was their mentor at the Academy. She didn't know another person who carried the same energy, whimsical and wise in the same moment; she didn't know anybody who had the same impish sense of humour. She smiled, remembering the Yarnbard leaping out from a tree and spurting Fletcher with Inspiration Ice. How furious he'd been, and yet, how much he'd droned on about the sonnet he'd penned afterwards.

She looked back. The three bodies lay unconscious – the three people she trusted most in the world, the three people she relied upon for everything.

Not just me, she thought, glancing at the Storyteller again. *The whole of this world depends on you. You're its life, its guide. We must get to the Threshold. We must wake you from this sleep, even if it costs our lives.*

As Scoop left the captain's cabin, the wind sweeping her into the battle to reach safer waters, the three bodies were left alone to be rocked by the restless sea.

* * *

On the other side of the Uncrossable Boundary, two women stared at different tracks of water. They were mother and daughter, but separated by hundreds of miles, and by having spent many months apart. The younger of the two, Libby Joyner, watched a river flow past and disappear over a weir. The older, Ms Speller, sat and stared at the grey, flecked sea. Although they were separated by time and distance, they shared the same state of mind: their hearts ached with loss.

It's strange how an object, something ordinary, can be imbued with emotion, linked to memory. Libby and her mother pictured such an object. For both, it was the same – it was a pen. Two pens that had been thrown into those different tracks of water, one in anger, the other in despair. The pens reminded each woman of the other. Both imagined them sinking through the water to be covered by layer upon layer of silt, and as they did, both buried their grief and allowed their hearts to harden.

Chapter 2

The Guardians Flee

On the moor, to the north of the Creativity Craters, three figures – a man, a woman and a girl – moved hurriedly along a rocky ridge. The first, a rugged fellow, wearing a grimy shirt and carrying a leather backpack, leapt over a boulder. He landed on a pathway that had been hidden by gorse bushes. Stooping, he studied the track.

'Quickly, this way,' he whispered.

Turning back, he held out his hand. An older lady, white hair pulled back into a bun, seized it and heaved herself over the rock, panting with the effort. 'I wish I'd worn better shoes for this.' She laughed nervously, nodding at her wellies.

'It's not as if we had much time to prepare for the journey now, Felda, is it?'

'No, Christopher, we certainly didn't.'

Felda looked over her shoulder at the girl who was following them, jumping from rock to rock. 'We're with the right person though, aren't we?' she called, trying to sound upbeat.

'If you say so,' the girl replied. A little bird settled on her shoulder and she stroked its feathers.

'I guess we need some luck.'

'I'm not used to relying on luck,' Christopher said, beginning to push through the gorse bushes along the path. It zigzagged down the steep slope of the moor.

Felda shook her head. 'None of us are.'

The girl looked down from where she was balanced on a boulder. 'Do we have to go that way? The bushes will sting my legs!'

'This is the way,' Christopher replied, not looking back.

'Who made you leader?'

'He is the Guardian of the Highways, dear,' Felda said, and began to follow him. 'We should probably take his advice.'

'And I'm Wisdom. You should listen to me too. And I don't like my legs being stung.'

'You'd think Wisdom would know better than to keep shouting and that she'd get a move on,' Christopher said, testily. 'They'll be after us, you know. And they move quicker than we do.'

Felda's face flushed. 'I'm sorry. I'm slowing you down. You go on without me. I'll catch you up.'

'We're not leaving you,' Christopher snapped. 'We've left too many already.'

Wisdom leapt down from the boulder and the little bird flitted away. 'At least we agree on *one* thing.' She started to skip and jump along the pathway. 'Ouch!' she yelped as the gorse scratched her legs. 'Ouch! Ouch! Ouch!'

'Shh!' Christopher hissed.

'But it hurts!'

'Well if you have to wear such flimsy clothing!' He waved at her green tunic. It looked as fragile as a leaf.

'These clothes are as tough as I am, I'll have you know! And they help me move with the wind.'

'They don't look very practical to me.'

'And you don't look very elegant to me. Ouch!'

Felda stopped. 'Will you two stop arguing! If it isn't enough to be ambushed by Red Hawks and imprisoned by that ghastly woman, I must put up with you two constantly bickering. It's too much, too much!'

'Sorry,' Wisdom muttered.

Christopher grunted.

'Oh, it's alright.' Felda sighed. 'It's just a lot to take in.' She paused. 'What do you think happened back there, to the Red Hawks I mean? They just...'

'...vanished,' Wisdom said, staring out across the valley.

'Disintegrated to dust.'

'Such an eerie sight. Though quiet somehow, almost peaceful.'

'Until all hell broke loose,' Christopher added. 'And I don't have to remind you that only half of them vanished. The others are still there. So, let's not get carried away.'

Felda nodded. 'It was chaos after, wasn't it? Soldiers running, shouting. It was when I saw them abandoning their posts and fleeing into the forest that I knew I had to take a chance. I just ran. I didn't have time to think, though. To take it in.'

'Some of the soldiers had the wherewithal to stay,' Christopher said. 'To keep their guard. Otherwise more of us might have escaped.'

'Is it really only the three of us who made it?' Wisdom asked.

Christopher nodded. 'From what I could see. The others were still being held.'

Felda stared at the ground and shook her head.

For a moment, the three walked in silence.

'I thought,' Felda said, quietly, 'that maybe our powers would return, you know, after the Red Hawks vanished, but...' She stopped and gingerly stretched out a green-gloved hand, touching a nearby bush that looked withered and brown. She closed her eyes and waited for a moment, as if willing life to pour from her fingers. Then she opened her eyes again. Seeing that there had been no change in the colour of the bush, she quickly withdrew her hand, a look of panic on her face. 'Nothing,' she whispered. 'What's to become of us? What's the use of being Green Guardian if you can't restore life to things?'

Christopher looked grave. 'What's the point of being Guardian of the Highways when you must navigate by your eyes, just like everybody else?'

'And what's the use of being Guardian of Hidden Treasure, when you're unable to call help from the deep?' Wisdom added.

'We might be free,' Felda said, 'but our home is still in terrible danger. The Red Hawks may be diminished, but our ability to maintain the balance of the island has gone. We need help. We need to consult something greater than us, something beyond even our power.'

'I agree,' Wisdom said. 'And I think we know what.'

Christopher nodded. 'The Well Whisper.'

'Yes.'

The Well Whisper was the voice of the island itself, constantly guiding the stories of its inhabitants to their conclusions.

Wisdom stared across the valley. In the distance, the Three Towers of the Academy rose from the jumble of streets that made the village of Bardbridge. 'That's where we need to go,' she said, pointing. 'The Well Whisper rises from the Central Chasm, right there in the centre of the Three Towers.'

'But the Red Hawks,' Felda said. 'Grizelda. They'll still be there. It would be madness for us to try and sneak into the heart of the Academy when the village is under their control.' She looked at Christopher for assurance, but he shook his head.

'The girl's right,' he said. 'What choice do we have? We could try to hide, but what good would that do? Perhaps they'll be too distracted by whatever's happened to notice us.'

Felda nodded nervously.

Wisdom looked at Christopher. 'Then what are you waiting for?' she said. 'Lead the way.'

With the trace of a smile, Christopher began along the path again. Wisdom and the Green Guardian followed, the three of them heading towards Bardbridge and the Academy's Three Towers, unsure what dangers they might find when they got there.

Chapter 3

The Parley

Alfa wrapped her fingers around the cup. It was warm.

'Spiced Poppin Brew,' a rake of a man with a pencil moustache said, smiling toothily. It was the ship's cook, Pierre. He spoke with a flourish. 'It will make you feel good. It will make you want to laugh until you float, or to run out and fly a kite.'

Alfa smiled back. She didn't believe Pierre, but the smell of the drink was comforting. She breathed in deeply, for a moment catching the scent of autumn leaves and log fires. Another of the crew, Freddo, was playing the accordion softly. Its notes flitted on the crisp sea air. Alfa took a sip of the drink and let her body relax, attuning to the gentle rhythm of the sea. For a moment, she allowed herself to forget the challenges ahead, and imagined dancing on a rooftop, chimneys puffing merrily around her.

She opened her eyes again and looked up. Through the rigging, the night sky sparkled with unnumbered stars. They were so much brighter in the ocean. Those on the horizon looked like diamonds, almost close enough to touch. Alfa breathed out and watched her breath swirl into the air, making the starlight hazy.

Tonight, the crew of the Black Horizon were gathering on deck. Gradually, they emerged from the cabins or stalked down the ropes to take their places in the circle that was forming in front of the mast. Knot and the Boatswain perched on one of the hatches. Fletcher, Scoop, Sparks, Nib and Rufina sat cross-legged on the timbers. Above, lanterns threw dancing light across the ship, making the mainsail flicker. It looked like a burning ember on the black ocean.

As the crew gathered, they glanced apprehensively at one another, exchanging half-smiles. The Boatswain sat awkwardly, as if he might get up at any moment. Sparks's legs jittered. Scoop studied her nails.

Alfa tried to ignore the others. The glow of the lanterns, the soft sound of the accordion, the twinkling stars and the scent of the Poppin Brew, reminded her of lazy winter nights on the verandas of the Botanical Gardens back on Fullstop Island.

The Dark Pirate's voice shattered her daydream. 'Well,' he growled. 'We all know why we're here.'

Alfa glanced nervously at Sparks. They did know why they were there, why they had been summoned for a Parley. Over the past two days, ever since the Black Horizon had made it out to the open ocean, there had been rumblings aboard, mutterings of discontent.

The cook sat down, having finished handing out the mugs of Poppin Brew. The smell of the spices was thick in the air.

Freddo stopped playing the accordion.

'Well?' the Dark Pirate said. 'Who has the guts to speak it out in an open assembly, rather than whispering behind my back?'

Alfa listened to the sound of waves slapping the hull as the ship cut through the water.

After a moment, Freddo stood. 'Okay,' he said, 'I'll say it. I'll say what most of the crew on this ship are thinking.' He looked from Pierre to Mr Snooze. The old man turned quickly away. The Dark Pirate glared at Freddo. The accordion player was a short man with long ginger hair and gin-soaked whiskers.

I bet he punches above his weight in a fight, Alfa thought.

'Many of us,' he began, 'think we're heading in the wrong direction. We believe we need to plot an alternative course, one that considers we don't have unlimited supplies.'

The Dark Pirate grunted.

'We don't even have enough supplies to make it to the South Bookend Seas. The course we are on is ill-advised at best. At worst, it is—'

'I've heard enough of these complaints,' the Dark Pirate

interrupted.

Freddo shook his head. 'They are not complaints! I'm voicing an opinion many have. I have the right to speak!' Sparks shifted uncomfortably. 'I should *not* have to remind *you* that the Black Horizon is free from a captain's command. You said yourself – we are equals.'

'Equals, yes!' The Dark Pirate raised his voice. 'Equals in terms of value, but not in terms of experience! And, I should *not* have to remind *you* how long I have been sailing these seas, what challenges I've faced and what obstacles I've overcome in this very vessel.'

'We are all *very* aware that you are the most experienced sailor —'

The Dark Pirate thumped the mast. 'Pirate!' he growled.

'Yes, pirate!' Freddo corrected. 'You are the most experienced pirate among us. But that does not mean you are always right! Myself, Pierre and the Boatswain have also risked life and limb at the mercy of the sea!'

The Dark Pirate looked at the Boatswain. 'You as well?' he snarled.

The Boatswain leaned forward, his face kind beneath his bushy beard. 'Yes,' he said. 'I'm afraid so. I've taken an inventory of our stocks. With the best will in the world, we will not make it beyond the Basillica Isles without rationing food. We risk falling into a state of hunger and —'

'Hunger?' The Dark Pirate snorted. 'What have I done to be lumbered with such weak-willed landlubbers.'

Freddo stepped forward. 'Landlubbers?'

The Boatswain's face reddened. 'We have children aboard, I will not—'

'Don't bring us into this!' Fletcher said, springing to his feet. His fists were clenched. 'I can go hungry if that's what's required!'

'You should listen to the boy,' the Dark Pirate said. 'He has more bottle than the lot of you.'

There was a murmur of outrage. Freddo pointed. 'You are *not* the captain of this ship!'

The Dark Pirate stood, followed quickly by the Boatswain, who stepped between the two men spreading his hands to hold them apart.

'No, I am not the captain,' the Dark Pirate snarled. 'That is why I called this Parley. That is how we make decisions aboard the Black Horizon – in an open assembly.' He stepped back and scanned the circle. 'We will hear each speak in turn. State your opinion and the decision will be made by the majority. Do we sail directly to the Threshold, as the Storyteller charged, or do we take the soft option and look for somewhere to restock before completing our mission?'

'I wondered when we'd get to speak,' Alfa said under her breath. Her voice was obviously louder than she'd intended. She blushed as all eyes turned to her.

The Dark Pirate grunted again. 'Very well. You speak first, young lady.'

Alfa looked momentarily thrown, but then composed herself. 'Well...' She hesitated.

'Out with it, girl. Do we sail or do we stop?'

'Sail. I agree with Fletcher. This is too important for us to be faint-hearted.'

Sparks sighed. The Dark Pirate turned on her. 'Do you have something to say?'

She shrank back.

'Speak, girl!'

Sparks folded her arms and pursed her lips. 'Well, I think we *should* stop for supplies. If the Boatswain says we need them, we need them.'

'Well said!' Freddo exclaimed. 'Better to get there a few days late than not at all!'

'I think we know which way *you* are going to vote,' the Dark

Pirate said.

'You do.'

In turn, each of the circle spoke. Rufina was for sailing on. To her consternation, Nib voted to restock. The Boatswain and Pierre agreed with him. Knot looked unsure, but after a few minutes of hectoring by Fletcher and the Dark Pirate, he voted to sail. Mr Snooze, who looked as if he were about to cry, registered his vote in favour of stopping.

'Well,' the Dark Pirate said, 'that's six votes to five. It looks as if we'll be plotting a new course for—'

'This is crazy!' Fletcher interrupted. He turned to Freddo. 'This isn't your quest! It's ours!' He signalled to Scoop. 'We're the ones who've been told to sail to the Threshold. We're the ones who must cross it. We're the ones who have to give up everything to try to save this world from the sickness. And you're worried about a few missed breakfasts!'

The Boatswain stepped towards him. 'It's not just a case of missed breakfasts, laddie!'

'I don't care! This is our quest, not yours! We must get to the Threshold. Have you forgotten who's in there?' Fletcher pointed at the captain's cabin. 'Have you forgotten what's at stake?'

'Nobody's forgotten anything!' The Boatswain raised his voice. 'We all have friends, people we hold dear, who have fallen under the curse of the sickness. I won't be lectured by—'

'Excuse me!' a voice cut in. Scoop was standing in the centre of the circle. 'I haven't been given my opportunity to speak yet.'

'Sorry, missy,' the Boatswain said. Shaking his head, he retook his seat.

'Good!' Fletcher said. 'Perhaps you can talk some sense into these numbskulls!'

Scoop composed herself. 'You're right, Fletcher. This is *our* quest. But it's not just yours and mine. This is bigger than us. I won't risk the lives of the people on this ship. I won't risk the life of Sparks or Mr Snooze—'

'What are you saying?'

'I'm saying I agree with the Boatswain. We should stop for supplies.'

Fletcher opened his mouth to speak but the Dark Pirate held up his hand. He turned away in disbelief.

Annoyed, Scoop crossed to him. 'It's like Freddo said, it's better to get there alive than dead. Who's that going to help?'

Fletcher glared at her. But Scoop stared back, resolutely.

Behind them, the Dark Pirate spoke. 'Then it is decided,' he said. 'We'll stop for supplies on the way to the Threshold.'

The ship fell into a tense silence. Fletcher broke Scoop's gaze and looked away, staring out to sea. The quest had not started well. They were already at each other's throats. Scoop recalled something the Yarnbard once said: "A house divided against itself will not stand."

I hope that doesn't apply to ships too, she thought, as she walked away from her brother.

Chapter 4

Last Song of the Fable Fish

Having made the decision that the Black Horizon should stop for supplies, the Dark Pirate pulled a scroll from his cloak. Crouching, he unrolled it on the deck. It was a beautifully decorated map of the Oceans of Rhyme. He looked up. 'The next question is, where should we stop?'

'I've been thinking about that.' Freddo walked forward and crouched next to him. 'I think we should plot a course east, to the Storyless States.' He traced his finger across the map. 'We can restock at Beurocropolis and then follow the coast until we're south of the Basillica Isles. From there, we can head west.'

The Dark Pirate shook his head. 'No. If we are to stop, we stop here.' He jabbed the map.

Freddo rose. 'The Basillica Isles?'

'No!' the Boatswain exclaimed. 'That's madness!' He joined Freddo.

Pierre got to his feet. 'Are you crazy? That's where the Red Hawks are from! It will be swarming with them!'

The three men stood in a line, facing the pirate. He straightened up. 'It's the fastest route.'

'I agree,' Fletcher said, joining the argument. He jabbed a finger into the Boatswain's face. 'We have to take the fastest route!'

The Boatswain knocked Fletcher's hand away.

'Don't touch me!' Fletcher yelled. It was like a spark to kindling. The whole ship exploded into a fire of passion. The pent-up fear and anger that had simmered for weeks erupted into a full-blown argument. The Boatswain, Freddo and Fletcher surrounded the map, hollering at one another. The fire spread as arguments broke out between Nib and Rufina, Alfa and Sparks.

The ship was engulfed in an inferno of pointing, thumping and shouting. Knot covered his ears and began to moan.

In the chaos, Mr Snooze backed away. He looked ghost-like in his nightgown. Reaching the edge of the ship, he turned. The sight that greeted him was overwhelming. He gripped the ship's rail, his legs almost buckling. Around the Black Horizon, the ocean sparkled with a million points of light. It was the most beautiful thing Mr Snooze had ever seen. The hubbub behind him muffled. He stared across the water, unsure where the ocean ended and the star-strewn sky began. All around, flecks glinted green and blue, violet and amber. The sea was shining. Mr Snooze could see the depth of the water, plunging down, the aurora stretching, deep as a mountain beneath him. Unable to cope with the sight, he looked up. Above, the sky exploded with starlight. Mr Snooze was overwhelmed with a sense of his own smallness. The ship he trusted was just a speck on a vast ocean, this moment just surf on a boundless wave, rolling through the universe.

'Look,' he gasped.

There was a gentle tinkling coming from the lights. It was barely audible above the fight. It was otherworldly, delicate and rich. The old man's heart leapt, as stories danced to life in his imagination. They made him want to dive into the sea, to become one with the lights. And yet, at the same time, the music was sad, weaved through with loss.

'Listen,' he said, stumbling backwards. Around him, the ship broiled with the quarrel.

'Listen,' the old man repeated. He staggered into the centre of the circle. 'Listen. Listen!' He grabbed the Dark Pirate's arm. The pirate swung round, mid-rant, his fist raised as if to strike Mr Snooze. The old man cowered. Realising what he was about to do, the Dark Pirate stepped back, shaken. His hand fell to his side and he collapsed onto one of the hatches, breathing heavily.

Becoming aware of what had happened, the rest of the crew

fell still.

Mr Snooze looked at them, wide-eyed. 'Listen.'

The crew looked at one another, unsure what the moon-faced man meant.

'The sea – the sea is singing.'

Sure enough, over the slap of the waves, Alfa became aware of a mysterious hum that hung in the night. Slowly, the crew moved to the side of the ship and looked out.

'Woah,' Rufina said.

The sea was ablaze.

'What's happening?' Sparks asked.

The Dark Pirate closed his eyes for a moment. 'They are the Fable Fish,' he whispered. He didn't often sound shaken, but Alfa could tell that even he was taken aback by the glowing ocean. 'But…this is the biggest shoal I've ever seen. This must be the whole of the Fable Fish population…all in one place. It's… it's unheard of.'

Scoop stared into the water. She could see the outline of one of the fish, just below the surface. Its scales shimmered. Suddenly, the fish leapt out of the sea, rainbow colours flashing through the air. 'Look!' She pointed.

One by one the fish began to jump. The ocean around the ship began to fizz, stirred by the display.

As the fish leapt, the music grew louder.

'I think they're singing,' Mr Snooze whispered.

The Dark Pirate nodded.

Mr Snooze closed his eyes. He could *see* the song. It formed pictures in his mind, made words flow through him.

As the fish leapt, the music swelled. Slowly, Mr Snooze began to speak.

'Moonlight wanes,
Starlight falls,
The world begins to fade.

Rainbows dim,
The Great Light ebbs,
The world begins to fade.
Last song of the Fable Fish,
Last song of the Fable Fish,
Swimming to other shores.
Last song of the Fable Fish,
Swimming to the world beyond.'

'Look.' The Boatswain pointed. 'That fish, it just disappeared.'

Scoop watched as around them the lights began to dim, dissolving into the sea.

'They're fading,' Rufina whispered, her voice faltering. Scoop knew why. The spectacle was heart-breaking.

'The last song of the Fable Fish,' Mr Snooze said again.

'They're saying goodbye,' the Dark Pirate said. 'We're witnessing the passing of a whole species.'

'But they can't,' Sparks whispered. 'They're the Fable Fish. They've always been here. We learnt about them at the Academy. They're part of this world.'

They watched as light by light, glimmer by glimmer, the sea began to darken. Nobody spoke. This was a sacred moment.

'It's a song that signals the end of all things,' the Dark Pirate whispered. 'Our world is beginning to fade.'

The Boatswain looked at him, his eyes red. He laid a hand on his friend's shoulder. 'I've changed my mind,' he said. 'We cannot delay any longer than absolutely necessary. We must take our chances on the Basillica Isles.'

The crew nodded in agreement, their hearts one. They watched, as slowly the sea fell still, the final song of the Fable Fish dissolving into the moonlit waves.

Chapter 5

The Time Terminator

Wisdom grabbed Christopher's arm and yanked him into a narrow alley at the back of Mr Snooze's Bedtime Story Slumber Shop. They were in the village of Bardbridge. Felda stood behind her, already concealed. The windows of the little cottage were shuttered, the air around the shop, usually rich with incense, was cold and still. Christopher opened his mouth to object, but Wisdom held a finger to her lips and pointed at the cobbled street beyond the alleyway. A squadron of Red Hawks ran into view, heading towards the Three Towers.

'She's called the entire fleet to gather at the Scythe,' one of them said.

'I heard they found her floating in the ocean, yelling into the mist,' another replied. 'She was alone on the boat.'

'Mad old witch. She's lost her grip on this place good and proper. Captain says we'll be back on the Basillica Isles before the week's out.'

'Better had, I'm sick of this place.'

The sound of boots faded.

The Guardians knew who the Red Hawks were talking about. 'Grizelda,' Felda whispered.

'Must be,' Wisdom said. 'Come on, let's follow them.'

'Follow them? But if we get caught—'

'They're not looking for us,' Christopher interrupted. 'Did you see the squadrons we passed on the way? They're in disarray – uniforms dishevelled, arguments in the ranks; I saw a fight break out in one of the brigades. The captain didn't even pull them into line, he just joined the rabble, baying for blood. It's anarchy out there. I think we could walk straight up Bridge Road and nobody would bat an eye.'

'And,' Wisdom added, 'we have to go that way to get to the Central Chasm. We may as well see if there's any information we can glean along the way. If the whole fleet has been summoned, it must be important.'

Felda looked unsure, but nodded.

The three Guardians slipped onto the street, the sign above Mr Snooze's shop swaying in the wind. Keeping close to the edge of the road, they began to move from door to door, following the soldiers.

* * *

A chaotic scene greeted them when they reached the little square that hugged the base of the Three Towers. They watched from a covered snicket, peering out from a low door that opened onto the square. On their way, they'd grabbed cloaks from the baskets outside Dénouement's Disguise Emporium and now looked like forest travellers.

The plaza was packed with Red Hawks, shouting, laughing, gambling and trading. A large group of soldiers had just tumbled out of the Wild Guffaw, swigging tankards of Fool's Paradise. Another group had set up a green baize-covered table, now scattered with playing cards. Other soldiers were trading arms. In the centre of the square, two beefy Red Hawks strained to hold Baskervilles back, their leads taut as the beasts clawed the ground, spoiling for a fight. Around them, a battalion egged the dogs on, whooping and clapping as the creatures bared their teeth.

Christopher looked up at the turrets of rock that rose from the tiny square. They had always struck him as being at odds with the gentle valley in which Bardbridge nestled. Over the years, the inside of the towers had been hollowed out, creating a labyrinth of tunnels and rooms that now housed the heart of Blotting's Academy – the place where all Story Characters trained. Between the two closest turrets, the Giant and the Scythe, a path led to the Central Chasm. But it was at the other side of the square, beyond the sea of Red Hawks.

'That's the way,' Christopher said, 'but we can't get through this crowd now. We'll just have to wait and watch until our chance comes.'

As he was speaking, Wisdom noticed a large flock of crows. They were perched on the ledges of the Scythe. Every so often, a crow would dive, disappearing behind the Red Hawks, before emerging again, flapping and cawing.

Wisdom caught sight of what looked like a stump of rock covered in black hessian, standing on the steps of the Scythe.

'Look,' she said, pointing at the strange shape. As she did, two eyes appeared beneath the folds of the fabric.

'Grizelda!' Felda whispered.

'Yes. My sister always knew how to glare.'

Christopher shook his head. 'Those soldiers don't know what's about to hit them.'

The Guardians studied the old woman. She stood, stock still, glaring at a troop of Red Hawks to her side. They were pulling a rope attached to a wire that had been fixed between two of the towers. The rope ran through a pulley, back to the ground.

Whatever's on the other end of that rope is the focus of the crows' attention, Wisdom thought.

She could hear the squeak of the wheel. There was another sound too. It was muffled, but it sounded like someone crying out in pain. And it was perfectly synchronised with the diving crows.

Felda gripped Wisdom's arm. 'There's somebody there.'

Wisdom watched as a booted foot came into view above the Red Hawks. Somebody was being hoist into the air.

A crow flew past and there was another cry of pain.

The soldiers nearest the Scythe turned to watch. Slowly, a wave of hush rolled across the square. Red Hawks froze, tankards in hand, playing cards half-dealt and muskets mid-trade. The Baskervilles retreated to their masters' legs, whining.

Slowly the man was hoist higher, dangling by his foot. He was a Red Hawk sergeant, his scarlet coat hanging behind his head. He had been bound and gagged. His free leg thrashed, making him spin on the rope. As he did, Grizelda's crows dived, pecking at his face. Christopher watched in horror as one of them tore a little clump of flesh from his cheek. The man screamed through his gag. Blood dripped from his forehead, forming a little pool of red on the cobblestones below.

'Well, that seems to have got yer attention now, don't it?' Grizelda said, the rasp of her voice carrying across the square. 'Now, it seems some of you, including our friend here, are under the misapprehension I'm not in charge anymore. You've got it into yer tiny little brains that I've *lost it*.' She spat the words, jabbing her temple. 'Now, it might seem like I'm immune to such remarks – Grizelda the thick-skinned you might have heard me called. It might seem like such *nasty* little lies wouldn't touch my poor old heart, but I'd like to make it clear to you that such talk is –' the old woman sniffed – 'upsettin'. You hear what I'm sayin'?'

The Red Hawks nearest the Scythe recoiled, as one of the crows plunged its beak into the hanging man's eye. His body shook with the impact.

Grizelda didn't pay any attention. 'Now, I believe this little misunderstandin' has been a…slip, shall we call it, a stumble in an otherwise quite fruitful relationship. I know it's never been your intention to upset me, has it?' A flurry of crows dived, beaks and claws tearing the hanging man's flesh, until his body fell still, his breathing barely visible. The Red Hawks shook their heads.

The crows quietened, some feeding, others returning to the towers with clumps of meat.

'Good,' the old woman purred. 'Well, I'm glad we've got that bit of nastiness out the way. So, I take it you'll all be going back to your duties like good little boys?'

The Red Hawks nodded.

'Well, that show of respect lifts a poor old woman's heart,' Grizelda said. 'That's yer good deed for the day, right there. And it's just as well, because there are bodies in there that still need guarding.' She pointed to the Scythe. 'I've still got floors of sleeping islanders under the curse of the sickness...'

The old woman carried on speaking, but a commotion had broken out at the other side of the square, among the soldiers nearest the Giant. They were moving backwards, away from the tower, pushing into those behind them, causing scuffles in the ranks. Wisdom peered at them.

What's going on?

They seemed to be reacting to something just out of view, something between the towers.

Grizelda had noticed the disturbance too. 'Oh, you poor pussycats. I'm not that scary now, am I?'

A few of the soldiers broke into a run.

'Where d'ya think yer goin'?' Grizelda cried. 'I'm not finished talkin' to yer yet!'

But her words had no effect. A wave of chaos broke across the square. It spilled from those nearest the Giant, fanning out. Soldiers started to run, pushing past each other, panic on their faces.

Grizelda yelled over the noise, 'I'll have you up there like him!' But the soldiers weren't listening. 'Come back! Come back here, immediately!' She continued to scream, but her voice was swallowed by the ruckus.

'Now's the time,' Christopher said. Before Felda or Wisdom could reply, he plunged into the crowd, pushing in the opposite direction.

'Oh my,' Felda said, as Wisdom followed. Taking a deep breath, she ran after them, scared to lose sight of her friends. The heat of the crowd was stifling, soldiers thumped into her as she pushed past them. Felda kept her eyes trained on Wisdom, flashes of her green tunic in the sea of red.

What could be scarier than the old woman? Her mind was racing. *What on earth are they running from?*

Then she saw it. A leg, as tall as a ship's mast, poking out from the gap between the towers. It was leathery and black and covered in thick hair. It wrapped around the Giant, clinging to the rock. Slowly, it stole around the edge of the tower, its spindly claw twitching. Other legs appeared. They rose and fell in staccato beats, crossing silently, feeling out clefts in the rock. The creature's body slid out, hovering. Its abdomen was a bulbous black sack. Four great eyes filled its head. The beast ticked as it moved. Each high-pitched strike sent a shudder through Felda. She wanted to join the soldiers and run. But ahead, she could see Wisdom and Christopher – they were sprinting towards the monster.

The beast stopped, utterly still, straddling the gap between the towers, its pincers swaying. Below, the last of the Red Hawks scattered.

Grizelda had advanced up the stairs of the Scythe, her back pressed against the rock. She was surveying the great spider with a mix of rage and grudging respect.

Christopher stopped.

'How are we going to get past it?' Wisdom panted as she caught up to him.

'I'm not sure.'

Felda joined the others. 'What on earth is it?'

'If I'm not much mistaken,' Christopher said, 'it's a Gigan Tick – a Time Terminator.'

Wisdom and Felda exchanged a dark look.

'I know,' Christopher said. 'That's why we have to get to the Central Chasm. If it is what I think it is...'

Before he could finish speaking, the giant spider sprang forward, its pincers ticking.

Christopher grabbed Felda, the three Guardians jumping backwards. To their side, Grizelda edged higher up the steps of the Scythe.

The great arachnid made for the Red Hawk hanging from the rope. It reared up, its front legs landing on the wire. The soldier's body bounced as the spider slipped, but in a matter of seconds it had secured its position. It lifted its head, its hairy underbelly exposed. Felda gasped. There was a thick fang beneath it. She turned away, burying her head into Christopher's chest. There was a sickening thud as the creature punctured the Red Hawk's chest. With lightning speed, the spider closed its legs around its prey. Swinging from the rope, it began to turn the body. Thread flowed from its abdomen, wrapping the man in a white cocoon.

'Quickly, now!' Christopher hissed. 'While it's distracted.'

The Guardians dashed forward, heading for the gap between the towers. Felda's stomach turned as she glanced at the spider. The Red Hawk's body was now encased in a thick substance, sticky with venom. The spider finished wrapping the body and climbed up to the wire to guard its prey.

The Guardians slipped between the Giant and the Scythe, entering the dark space between the three towers. The Central Chasm opened before them, a large pit that plunged into darkness. They reached the edge of the hole and stopped, their breathing heavy.

'Now,' Christopher said, 'we listen.'

Felda waited, trying to push thoughts of the giant spider from her mind. She needed to listen. It was a Guardian's job to listen to the Well Whisper, to sense its rhythm, its sighs, to follow its lead. Usually, it was an instinctive task. The Well Whisper was always present. It flowed from the Central Chasm across the island, out across the Oceans of Rhyme. Listening to its call was like breathing, vital but unthinking. To come to the Central Chasm itself was a different matter. Felda had only stood here twice in her life – the first time had been to accept her

Guardianship. This was the second.

Wisdom's face was pale, her hands were shaking.

Felda knew why. 'Nothing,' she whispered. 'The well is silent.'

A little bird flitted down and perched on Wisdom's shoulder.

'It's as I feared,' Christopher said. 'The heartbeat of the island has stopped. Its source has run dry. That creature *is* a Gigan Tick – a Time Terminator. They are creatures of the end, tasked with bringing the island into a place of stasis for the Great Waiting, in hope that one day this world will be awoken again. That creature may not seem it, but it's our friend. It'll protect the things we love, the people we love. It will wrap them in a protective shell, saving them for the future. More of its brothers will join it soon. Before long, an army of Gigan Ticks will emerge from this gorge, released from the very place the Well Whisper once sounded. They will drag the island into a state of hibernation.'

Felda thought she could hear the terrible sound of ticking coming from the chasm below. 'What are we to do?'

'We have to escape,' Wisdom said. 'Find a place of safety.'

Christopher shook his head. 'Is there anywhere safe?'

'I think, perhaps, there is one place. Come, follow me.'

Quietly, the Guardians sneaked away from the Central Chasm, careful to avoid the Gigan Tick still perched on the wire, careful not to be spotted by the few Red Hawks still patrolling the streets. Felda wondered if she would ever see Bardbridge again. As she followed Wisdom away from the Three Towers, a fear gripped her, the fear that Bardbridge had been lost, that she would never walk these streets again, that this was the last time she would set eyes on the village she loved.

Chapter 6

Digging Down

'Can you tell me what happened?'

Libby stared at the pile of kids' toys in the corner of her counsellor's office. There was one of those "Don't Buzz the Wire" games, shaped like a tiny rollercoaster.

'You were in some sort of incident at school, Libby. Can you tell me about it?'

And there was a Lego house, with lots of little characters. There was always Lego.

Libby was used to sitting in this room, willing the time to pass. It was an old Victorian house that had been converted for use by CAMHS, the Children and Adolescent Mental Health Service. The carpet was green, faded and patchy. The walls were off-white. A desk was pushed into the corner, a computer on it, containing client files. Libby thought about the notes that must be stored there from her previous sessions. In the centre of the room was a little round coffee table with a small vase of flowers on it. Libby sat in an armchair next to it, her counsellor, June, opposite. June's straggly blonde hair and flushed cheeks made her look tired. She cocked her head to one side.

Libby sighed. 'It was just a fight.' She didn't look up. 'They happen all the time.'

'Okay. Well, can you tell me how you were feeling just before it happened?'

'I don't want to talk about it.'

June paused. 'Okay, that's fine.'

The two of them sat in silence for a moment.

'How's your writing going?' June asked, changing tack.

Libby felt a twist in her gut. 'It's not.'

'No? You were finding it helpful a few months ago.'

'Well, I'm not now. It's stupid.'

'Stupid? Why do you say that?'

'I dunno.' Libby could feel her cheeks burning. 'Dad's right. I've spent too long living in a fantasy world.'

'Lots of people use writing as a way of processing their emotions.'

Libby shrugged. 'Yeah. I dunno. I think it was childish – just a childish dream.'

Her counsellor paused again. The silence was awkward.

'And what about dreams, Libby?' June asked. 'Have you had any recently? You've spoken about them before.'

Libby glanced up. Sometimes it felt as though June could see straight through her with those kind eyes.

I hate that kindness, Libby thought. *It's so intrusive.* 'Yes, I've had one,' she said, looking away again. She didn't know why she was talking.

'Tell me about it.'

Libby shrugged. 'It's just about spiders. Lots of spiders in a sort of pit.'

Her counsellor waited.

'That's it,' Libby said. 'I've dreamt about it a few times.'

June nodded. 'What do you associate with spiders?' she asked.

'I dunno.' Libby paused. 'People are scared of them, I guess.'

'That's true. It's a very common phobia. And what about the pit?'

'I dunno. It's just a hole, isn't it?'

June paused. 'Often in dreams, or stories, underground places are connected to our subconscious, to things we don't see on the surface, perhaps things we don't want to see or acknowledge. Think about going down the rabbit hole in Alice in Wonderland or the Minotaur in the labyrinth.'

Libby glanced up again. She and June had talked about dreams and symbols before. She could tell it was a subject that interested June. Despite herself, Libby was intrigued.

'So perhaps,' June continued, 'there are things going on underneath, in your subconscious – feelings and emotions that, perhaps, you're afraid of – like the spiders.'

Libby shrugged again, but she was aware her hands were clammy.

'We all have those feelings, you know,' June said. 'We all have parts of ourselves we don't feel entirely comfortable with, that we aren't in control of. Sometimes they make us feel afraid.'

June glanced at the clock. The session had almost finished. She linked her fingers, twiddling her thumbs for a moment. 'I wonder if, perhaps, a goal for the next few weeks might be to allow yourself to be aware of any emotions that arise – not to push them away too quickly, just to be aware of them, without judging or trying to analyse. If you're able, you could make a note of anything you do become aware of and we could pick it up in our next session.'

Libby nodded.

'Okay,' June said, standing. Libby followed her lead. 'I'll see you in a few weeks' time, yes?' Libby turned to leave the office. 'Libby,' June said. Libby looked back. 'You're doing well, you know. Don't be hard on yourself.'

Libby nodded again, but as she walked out of the room, she kicked herself for having told June about her dream. She'd said too much. She didn't want to talk about it. She didn't want to think. She just wanted to lie down and sleep, sleep and never wake up.

* * *

Two hundred and fifty miles south, Libby's mother, Ms Speller, sat on a camping chair on the beach. It was cold. She wore an old puffer jacket and had a blanket thrown over her legs. The beach was deserted now the weather had turned.

It's quiet, she thought. *Too quiet.*

She stared out across the restless sea, muttering to herself. The wind whipped sand at her, making her skin prickle.

Ms Speller listened. She was used to hearing them, seeing them – Mortales, the Story Characters that plagued her. They appeared unprompted, unwelcome visitors to her imagination, disturbing her, not letting her get any peace. But no matter how she railed against them, she had become accustomed to them. Since she had thrown her pen into the sea, since Falk had disappeared, her mind had just been...empty.

Too quiet, she thought. She tapped her foot, nervously. This silence put her on edge. But when her mind was noisy, she couldn't cope. She couldn't win. She couldn't live with them, but she felt lost without them.

I'll never have peace, she thought. *I'll never have peace.*

Chapter 7

Gigan Tick Attack

Grizelda backed up the steps of the Scythe. She was being pursued by a Gigan Tick. 'Get back with ya!' She lashed out with a pike she'd found abandoned on the steps. Tripping over it had been a stroke of luck. Secretly, she thanked the guard who'd left it, although she vowed that if she ever saw him again, she'd kill him for abandoning his post.

The old woman lunged forward, swiping with the pike. It struck the Gigan Tick in the eye. Grizelda cackled as it recoiled, its legs slipping from the steps, sending lumps of rock crashing down.

'Go on, back with ya!' She lunged again. 'Take that! Don't yer know who yer messing with? Don't yer know who I am? I'm Grizelda! Grizelda, you hear? *You* should be afraid of *me!*' She struck out again, knocking one of its legs away. The creature scrambled wildly, trying to gain purchase, but it was enormous, its orbed body squashed against the side of the tower. The steps were ancient and crumbling, and the more the spider struggled, the more debris it dislodged.

Grizelda raised her free hand and brought it down in a sweeping motion. Her crows dived, madly. They struck the creature like a volley of darts. The great arachnid reared up, catching one in its mouth. There was a crunch as it snapped its jaws shut. Other crows fell from the Scythe, their bodies broken by the impact. Birds bounced down in a flurry of feathers and blood. The enormous spider ticked rapidly, its pincers thrashing.

'Argh!' the old woman yelled, dashing down the steps. She brought the pike down on the creature's head with a thwack.

It let out an ear-piercing screech.

'Take that, yer hairy monstrosity!'

The beast reared up again, its body swaying. Pressing her advantage, Grizelda struck it in the eye again. It jerked away, losing balance. Its back legs slipped, pulling its bulbous torso with them. It flopped over the rocks, clawing, but it was too heavy. Its body toppled over the ledge. It clung on, two claws hooked onto the pathway, its other legs hanging down, flailing wildly. They thumped the tower. Great chunks of rock fell from the Scythe. The spider screeched again, its ticks like gunfire. Grizelda's crows dived once more, trying to dislodge the creature's grip. One of its leg slipped and it lurched to the side, leaving it hanging by a single claw.

Grizelda stepped forward.

'Send my love to yer maker, won't you?' Crouching, she prized the Gigan Tick's claw from the ledge. It let out a high whine as it lost its grip. It fell, legs swimming through the air. Grizelda brushed herself down as she watched it plummet. It hit the ground with a dull thud, splattering black goo across the square below.

'That'll teach yer,' the old woman said.

She looked out over the village. An army of Gigan Ticks spilled from the Central Chasm. Black legs and bulbous bodies swarmed through the streets. A frenzy of ticking filled the air. The great arachnids scuttled along the cobbles, spinning sticky webs between the houses, climbing onto their roofs, ready to pounce.

Villagers fled their homes, scurrying to the edges of the village, but it was no good. One by one the Gigan Ticks picked them off, darting from their hiding places to snare them in their web. Gradually, little pouches of white appeared, bodies wrapped and stored, guarded by the giant beasts, victims or valuables, waiting to be woken.

From the corner of her eye, Grizelda caught sight of another enormous spider beginning to climb the Scythe. Across the way, others were scaling the Giant and Needle too.

'Well, I never did like the place, anyway,' she muttered.

She spun round, her cloak fanning out. With a swirl, Grizelda transformed into a large, black bird. It leapt from the Scythe, the few crows that were left following. Up they flew, away from the Three Towers, until Bardbridge, infested with Gigan Ticks, covered in cobwebs, faded, as Grizelda and her flock disappeared into the clouds.

Chapter 8

The Venus Flower

In the wetlands, where the wind from the Marshes of Ersatz meets the shallows of the Puddles of Plot, the Everafterglade thrives. Here, the sun hangs orange all year round. Even in winter, a warm breeze drifts through the eucalyptus trees, making the long grass wave.

Christopher, Wisdom and Felda pushed through the palms, their feet swirling the shallow water. The carpet of flat leaves that floated on the swamp, parted as they moved. Around them, sleepy geckos flitted from their logs, disappearing into the shade of the ferns.

The Guardians' faces were spotted with mud, the bottom of their clothes heavy and sodden. Christopher swatted another fly from his face. He was irritable. There were no paths in the glade. It made him nervous.

Wisdom, however, moved through the everglade like a butterfly tracking the scent of a rare flower. A little bird flitted ahead of her, darting from tree to tree. She ran her hand through a mass of blue buds, then stopped to smell a cup-shaped flower. It looked as if it had been set at a table of white goblets.

Felda was the last in line. She was jittery. She kept spying creatures on the edge of her vision and couldn't shake the feeling the Gigan Tick was following them.

'How far?' she asked.

Wisdom held up a finger. 'Listen.'

A distant whirring vibrated through the trees, peppered with melodic chirrups like the broken chords of a wind chime. It was peaceful, hypnotic.

'What is it?'

'That's where we're going,' Wisdom said. 'It's not too far

now.'

They moved on, following the sound. As it got louder, the Everafterglade closed in around them. Felda could feel the hum in the air. It made her skin tingle. The noise was soothing, like a blanket being drawn across her shoulders. Her mind quietened and she found herself stepping without thought.

A white flower floated across her path. She smiled, dreamily. *Trillium*. The three-petalled buds had always been one of her favourites.

Slowly, more flowers gathered around her feet, until she was surrounded by a carpet of white. It spilled through the trees, forming a pathway. Tall, scarlet flowers lined the way like torches from an enchanted forest.

The Guardians followed the pathway until the glade opened into a cathedral-like clearing. Light shot through the trees in hazy beams, the sun hanging behind their branches like a dreamcatcher.

In the centre of the clearing, a colossal flower blossomed. It sat on the ground, its tulip-shaped bowl surrounded by Trillium buds. Its petals looked as soft as swan feathers, but it was four times the height of Felda. Around the flower, tiny birds hovered, their wings flashing green and blue. They hummed as they beat. The birds seemed to be tending the plant, their beaks stroking its petals, before flitting away to the surrounding branches. As they tended the plant, they chirruped and whistled. A rich scent like sugared almonds and honey lingered in the glade.

'Lullaby birds?' Felda asked.

'Yes,' Wisdom replied.

'Then this must be...'

'The Glade of the Setting Sun.'

'And that's the Venus Flower. So, this is where you've been leading us. I've heard stories, but...'

'We'll be safe here.'

'Where?' Christopher said. He sounded nervous.

Wisdom pointed at the flower.

'Inside the plant?'

'Yes.'

'No! I'm not stepping a foot in there.'

'There's nowhere safe from the Gigan Ticks. You said it yourself. We cannot stay on the surface of this world. We need to travel deep, to the roots of the land, to the world beneath.'

'DREAM?' Felda asked.

'Yes, this will be our carriage to the other side. The plant will keep us safe.'

'The plant will feed on us!' exclaimed Christopher.

'It will sustain us.'

'It will secrete a fluid that will knit our bodies into its vascular system and draw us into a hallucinogenic state. You can smell it now – that sickly scent.'

'You were always so literal, Christopher. I prefer to see it as a pillow, a bed to keep us safe as we cross into DREAM.'

'But how will we get out again?'

Wisdom paused. 'There's no telling how, or if, we'll ever leave DREAM.'

'Then how is this different to the Gigan Ticks? We're prey to both.'

'The difference is we choose this willingly.'

'Willingly? Pah!'

'Being taken by a Gigan Tick is like disappearing, swallowed by darkness until you are woken. This way, we will continue to have some level of consciousness. We will slip into the subterranean realm of DREAM where we will be together. Once there, we will be able to fight for our survival. This way we have a chance. The Gigan Ticks will gradually take every living thing – but they will not venture here.'

'For good reason!'

'Christopher, I am Wisdom, the eldest of the Guardians. This is our best chance. It is our *only* chance. Will you trust me?'

Christopher held Wisdom's gaze for a long moment, searching her eyes. Then, he gave a sharp nod. 'Very well. I will.'

'Good. Then, I bid you sweet dreaming.'

The little bird that had been flitting ahead of Wisdom landed on her shoulder. She stepped forward, Trillium buds like confetti around her feet. Reaching the Venus flower, she ran her fingers over the edge of its petal. It was silken and strong.

'Hello,' Wisdom whispered. 'Will you keep us safe?'

Finding the place where the petals overlapped, she pulled the flower to one side, revealing a doorway into the warm, dim heart of the plant. The sweet smell spilled out. Wisdom held up her finger and the little bird jumped onto it. She tucked it safely into her pocket and stepped into the plant.

Felda followed. The flower was spongy beneath her feet. She watched Wisdom sit down, leaning against the petals and stretching out her feet. Felda followed her example. She breathed in the sweet scent and her head swam. She was half-aware of Christopher next to her, breathing deeply. The muffled hum of the Lullaby birds filled the plant. She closed her eyes and allowed herself to slip into the sweet embrace of the Venus Flower.

For a moment, there was nothing. Felda felt as though she were floating. But then her body became heavy, uncomfortably heavy. She was being dragged down, down into the ground, deep into the earth, to where the roots of all things twisted together.

A voice spoke: 'Welcome,' it said. It was familiar. 'Welcome to the Halls of DREAM.'

Chapter 9

Towards the Basillica Isles

A blade flashed over Alfa's head. She raised her hands, sword and dagger crossed, as her opponent's weapon sliced down. She spun round. There was the scrape of foil on dagger and her rival's sword clattered to the deck.

'Take that,' she said, pinning her adversary to the mast.

Rufina, Sparks and Freddo broke into applause.

'You did it again,' cried Sparks. Freddo picked up his accordion and began to play.

Alfa grinned and spread her arms in a low bow.

'I let her win again, you mean,' Fletcher muttered. He stepped away from the mast, his cheeks flushed and picked up his sword.

'Fibber,' said Sparks. 'She disarmed you – just as she did the past four times.'

Fletcher grunted.

Rufina patted Fletcher on the shoulder. 'You're *all* getting better.'

Over the past few weeks, the Black Horizon had held a steady course towards the Basillica Isles. The sea had been calm and the winter days bright. Other than their regular duties, there hadn't been a great deal to do. Time at sea could be dreadfully dull, cooped up in a space no bigger than Scribbler's House, a watery wilderness surrounding them. As boredom set in, they each found different ways to occupy themselves. Alfa had asked Rufina, who worked for the Department for Overcoming Monsters, to teach her some new combat skills. Fletcher, Sparks and Freddo had joined the lessons. Training was a good way to let off steam, and the deck made an ideal sparring arena. They had spent a good few hours each day brushing up on their sword craft

'Just be careful to plant your feet,' Rufina said. 'A solid position is key. If Fletcher had been paying attention, he might have done this.' She shunted Alfa in the back of the knee. The young apprentice lurched to the side and Rufina pushed down on her shoulder, but pulled her up before she collapsed.

'I was paying attention,' Fletcher said. 'She's young though. I have to give her a chance.'

Alfa and Sparks looked at one another and giggled.

The Dark Pirate was passing. 'I've said it before,' he growled, 'the battle isn't here.' He held up Fletcher's sword arm. 'It's here.' He patted Fletcher's head. 'If you can master that, you'll defeat the enemy. It's about mind, not muscle.'

'Can't hurt to be able to do this, though.' Rufina spun round, pointing her sword at the pirate's throat. Quick as a flash, he grabbed Fletcher's sword. With a flick of his wrist, he lunged forward and Rufina's weapon clattered to the floor. She spread her hands, the pirate's sword at her throat.

'Better not try that again, missy,' he said, a gleam in his eye. Rufina bowed, holding his gaze, a small smile of respect on her face. The pirate lowered his sword. 'I might carry these –' he tapped one of the pistols strapped to his belt – 'but ours is the way of peace. I've only fired them a handful of times, always to distract or to draw attention, never to wound, and certainly never to kill. As I say, the real battle is here.' He tapped his temple and then threw the sword back to Fletcher. He strode away, his cape billowing.

Rufina raised an eye at Nib. He was sitting on a hatch watching the exchange. He grinned in reply and then turned back to his work. He was whittling a small piece of wood, the deck around his feet sprinkled with shavings.

'What are you making?' asked Scoop. She was next to him, also watching the combat lesson.

Nib smiled. 'Come on. I'll show you.'

'Okay.'

As Scoop followed him across the deck, the clink of swords resumed, Sparks trying her luck against Fletcher.

They ducked under the low doorway of the captain's cabin. Knot was inside, watching over the Storyteller, Princess and Yarnbard. Since the ship had reached calmer waters, he had hardly left their sides, maintaining a daily, often nightly, vigil. He looked up.

'Anything?' asked Nib.

Knot shook his head.

Nib nodded, gravely, but then smiled. 'I've come to show Scoop our little project.'

'Oh.' Knot sounded surprised. 'Yeah. Yeah, she can see.'

Reaching down, he pulled a narrow sheet of wood from beneath his seat. It was the length of a full-grown child and mounted on a series of small wheels.

'It's a...trolley,' Scoop said, unsure.

'Yeah.' Knot beamed. 'My idea!' He pointed at the Storyteller. 'It's for them.'

Scoop looked bemused.

'It's so we can take them out more easily,' explained Nib.

'They should have sun and air – fresh air,' added Knot.

Over the past few days, Knot had taken to carrying the bodies onto the deck and laying them in the sun for an hour or two. But he was the only one strong enough to carry them alone.

'Now you –' he pointed at Scoop – 'or Master Fletcher, or even little Alfa or Sparks can take them out – on this.' He pointed at the trolley, a satisfied look on his face.

'Knot asked me to help make them,' Nib added.

'Oh, Knot.' Scoop rushed forward and threw her arms around the giant. For a moment, he looked thrown, but then he wrapped his arms around her and hugged her back. 'That's such a kind idea. And a good one too!'

'I just thought they should have air.'

'Well, I think it's brilliant!'

Knot gave a nervous laugh. 'Nobody ever said anything like that to me before.'

'Well, they should have.' Scoop turned to Nib. 'So, this is what you've been up to the past few days.'

'Yes. I've almost finished whittling the rest of the wheels.'

Knot smiled. 'Three trolleys – one for each.'

There was a knock at the door and Pierre ducked into the room, holding his cook's hat to his head. 'It is dinner time.' He grinned. 'I have come for your order, Miss Scoop, Master Nib, Monsieur Knot.'

Nib and Scoop chuckled.

'I would like roast boar!' said Nib.

'Yes, with lashings of gravy,' Scoop added. 'And a rich, apple sauce.'

'Give us a bucket of Posyshire Roasts.'

Scoop giggled. 'Seasoned with your finest herbs.'

'Of course, of course!' Pierre replied.

'And Rainbow's End Trout,'

'And Plotted Shrimp.'

Knot licked his lips.

'And for pudding...Caret Cake!'

'Yes, and Rondeau Sorbet!'

'And treacle tart!'

'And your finest Jotted Cream!'

'Aha!' Pierre kissed the air. 'You shall have a feast fit for kings and queens. Dinner is served.' He held his fingers to his lips and kissed the air again, before ducking back through the door.

'I don't understand,' Knot said. 'He always asks, but he only ever serves gruel.'

Nib laughed. 'It's a game, Knot. I think he's trying to keep our spirits up. It can't be easy being cook on a ship where food is in such short supply.'

'Oh.' Knot looked disappointed. 'But, I wanted treacle tart.'

'I'm sure you'll get some...eventually.'

Knot was about to reply when there was a cry from outside. 'Land ahoy!'

Nib glanced at Scoop. 'We're here.'

They rushed out. The rest of the crew were gathering around Mr Snooze, who was staring at a slither of land on the horizon, no thicker than the side of a coin.

'The Basillica Isles,' whispered Scoop.

'Yes,' Nib replied. 'This is where the fun starts.'

Above his head, a large, black bird came to rest on the rigging. It had been following the ship, leaving enough distance to remain unseen. It fixed its eyes on the land ahead and let out a low, satisfied caw.

Chapter 10

Cathedral City

The crew gathered on deck. They were dressed in an array of mottled cloaks and wide-brimmed hats. Fletcher and Nib wore bushy, fake beards; the women carried sacks of fabric; Knot was dragging a large, wooden chest; and the Dark Pirate carried a staff.

Sparks tripped over her cloak and cursed under her breath. 'It's too long,' she said.

'Hitch it up like this.' Nib helped her tie it higher.

Fletcher huffed. 'You should try wearing one of these. The hair keeps getting in my mouth.'

'What's that?' Alfa grinned. 'I couldn't quite hear.'

Fletcher glared at her. 'Are these really necessary?' he asked the pirate.

'They are. We need to look like pilgrim traders. If they realise you're from Fullstop Island we'll be searched.'

Freddo, Pierre and the Boatswain stepped back and admired the disguises. The Dark Pirate had ordered that they and Mr Snooze stay on the ship.

The Boatswain laughed. 'I haven't seen such a bunch of ne'er-do-wells since I visited the Market of Miracles on Great Furnace. You'll fit in perfectly.'

Freddo tried to adjust Fletcher's beard. 'You wear it like this,' he said, pointing at his own. Fletcher looked up, his beard still wonky. What with his overlong cloak and big hat, he looked quite a sight. Freddo burst out laughing. It was infectious. Before long, the whole crew were doubled over.

'It's not funny,' said Fletcher, sulkily.

The Boatswain wiped a tear from his eye. 'You're not standing where I am, laddie.'

'The boy's right,' the Dark Pirate barked. 'This is a dangerous mission. I hope you haven't forgotten we're about to walk right into the heart of Red Hawk territory. This is the Falcon stronghold. We need our wits about us. Travellers from Fullstop Island are not welcomed here. And since Falk's alliance with these islands, the Storyteller has been declared an enemy. If they realise who we are, and who we have aboard this ship, the Hawks won't hesitate to shoot on sight.'

The laughter died away.

'I want to bring a full crew back,' the pirate finished.

Scoop studied the land. It was different to Fullstop Island. There were no rugged cliffs. Instead, a pale beach sloped up to arid hills, spotted with bushes and squat trees. Where the hills dipped down, a warren of tents and ramshackle huts spilled onto the beach. Behind, a city of golden domes and spires glistened in the sun. The harbour bustled with frigates and fishing boats, traders from places as far flung as the Furnace Islands and the Storyless States arriving to sell their wares at the famous Basillican markets.

The pirate moved across to the Boatswain. 'You know what to do if we're not back by sunset?'

The Boatswain nodded.

'Good. Then, let's make for shore.'

* * *

The crew travelled across the beach in nervous hush, every so often whispering and pointing at the magnificent city that rose beyond the village of tents. A large, black bird hopped after them.

Ragged children buzzed around them, offering scraps of rope, old coins and charm necklaces. The pirate had instructed them not to speak to the children or to give anything, but Scoop's heart went out to them. They looked so hungry.

'Here,' she said quietly, giving one of them an apple she'd been handed with her lunchtime rations. 'Don't tell anyone...' she began, but the child ran away, shouting excitedly, holding the apple high like a trophy. Before Scoop knew it, the crew were surrounded. A pack of urchins, arms outstretched, pressed in around her.

The pirate swung round, his staff raised. He bellowed in a language Scoop didn't understand and the children scattered, squawking like birds.

'Who did that,' he barked. 'Who gave the apple?'

Scoop raised her hand. 'I just thought...'

The Dark Pirate rounded on her. 'What did I tell you?' he snarled. Scoop stepped back. She'd never seen him look so angry. It scared her.

'I'm sorry,' she stuttered.

'Are you trying to get us all killed?'

She shook her head.

The pirate turned to the rest of the crew. 'You are to do *exactly* as I say from now on, do you understand?' They nodded. 'If you do as I instruct, we might just get through this alive.'

He stormed into the jungle of tents. Scoop and the rest of the crew followed silently.

They made their way along a dirt track that led through the heart of the makeshift encampment. Every so often, through the tarpaulins pulled between the shacks, Scoop caught a glimpse of the cathedral domes. The air was close, heavy with the smell of fried fish, sweet meats and waste water. Ramshackle huts of corrugated iron and scrap wood were squashed next to each other. Market stalls faced the track, boxes overflowing with spiked shells, grimacing fish and strange insects. Behind them, Scoop caught sight of camp beds and broken chairs. There were people everywhere: sailors drinking at roadside bars, merchants striking deals, pilgrims leading livestock along the carriageway. A single-toothed old man held out a handful of charm necklaces.

'Protect from Fade,' he said, his language broken. 'Protect from Fade!'

'Protection from the Fade?' Scoop whispered to Fletcher. 'Do you think that's what we saw with the Fable Fish – the Fade? Do you think other things are fading too?'

Fletcher nodded, not wanting to speak through his beard.

The pirate stopped by one of the stalls and whispered to a boy with a shell stitched into his ragged shirt. The boy nodded and disappeared into the forest of tents. The black bird that had been following them landed on a nearby water pump and watched with beady eyes.

Across the track, there was a commotion. A group of Red Hawks pushed their way into one of the huts. There was yelling. A baby began to cry and a moment later, the soldiers emerged, dragging a man. He was hunched over, pleading with them in the language the pirate had spoken. A woman appeared at the door, her face smudged with tears, the baby in her arms. She yelled after the soldiers as they dragged the man away.

'Come on,' the pirate said, 'we need to get out of here.'

Quickly, the crew pushed along the path. Scoop could see other Red Hawks questioning traders. They slipped through a narrow passage between a gambling den and a cluttered shrine. A few minutes later, they emerged into a small square, a dolphin fountain at its centre. It was the opposite to the village of tents in every way. The buildings were made of sandstone. They were tall and stately, decorated with pale blue frescos. Little cafés lined the plaza, their patrons dressed in bright clothes, some of them carrying parasols. The sound of polite conversation mingled with the quiet splash of water, making the square feel spacious and light. One side was dominated by the entrance to a cathedral.

'Whoa,' Scoop said, looking up at the spire. It loomed over them, carved with rank upon rank of statues. It made her dizzy.

An ornate door opened into the basilica. Inside, the air

was thick with incense. Sunlight passed through stained-glass windows, dancing on a gilded altar. Heavy golden lamps hung from an exquisitely painted ceiling. And the floor was polished marble. But, at odds with this, temporary scaffolding had been constructed along the walls. It held rows of beds. The structure must have been fifty bunks high and the length of the cathedral itself. It looked like a hive. The beds contained hundreds, perhaps thousands, of bodies. It was a shocking sight. From the door, a river of flowers, candles and pictures cascaded down, spilling onto the square in a pool of petals and light.

'It's a shrine,' said the Dark Pirate, reading the look on Scoop's face, 'a memorial to those taken by the sickness. And this is only one of the cathedrals. There are hundreds in the city and they're all filled with bodies. The sickness hit the Basillica Isles before it reached Fullstop Island. They have suffered greatly.'

Scoop scanned the bustling cafés. 'But it seems so busy…so alive.'

'The city is a shadow of its former self. In its days of glory, it thronged with processions, pageants, thriving markets, multitudes of pilgrims and travellers from across the oceans. Music spilled from these cathedrals, and artists painted and sculpted the most exquisite work. The theatricality of its rituals, its costumes and choirs, were a sight to behold. It was truly impressive, even to someone not inclined to pay attention to such shows of wealth and power. But even I could not fail to be impressed by its majesty. Now, the city creaks under the weight of its own edifice. It's decaying from the inside. The sickness, the displaced peoples who've sought shelter here, and the incapacity of many of its priests and patriarchs, has turned the city into a powder keg. The smallest spark could ignite revolution. That's why the Red Hawks have been given so much power and why they exert it so brutally. The Falcon Household are scared.'

A woman appeared behind the pirate. Sensing her presence, he spun round, his hand moving to his cutlass. But when he saw who it was, a broad grin broke across his face.

'Martha! It's so good to see you.'

'As it is you…' Martha embraced him, burying her head into his shoulder. Scoop thought she heard her speak a name, but it was muffled.

'You got my message from the boy then?' the pirate asked.

'I did. Everything is ready.' Martha took the pirate by the shoulders and examined him. 'Look at you. You've not changed a bit.'

'Perhaps not my features, but I have in here.' The pirate thumped his chest. 'I'm always changing, growing I hope, being enlarged.'

'You haven't changed in that you can't take a compliment!' Martha laughed. 'Always too serious!' Her smile was infectious. Despite the worry lines on her face, she was pretty. She wore a long, flowing skirt and a bright blue top, fastened with a shell broach. Her hair was curly and brown and she wore vivid lipstick. 'Anyway,' she said, glancing across the square, 'we mustn't stay here. You can introduce me to your friends when we're somewhere safe.' She smiled at Scoop, acknowledging the crew in turn. Then, taking the pirate's arm, Martha led them away.

* * *

At the other side of the square, an old woman watched, peeking from the folds of her hood. Keeping her distance, she followed the crew through vine-covered pergolas and cathedral colonnades. They passed up some wide stone steps, flanked with statues. After emerging from one of the crowded silk markets, they turned onto a narrow side street between two rows of tenements. Halfway along, they disappeared into one of the houses. A wicked grin twisted Grizelda's face. Finding the nearest Red Hawk, she curtseyed and proceeded to tell him who had arrived at the island and where they might be found. The soldier's moustache twitched as he contemplated the reward he would receive for informing his superiors of the Black Horizon's whereabouts, of the traitor's hideout, and of the Storyteller's presence on the Basillica Isles.

Chapter 11

Martha

Martha's home was a makeshift wooden cabin on the flat roof of a sandstone tenement. The next building along was three storeys higher, creating a corner in which the little shack nestled. The tenement stood next to one of the narrow river-streets that criss-crossed the city, the churn of water a constant thrum. It had once been the home of a wealthy patrician, vestiges of grandeur still visible. But the old house had been converted into apartments and was now occupied by a multitude of characters from across the Oceans of Rhyme: pale-skinned women from the Starlight Isles, swarthy men from the Furnace Islands, and everything in between. There were even camp beds squashed into the hallways. The house buzzed with half-spoken languages, its air heavy with the scent of foods from distant shores.

To get to the cabin, the crew had to climb through an apartment window. A bald man gave them a friendly wave, but didn't seem to understand their apologies or thanks. As they crawled onto the roof, Martha motioned to some tall, wicker baskets and told the Dark Pirate they were supplies for the Black Horizon.

The crew squeezed into Martha's cabin and she began to bustle about, preparing food and filling large earthenware jugs with water. The room was crowded but in a cosy way, the floor strewn with woven rugs and patterned cushions. There was a bed in the corner, a knitted blanket thrown over it. Dreamcatchers, ceramic pots and dried herbs hung from the ceiling, and the smell of freshly baking bread wafted from a large, clay oven. In the centre of the room a low, wooden table stood. Despite the lack of space, Martha ushered the crew around it.

Fletcher sat on the floor, cross-legged, squeezing himself between Alfa and Nib. Alfa was reclining, her elbow on the table. Fletcher nudged her and she shuffled up a little but was still uncomfortably close.

The Dark Pirate instructed Knot to start loading provisions from the wicker baskets. Knot busied himself, moving in and out, filling the large chest and packs with salted meats, apples, onions, cheese, sea biscuits, canvas and thread, lantern oil and sundries for the ship.

'You must be hungry,' Martha said, setting a bowl of steaming stew on the table. It smelled rich and sweet.

'Famished!' Fletcher replied.

Martha handed out wooden bowls. 'Go on then. What are you waiting for? Tuck in!'

Fletcher didn't need to be asked twice. Taking the ladle, he served himself a large portion.

'Leave enough for the rest of us,' Alfa whispered.

'There's plenty for everyone,' Martha said, setting down a freshly baked loaf of bread. 'There's more where that came from.'

'See!' Fletcher reached across and tore a large chunk of bread.

Alfa glared and shuffled up, squashing him again. He wriggled about, trying to push her back.

'Will you two stop that!' Nib said. 'You'll knock the table!' He raised an eyebrow at Fletcher and winked.

Fletcher's face flushed. 'You'd better tell her,' he muttered. But he stopped pushing and tucked into his food. Alfa caught Sparks's eye, and they giggled.

The Dark Pirate sat at the end of the table, reclining. 'What a feast, Martha. Fit for a king, as always.'

Martha smiled. 'Always for you.'

The Dark Pirate looked away. Was he embarrassed? He was obviously close to Martha.

'So, how do you two know each other?' asked Scoop.

The pirate frowned.

Martha laughed. 'Well, there's a question.' She laid a hand on the pirate's shoulder. 'Do you want to answer, or shall I?'

'You were always better at telling stories,' he answered, looking down. He began to eat.

'Well...' Martha sat at the table with them. 'Where to start...?' She thought for a moment. 'Before Leo—'

'Don't use that name.' The pirate looked up, his spoon clattering in the bowl.

Martha looked thrown. 'But it is your name. I can't tell the story without—'

'Dark Pirates do not use their given names. You know that full well.'

'You can't pretend there was no before. You are who you are.'

'I'm not pretending. I fully accept who I am, past and present. But when I vowed to forsake the ways of the land, I chose to lay down that name. I chose to identify with the sea, with something bigger than any individual identity.'

A trace of sadness passed across Martha's face. 'Then what should I call you?'

'*Him* or *the Dark Pirate*. Anything but *that*.'

'What about *my friend*?'

The pirate met her eye. 'Yes. That will always be true.'

A smile flicked across Martha's face. 'Well then...before *my friend* was a Dark Pirate—'

'I'd assumed he'd always been a Dark Pirate,' interrupted Scoop. 'I mean, we've never known him any other way.'

Martha laughed. 'Oh no. No, he certainly had a life before.'

The pirate carried on eating, as though he were not being talked about.

Martha continued: 'Before my friend was a Dark Pirate, he lived just a stone's throw from where we are now.'

Scoop interrupted again. 'You lived on the Basillica Isles?'

Fletcher sighed.

'I did,' the pirate said. 'I was born here.'

'You're Basillican?'

'I am. Or at least I was, before I left the land.'

'We both were,' Martha said. 'Well...I still am. We were childhood friends. Leo—' She stopped herself. '*My friend* lived two houses from here. I grew up in this house.'

'She lived inside, back then,' the pirate added, 'before the house was given for the care of refugees and the homeless, before she moved into this cabin.'

'Yes, it was different back then. My parents owned the house.'

'All of it?' asked Scoop.

'Yes, the whole house. I come from one of the oldest Basillican families, a very wealthy family.'

The pirate slurped his stew. 'Her parents used to throw grand parties for the great and the good.'

'Do you remember? You used to steal the canapés.'

'I do. Who could forget your father's farfetched stories. And his laugh. It was like the bellow of a walrus.'

'Ha!' Martha looked delighted. 'Yes.' A faraway look passed over her face. 'He was a generous man. They were good times, weren't they?'

'They were. But they were a lifetime ago.'

'Yes, before things changed.'

'What changed?' asked Scoop.

'The Falcon family. They gradually consolidated their power. So many people came here to find a better life, drawn by the city's wealth. The Basillicans began to resent those who came, to fear them. Conflicts broke out, ugly scenes, unbecoming of this great city. And with fear came the clamour for a strong leader, someone to protect the city's wealth, its status, to return it to its great past. Gradually, people turned to the Falcons and their militia, the Red Hawks. Slowly, they undermined the city's traditions of shared decision making, the way of the shell—'

'I've seen people wearing shells,' interrupted Scoop, 'stitched to their clothing.'

'Yes. It's a sign of the old ways. The shell is a symbol of protection for the weak, one of the city's founding principles.

Sadly, not one shared by the Falcon family or the Red Hawks. Many still hold the old principles though, and hope one day we might return to them.' Martha sipped her drink. 'Well, by the time my friend and I came of age, young and idealistic as we were—'

'Don't,' the pirate interrupted. He looked uneasy.

Martha turned to him. 'I'm at peace with all that has come to pass. I wouldn't change the way things are, the choices we made. We've both taken our stand in different ways. I don't regret the people we've become, even though we've both lost many things in the process. I think your companions should know the man they travel with. This is a story you would never tell yourself, so allow me this one indulgence – please.'

The pirate paused, his spoon midway to his mouth. Reluctantly, he nodded.

Martha gave him a sad smile. 'By the time we had both come of age, we had become fond of each other – very fond. We had imagined a life together, a home, children...' Her voice trailed away.

Scoop stared at Martha. 'You were...'

'We were betrothed, yes. But, for the very reasons I loved him – I still love him – my friend decided he was not able to settle for such a life. At the time, the city had all but collapsed. The village of tents you travelled through had begun to form. The Red Hawks were given complete authority. My friend decided that something had to be done, that we could not continue as if nothing had changed. And I agreed. He decided to embark on a journey I could not share, to forsake the ways of the land, the wealth and status he'd been given by birth, and take to the sea. He decided to become a Dark Pirate. He chose a lonely call, one I respected, one I respect now, even if at the time, it broke my heart.'

A heavy silence fell.

The Dark Pirate began to speak. 'I...'

'You don't need to say anything,' Martha whispered. 'You did what you thought was right. *We* did what we thought was right.' She looked back at the crew. 'That day I decided that when this house came into my possession I would move here, into the old cabin we used to play in as children. I decided to open my home for the care of those in need. I've lived this way ever since. It's been my own attempt to shed my status and live for something better. I don't regret it for a moment. I've been showered with riches, so many good friends, such beautiful community...'

As Martha was speaking, there was a whistle outside. She flinched. 'Stay here,' she said, her manner changing. Rising, she dashed out of the cabin.

The pirate put down his spoon, his features hardening. 'Get ready. I think we may need to—'

'They're coming,' Martha said, rushing back in.

The pirate rose. 'Quickly. We need to move.'

'Who's coming?' Scoop asked, getting to her feet.

'Red Hawks,' Martha replied. 'Someone must have told them you're here. You're in danger. You need to leave. If you're caught—'

She shot round, startled by shouting from the house.

'Quickly. They'll be here any moment.'

The crew scrambled for their cloaks, picking up their packs. Knot lifted one end of the chest, dragging it onto the rooftop.

As they were leaving, the pirate turned. 'Come with us,' he said to Martha. 'I know the sea is a hard life. I cannot offer all I may have hoped, but—'

'I can't!' interrupted Martha. 'My home is here.'

The sun was beginning to set, making the sandstone garish red. The pirate paused, but then nodded. Scoop could feel the tenderness between them, the ache of being pulled in different directions, the ghost of a hope, a desire lost.

'That way,' said Martha. She signalled away from the window. The sound of a scuffle echoed through it. 'Go around that corner and through the second window. The stairs there lead directly to the river-street below. I'll delay them as long as I can.'

'No, Martha. I won't have you put your life at risk—'

'Don't argue. This is my house. I deal with Red Hawks all the time. I know how to handle them.'

'Martha, be careful—'

'Go, will you! I will not allow you to be caught – not here!'

For a moment, the two old friends gazed at one another. Then, Martha planted a kiss on the pirate's cheek. 'Go,' she whispered. 'I'll be here next time you visit. If you don't leave now, you'll be putting your crew at risk.'

The sound of heavy footsteps echoed through the window.

The pirate gripped Martha's hand for a moment. Then, releasing it, he turned and dashed away.

Chapter 12

A Dark Day

Scoop darted after the pirate. She glanced back. Through the window, she could see a Red Hawk arguing with the bald man they'd passed earlier. The soldier knocked him out of the way.

'What are you doing in my house?' Martha demanded, blocking the window.

'We've been informed there are fugitives here.'

'Nonsense! Everyone in this house has the correct papers. I work with the authorities. You know that full well.'

'I have my orders. We've been told to make a full search. Move out of the way.'

'No!'

The argument continued as Scoop rounded the corner and clambered through the window to the river-street.

The crew ran down the stairs, their boots pounding. Scoop zigzagged after them, jumping down a few steps at a time. When they reached the bottom, the pirate pulled open a rickety door and they tumbled onto a narrow ledge. Knot began to drag the chest along it, Rufina, Alfa and Sparks following. Scoop was about to follow when a shot rang out. She froze. The blast echoed along the narrow corridor. A look of horror spread across the pirate's face. Swinging round, he pushed past Scoop and ran back into the building.

'What's he doing?' cried Rufina. 'We have to get out of here!'

'He's going back,' called Scoop. 'He's going back for her!'

Nib met Fletcher's eye. 'Come on!' The two of them pushed past Scoop, dashing after the pirate. 'You carry on,' Nib called over his shoulder. 'We'll meet you further up.'

'Be quick!' yelled Rufina.

Fletcher followed Nib back into the building. They bounded

up the stairs. They could hear the pirate ahead. He was quick, but the boys were agile. They caught up to him just as he was climbing back onto the rooftop. Nib grabbed his cloak but the pirate struggled free and disappeared. The boys clambered after him, desperately trying to catch up. As he rounded the corner to Martha's cabin, Nib managed to seize his arm. The pirate tried to shake him off, but Fletcher lunged forward and caught his cloak. The boys hauled him back.

'Let me go,' he snarled.

'No! We need to get out of here,' Nib hissed. 'You're not thinking straight.'

'I won't leave her!'

'Martha wanted us to get out of here,' Fletcher gasped. 'She wanted us to help the Storyteller.'

At the Storyteller's name, the pirate's struggle weakened. The boys pressed their advantage, grabbing him further up the arm and dragging him back. But with a huff, he yanked them forward. The three of them stumbled out around the corner.

A group of Red Hawks stood in a tight knot outside Martha's cabin. Fletcher could see a bright skirt through their legs. One of the soldiers shifted and Martha came into view. She was sprawled on the ground, her body twisted. A pool of dark blood was slowly spreading.

'She's been shot,' whispered Fletcher.

'No.' The pirate's voice was hoarse.

Martha wasn't moving.

'She's dead,' Nib said, blankly.

'No!' The pirate moved forward, but the boys grabbed him.

'She's gone!' Nib hissed, pulling him back. 'There's nothing we can do! We need to get out of here!'

The pirate struggled, but his strength had gone. He thrashed, but Fletcher and Nib managed to pull him back.

As they disappeared around the corner again, one of the Red Hawks looked up. 'There,' he barked. 'It's them!'

Without thinking, Fletcher and Nib ran. Dazed, the pirate followed.

They flung themselves back through the window and hurtled down the stairs. If the Red Hawks had shot Martha, they certainly wouldn't spare them. Fletcher could hear soldiers scrambling through the window above. Glancing up, he saw a face appear through the railings.

'There!' a soldier shouted. A musket appeared. Crack! The shot vibrated through Fletcher's body, the plaster next to him exploding.

The threat seemed to shake the pirate into action. He grabbed Fletcher, pulling him to the side of the stairs. The three of them leapt down. Reaching the door, they threw it open. There was another shot as they dashed onto the ledge.

Scrambling along the narrow walkway, Fletcher's foot slipped, almost sending him into the water. Nib caught his arm and they hurried on, their hearts thumping. The tenements rose either side of them, their tops stained red with the setting sun. Any moment, Red Hawks would emerge onto the path and there would be nowhere to hide. Behind them, Fletcher heard the door bang open.

'Halt!' one of the soldiers shouted. 'Halt, or we fire!'

Fletcher heard them raise their muskets.

An arm reached out and grabbed him. 'Quick, over here!' He was dragged onto a second river-street that cut away to the side. There was a shot and a bullet whizzed past. He turned to see Rufina staring at him. She released his arm.

'Thanks,' he panted.

Below, a motorised gondola bobbed on the water. Knot, Alfa, Sparks and Scoop were already on it, the chest and packs stowed at one end. A long-faced ferryman stood at the tiller, a shell pinned to his hat.

'Quick, give me your pack,' Rufina said. Grabbing it, she threw it down to Knot. 'Now, get in.'

Behind, the sound of heavy boots was growing louder.

Fletcher jumped into the gondola, helping Nib down. The boat rocked dangerously as the pirate jumped aboard. As Rufina leapt down, the ferryman started the motor.

The little boat zipped away as the Red Hawks appeared.

'Duck,' yelled Nib.

Fletcher threw himself facedown as a shot cracked out. The blast ricocheted from the narrow walls, followed quickly by another. Fletcher could feel Scoop pressed next to him, her breathing heavy.

With a loud buzz, the boat tipped to one side. There was another shot, but it was muffled. The pirate stood up. 'We're out of range now,' he said.

Fletcher pushed himself to his feet. He was dirty and wet. They'd turned onto another narrow channel. The Red Hawks were out of sight but he could still hear them shouting.

He looked at Scoop. His thoughts were reflected in her eyes – they were lucky to be alive.

'We're not out of danger yet,' the pirate growled. 'Don't relax. They will commandeer the next vessel they see. The city is cut through with river-streets. Keep your eyes peeled. We don't know where they might emerge.'

'Where to?' the ferryman asked.

'Take us to South Bay.'

'South Bay? But I saw your ship at port.'

'I instructed those left aboard to weigh anchor when the sun set. They'll meet us to the south of the island. I had a feeling we'd need to make a hasty escape.' The pirate sat down, his head in his hands. 'We should never have come here. I knew it was a mistake to stop for provisions.'

Nobody replied. Scoop wished she could say something to comfort him, but there were no words.

For the rest of the journey, everyone sat in silence. Every time they crossed another river-street, they looked along it for a flash of red, for a boat of soldiers in pursuit. But no Red Hawks emerged.

Finally, after passing through the backwaters of the fishing district and navigating some foul-smelling tunnels, the river-street opened into a quiet bay. The sight that met them lifted Scoop's heart a little. The Black Horizon was silhouetted against the last of the setting sun, its sails billowing. The gondola rocked heavily as it pushed out into the sea. The ferry buzzed towards the ship, buffeted by the breeze. Scoop looked back at the golden domes. On the beach, a single Red Hawk was watching them. He turned, running back towards the city. Scoop knew it wouldn't be long before he alerted his superiors of their whereabouts. If they knew the Storyteller was aboard the Black Horizon, they would hunt them across the Oceans of Rhyme. The clock was ticking; they had to make their escape.

Chapter 13

Horizon's Broken

Fletcher had long heard tales of the Basillica Isles. The domed city was famous across the Oceans of Rhyme. He never imagined coming here would be filled with such sadness. Behind him, Freddo, Pierre, the Boatswain and Mr Snooze had just been informed of Martha's death. A heavy gloom hung over the ship.

Fletcher looked up to see a large, black bird perch on the rigging. *Strange,* he thought, *to see a bird like that out here at sea.* But he was distracted and thought no more of it.

That night, the crew slept in shifts, taking turns to keep watch as they sailed through the darkness. As the first glimmer of dawn seeped across the grey sky, there was a cry from the Boatswain.

'Ship ahoy!'

Fletcher, who has been on duty through the first watches of the morning, ran over to him. He looked out, bleary eyed. The dawn was insipid, banks of heavy rain smudging the sky, but through the murk, he could see a speck on the horizon. The Boatswain handed him the telescope. Raising it to his eye, Fletcher could make out the black-winged insignia of the Falcon crest against red flags flying from the ship's stern and masthead. It was a galleon, three masts in full sail. And it was fully armed, rows of cannon lining its sides.

Fletcher lowered the telescope. 'Red Hawks?'

'Yes. And it's likely they'll catch us before nightfall. We have little chance of escaping under cover of dark and no chance at all in open combat. They'll blow us out the water.'

'What will we do?'

'I don't know. I need to speak to *him.*'

Fletcher gave the Boatswain an apprehensive look. The Dark Pirate's mood had steadily worsened. This wasn't a good time to bring him bad news.

* * *

Fletcher was relieved from duty by Nib as the sun languished in the morning sky. Only a couple of hours had passed since the Red Hawk galleon had been sighted, but it was gaining on them.

There were mutterings aboard. The pirate was refusing to receive counsel. He was so angry they'd stopped instead of heading straight for the Threshold, he was now refusing to countenance any other option. There had been raised voices and he'd sent the Boatswain away with a flea in his ear. The usually good-natured fellow now thumped about the ship, a thunderous look on his face. The pirate also refused to accept the Red Hawk galleon was gaining on them, despite clear evidence to the contrary.

'He's going to get us all killed!' Fletcher whispered to Alfa. 'Somebody needs to do something.'

Sparks was listening. 'He's grieving,' she said.

'Maybe he is. But we'll all be grieving soon – for our own lives!'

She shook her head and stormed off.

'What's up with her?'

'She's upset about Martha,' Alfa replied.

'We're all upset about Martha. That doesn't mean we should throw away our critical faculties. We're going to be blown out of the water by Red Hawks. Doesn't anybody care!'

'Of course we care, Fletcher. What a stupid thing to say! But what can we do?'

'I don't know! We need the pirate to snap out of this malaise and come up with a plan!'

* * *

By midday, the Red Hawk ship had closed the distance further. The Falcon flags were now visible to the naked eye. As the sun climbed to its highest point, causing dramatic rays to shoot through the stormy clouds, Sparks emerged from below deck. She was dragging Freddo by the arm. He was carrying his accordion. She walked to the centre of the deck and stood in front of the mast.

She cleared her throat. 'I'd like to say something,' she called.

Nobody paid any attention.

Shaking her head, she pulled something from her coat.

'Woah!' Freddo said, stepping away. 'What are you doing? Be care—'

Before he could finish, Sparks raised her hand and fired the pistol she was holding.

Freddo ducked. The force of the gun knocked Sparks from her feet.

Everybody spun round, hands raised to protect themselves. They stared at Sparks. She lay sprawled on the deck, the pistol smoking in her hand.

The pirate bounded out. 'What the hell is going on!'

Sparks scrambled to her feet, obviously taken aback by the power of the blast. 'I was just—'

The pirate rounded on her. 'Is that mine?'

'Yes, I was just—'

'You stupid girl!' He grabbed the pistol, knocking her back to the ground again. 'You could have killed someone.'

'I fired it upwards,' said Sparks, her voice trembling.

The pirate pointed the butt of the pistol into her face. 'Never, ever take anything of mine again! Do you understand?' Sparks looked terrified. 'I have half a mind to lock you in the hold! Get back to your post before I do!' He turned. 'That goes for the rest of you, too! Get back to work! I will not have this ship put at risk!'

Behind him, Sparks got to her feet. 'I just wanted everyone

to listen!' she screamed. 'I have something to say – something important! Why don't you listen to me?' Her face was red. 'I have something to say,' she said again, trying to control her voice.

'What?' the pirate barked. 'What's so important you put the lives of my crew at risk?'

'Nobody was at risk and you know it.'

The pirate stared at her. 'Just say what you have to say and make it quick.'

Sparks closed her eyes for a moment and breathed deeply. 'I think we need to remember Martha.'

'What?'

'I think we need to mark her passing, remember her life. We need to allow ourselves to mourn.'

The pirate shook his head and ran his fingers through his hair. 'We don't have time.' He pointed at the Red Hawk galleon. 'Do you think they're going to stop their pursuit while we indulge in such sentimentality? We can't. We have to keep going.'

'It won't take long,' Sparks said. 'I've written something, something to help us mark her passing, something to honour her.'

The pirate frowned. 'You've written something?'

'Yes.' She pulled a piece of paper from her pocket. 'It's a song. It's not that good. But I didn't have much time. Alfa and I are Apprentice Spell-Shakers. We've learnt lots of songs of transformation from across the Oceans of Rhyme. I've written some new words to the tune, *The Breaking Day* – the song the mermaids of Dawn Rock sing each morning. Do you know it?'

The pirate nodded.

'If it's alright, I've asked Freddo to play it? I'll sing.' She looked around the ship. 'And if anyone wants to join me, they can. I'll sing it twice…but you don't have to,' she added.

The pirate nodded again, unable to speak.

'I'm nervous now,' Sparks muttered.

The Boatswain stepped forward and laid a hand on her

shoulder. 'It's a remarkable thing you've done. Don't be nervous.'

She gave a timid smile.

Slowly, the company came forward, leaving the things they'd been doing. Pierre took his hat off.

Sparks nodded at Freddo. Quietly, he picked up his accordion. The bellows hissed as he opened them. Gently, he played a single note. It carried through the air, piercing the silence, bittersweet.

Sparks held up the paper. Her hands were trembling. Tentatively, she began to sing, her voice fragile.

'Her light has set,
The sky's jewels darken,
Sea spills into night,
Horizon's broken.'

The song cut through Scoop, touching her deeply. Sparks was so open, her voice raw. It was impossible to hide. Scoop brought Martha to mind. She closed her eyes and imagined her: her warmth, her beauty, her strength and passion. She thought of her relationship with the pirate; the way they had chosen to sacrifice their own dreams for something bigger, something they hoped would be better. She smiled as she remembered Martha's house, the colours, the smells, the beautiful diversity, the love that seeped through the fabric of her home.

'The sky's a map,
But the stars are ravens,
We're lost at sea,
And we are broken.

Dreams filled her night,
Her life was spoken,
A better word,
To heal the broken.'

Sparks' voice swelled. Alfa stepped across to her and reading the words joined her friend, the two girls weaving delicate harmonies.

The pirate began to sob. The Boatswain moved to stand next to him. Together, the two men cried.

'Her thorn inside
Is our hearts' token
That all's not lost.
Her day has broken.'

Tentatively, the company began to sing together, their voices fractured at first, but growing in confidence.

When the song ended, they stood quietly, listening to the slap of the waves on the hull. Sparks folded the paper and put it back in her pocket. She looked around, nervously.

The gloomy atmosphere that had hung over the ship had dissipated. Instead, Scoop felt cold, clear, stillness. The company's grief was palpable, but somehow the song had given a sense of strength, of clarity.

The pirate wiped the tears from his eyes. 'Thank you,' he said. Sparks gave a shallow nod. 'I'm sorry I—'

'You have nothing to be sorry about,' she interrupted.

Pausing, the pirate nodded.

He turned to the rest of the crew. 'I'm sorry for being stubborn. It's clear we will not outrun the Falcon ship. We do need to change course.' He looked at the Boatswain, apologetically. There was a murmur of approval. 'I do have an alternative plan, if you'll hear me, but there's no easy answer to our predicament. Whatever we do, risks will have to be taken.'

'Better to take a risk than to sleepwalk into danger,' the Boatswain said.

'Yes,' the pirate agreed. 'I'm sorry for not listening to your counsel earlier. We've wasted much needed time.'

The Boatswain lifted his hand to dismiss the apology.

Freddo stepped forward. 'What do you think we should we do, then?'

All eyes turned to the pirate. A wave slapped the hull and he stumbled. Behind him, the Red Hawk galleon came into view. It was gaining on them. Whatever the plan, they would have to put it into action quickly. The Black Horizon would have to take its chances, whatever the risk.

Chapter 14

Curse of the Southern Ocean

'In my opinion, there is only one choice,' the pirate said. 'We must change course and head directly towards the South Bookend Isles.'

There was a murmur of disquiet.

'Yes, I know the stories,' he said, seeing the crew's reaction. 'I know the people of the Basillica Isles fear them – and with good reason. But their *fear* is our best weapon. As we sail south, there will be unrest aboard the Falcon vessel. The crew won't want to enter the Southern Ocean. I've seen mutinies aboard ships that have tried to cross those waters. I believe the Red Hawk commanders will give up the chase, in order to maintain discipline aboard their vessel. They'll hope to resume the pursuit west of the Bookend Isles.'

The Boatswain looked grave, but nodded.

Sparks spoke up, obviously feeling emboldened. 'Um...If you don't mind me asking, why do the people of the Basillica Isles fear the Southern Ocean?'

The pirate considered for a moment. 'The South Bookend Isles mark the edge of our world. Just as Mortales pass through the North Bookend Isles as they enter the world, so the south is a place of leaving. Beyond them are only the Un-Dead Lands and then, infinite sea. Very few have ever sailed into the Southern Ocean of their own accord. But the stories that have found their way back from those who have, speak of...' the pirate paused, searching for words, '...an enchantment that troubles the waters.'

'An enchantment?'

'Well, records are patchy, often unintelligible, but those who return speak of being caught in a sort of...time vortex.' The pirate stopped. He looked uncomfortable.

'What does that mean?' prompted Fletcher.

'It's hard to say. Those who've returned are...how should I put it?'

'Just say it. We need to know what we're sailing into.'

'They are changed.'

'How?'

'They're older. In some cases, many years older and their minds...well, many have found their testimony easy to dismiss.'

Sparks shifted uneasily. 'An ageing curse?'

'In a way, perhaps. I think time itself operates differently there. Even if a vessel strays into the Southern Ocean for a matter of days, on returning, those aboard look and feel as though years have passed, their beards long, their skin grey. Because of this, the Southern Ocean is feared. It holds a solemn place in the mind of Basillicans, who view it with a mixture of holy awe and primal fear. They launch their dead into that sea and carry charms to protect against it. They do not venture there willingly. And Red Hawks are no exception.'

Fletcher coughed. 'But you're suggesting *we* venture there?'

'I am. It's either that or wait to be blown out the water.'

'Not much of a choice, is it?'

'No, it isn't. But it's a choice we need to make.'

Fletcher sighed. 'Well, I never was fussed with being this age. And I'm not too fond of the idea of being blown out of the water, either. So, all in all, I guess I'm in.'

'That's the spirit,' the Boatswain said. 'I'm in too.'

'And me,' said Alfa.

Sparks frowned. 'You always want to walk headlong into danger, don't you?'

Alfa grinned. 'What's life without a little adventure?'

Sparks shook her head and sighed. 'Okay, me too.'

One by one, the crew gave their assent. It was unanimous.

'Then it's agreed,' said the pirate. 'Set our course for the South Bookend Isles, Boatswain.'

'Right away, sir.'

Sparks raised her hand. 'Um, how long will it take to get there?'

'A matter of hours,' the Boatswain answered. 'We've been sailing west, along the northern edge of the Southern Ocean. We need only adjust our course a little and we'll cross into it. Then we'll see what the Red Hawks do.'

'We will,' said the pirate. 'And let's hope for all our sakes that I'm right and their galleon turns back.'

* * *

Over the next few hours, the crew busied themselves adjusting the ship's course. Once the new direction had been set, Scoop looked for things to occupy her. She didn't want to linger on what might happen once they crossed into the Southern Ocean.

She was scrubbing the steps to the forecastle, when she felt something like a cold wind rush through her. She straightened up, feeling nauseous.

Fletcher was passing with a bucket of water. He frowned. 'Did you feel that?'

'Yes…it was like something passed through us.'

The Dark Pirate called Fletcher. 'Or perhaps,' Fletcher said, beginning to move away, 'perhaps *we* passed through *something*.' They exchanged a nervous glance.

'You mean we just passed into the Southern Ocean?'

The pirate called Fletcher again. 'Exactly.' He dashed away.

Scoop looked around. The sea here didn't look any different. She was just about to continue her task, when there was a cry of surprise from the deck above. She looked up to where the Boatswain was studying the marine chronometer (a timepiece he used for navigation). He stepped away from it. 'That's peculiar,' he said, scratching his head.

'What is it?' Scoop asked, moving up the steps.

'See for yourself.' The Boatswain pointed at the wooden box. It was set with golden wheels and little cogs.

Scoop looked. The wheels were spinning erratically.

'They just started to turn,' the Boatswain said. 'They usually move slowly. I've never seen anything like this before.' He ran his hand through his hair.

'What do you think is making them—' Scoop began. But before she could finish, she blinked.

As she closed her eyes, she felt the cold wind rush through her again. It was stronger than before. In her mind's eye, the world flickered and began to change, speeding up. She saw the sun rise and set, the sea rage and quieten, winds strengthen and wane. She glimpsed the crew of the Black Horizon skimming across the ship, fleeting impressions, appearing and then vanishing. Sails were furled and unfurled, the deck was scrubbed, meals eaten, maps studied, lanterns lit, watches changed, all in the blink of an eye.

With a gasp, Scoop's eyes sprang open. Instantly, time slowed again. The stillness was unnerving. The world had transformed. It was night now, clear and cloudless. A high moon threw a pathway of light across the sea. Scoop stumbled backwards, looking for the Boatswain, but he'd gone. She stared at the chronometer. Its wheels were still spinning. 'What?' she said. It felt as though she'd woken from a deep sleep. Her stomach gurgled and she clutched it. She looked around, trying to make sense of what had happened. She was still on the ship, but the deck was deserted.

How's it night?

She tried to calm herself, to think rationally. *Something's going on with time, just like the pirate said.* She looked up to where she knew someone would be on watch. Nib was looking down at her from the crow's nest. His face was pale. He clutched the rails, looking weary.

'What just happened?' Scoop called up. 'A moment ago, I was

talking to the Boatswain. It was the middle of the day. We were on our way to the Southern Ocean—'

'That was days ago,' Nib interrupted. 'We entered the Southern Ocean days ago.'

'Days ago, but—'

'Listen – you won't have long before you jump again.'

'Jump?'

'Yes. From your question, I'm guessing that's the first time you've come up for air?'

'I don't know what you mean.'

'You will.'

'What are you talking about? You're scaring me.'

'I'm sorry. It's just…' Nib shook his head. 'It's hard to hold on.'

'Just tell me what's happening.'

'I don't know! It's just as the pirate warned. Somehow time is jumping. This is the third or fourth time I've surfaced – that's the best way I can describe it. A moment ago, I was studying a map with the Dark Pirate. He said we'd been sailing the Southern Ocean for days. And then the next moment, I found myself here in the crow's nest. I watched you come up from below deck.'

'Below deck? I don't remember coming up from below.' Scoop was panicking. Had she blacked out?

She felt another rush of wind. It roared. She doubled over, breathless.

The world sped past again. Her stomach lurched, as though she were being thrown forward. Frost spread across the ship and retreated, birds shot across the sky, stars appeared and then vanished, clouds skidded overhead.

Scoop opened her eyes again and gulped a big breath of icy air, coughing. She knew what Nib meant. This was like having her head forced into a vat of water, being held under and then yanked out again. It was like drowning.

She realised she was standing at the side of the Black

Horizon. Her hand was on Sparks's back. Without warning, Sparks doubled over and vomited down the side of the ship. Instinctively, Scoop rubbed her back. She couldn't take in what was happening. Everything was moving too quickly. It was daytime again. Icy wind bit her face. She was wearing a winter coat, snowflakes having settled on the fur around her hood.

'Urgh,' Sparks said, wiping her mouth. Scoop breathed deeply, trying not to vomit herself.

'What's happening?' Sparks snivelled. 'What's going on?'

'I don't know. Something's happening with time.'

'The ageing curse!' Sparks looked terrified.

Scoop wanted to tell her it wasn't, but she couldn't. 'I don't know. I was just with Nib. It was night. And now I'm here.'

'I'm scared.'

'Me too.'

Sparks shot round, scanning the ocean. 'Have we lost them – the Red Hawks?'

Scoop turned. Behind them, its sails billowing, was the Falcon galleon – it was still there.

'Oh no,' Sparks sobbed. 'The pirate was wrong! They've not turned back! They're going to catch us! We'll never escape.'

Scoop reached out to comfort her, but as she did, another blast of coldness hit. Again, she closed her eyes. Wind roared around her. She could see the Falcon galleon. It closed in on them. It was relentless. There was a large, black bird too, perching on the rigging, pecking crumbs from the ship's rail, flying in the Horizon's wake.

'Admit you were wrong!' a voice shouted. It was Freddo.

Scoop opened her eyes. The ship was in uproar. The whole crew were gathered on deck. An argument was raging.

'They're still following us,' Freddo yelled, his face red.

'We need to hold our nerve,' the Dark Pirate snarled. He looked tired. Scoop noticed grey among his mop of black hair. 'They *will* turn away. They will not be able to cope with the time instability.'

'I'm not sure we can cope,' Rufina said. There were dark rings under her eyes. 'How long has it been since we crossed into these waters?'

'We don't know,' said the Boatswain. 'It could be days. It could be months. We've no way of telling.'

Days? Months? What? Scoop noticed the snow had gone. It was now a warm, summer's day, the sails billowing against a clear blue sky.

'Could it be years?' asked Nib.

Everyone stared at him.

Years? It can't be. Surely! This is insane.

'Don't blink,' said the pirate.

Rufina shook her head. 'What?'

'Don't blink. That's when time leaps. Not every time you close your eyes, but that's the trigger.'

'Oh great.'

'Well,' the pirate corrected, 'to be precise, it's not actually time that's leaping.'

'What do you mean?' asked Nib.

The pirate thought for a moment. 'Imagine skimming a stone across a lake. The lake is always there but the stone only comes into contact with it every few feet. It's the same with us – time is still there – we're still sailing the ship, still fleeing the Red Hawks – but our consciousness only connects with that reality fleetingly.'

Nib nodded. 'So, when we blink, we disconnect from time. And when we open our eyes again we reconnect, but further on.'

'Yes.'

'Like when you've slept,' Alfa added. 'It feels as though only a moment has passed, but actually a whole night has gone.'

'Exactly.'

Scoop turned to Nib. 'That's why you saw me coming out from below deck just now, even though I couldn't remember it.'

Nib stared at her. 'That was ages ago, Scoop. That was last winter…'

'Last winter?' Scoop felt weak. 'But it was just a moment ago.'

Nib shook his head.

'A moment, a month, a year, we just don't know,' said the Boatswain.

'Will it ever stop?' asked Sparks.

'I think it will,' the pirate replied.

Freddo thumped the mast. 'You *think?*'

'I know as much as you! But yes, I think it will. Just as with the stone. The jumps will get shorter, more frequent, until…' He stopped.

'Until what?' Freddo asked.

Nobody spoke.

'Until what?!'

'Until we sink,' Rufina said, quietly.

The pirate shook his head. 'I don't know. We can't say what will—'

There was another rush of wind. Scoop gagged, doubling over. She'd been trying not to blink, but the more she tried, the harder it had become. With a cry of frustration, she shut her eyes.

As the world sped by, Scoop could feel something deep in her flesh. It prickled and throbbed. Something in her was changing. She looked at her hands. Her skin was darkening. She became aware of hair tickling her shoulders. She reached up. It was growing. *I'm getting older,* she thought.

She emerged from the maelstrom to find herself in a huddle of people around the mast. There was a commotion. Alfa was next to her. As Scoop saw her friend, her gut twisted. The First Year looked different. Her face was longer, her hair thinner. She was losing her youth. She reminded Scoop of how she herself looked.

'Get help,' Alfa said, seeing Scoop staring.

'What?'

'He's fallen again.' She signalled to where Mr Snooze lay awkwardly on the deck, his silver hair long and thin. He looked so much older than when Scoop had last seen him. Alfa pointed. 'Get the pirate!'

'Oh. Yes, okay.'

Scoop rushed off, but before she'd got very far, there was another rush of wind.

They're coming more regularly now – like waves.

'There they are,' said Fletcher. His voice was deeper than Scoop remembered. She looked at him and flinched. Time had jumped forward, almost without her noticing. Fletcher's skin was weathered and sun-stained, and there were new lines around his eyes and mouth. He was standing at the prow of the ship, staring across the ocean. Ahead, a thick storm cloud hung over the sea. It swirled and seethed, as if alive. Rising from it were two tall rocks, each perfectly flat on one side. The flat sides of the rocks faced each other, forming a corridor in the ocean.

'The South Bookend Isles,' Fletcher said.

Scoop shuddered. The cloud that clung to the rocks looked somehow familiar. 'That cloud...' she said, slowly.

'We've seen it before,' Fletcher finished.

'Yes.' With awful recognition, Scoop realised where. 'At the wedding banquet.'

'Yes.'

The two apprentices gazed in silence. Scoop recalled the night of the banquet. It seemed a lifetime ago. She remembered how the cloud had appeared in the Great Hall of Alethea, summoned by Grizelda, how it had morphed into a terrible creature that threatened to destroy the castle. That evening, it had been defeated by a firebird, forced away, out to sea. Scoop had hoped she would never see it again. Now, here it was. And they were sailing directly towards it.

'We're going to sail into it, aren't we?'

'We are,' replied Fletcher. 'The pirate says it's the only way to lose the Red Hawks.'

'Yes.' Scoop's voice was flat. The pirate was right. It was the only way to lose the Falcon galleon. They wouldn't follow them into the cloud.

She wanted this to be over. She stared at the seething mass and then deliberately shut her eyes.

The rushing knocked her from her feet, as the world slipped into blackness. The cloud was there. An eye appeared in its swirling ash. She saw claws form in the darkness. They swiped at the ship. The creature wanted revenge. And then from the shadow she heard a name. It hissed on the breeze.

'The beast,' it whispered.

Scoop could feel rain on her skin. It was icy. She opened her eyes again. Wisps of dark vapour slithered around the Black Horizon. Other than rain hammering the sea, it was deathly quiet. The ship drifted silently forward. They were entering the cloud. Scoop could see the Boatswain standing at the stern of the ship, staring back across the ocean. She joined him.

'The pirate was right,' he said. 'They're not entering the cloud.'

Scoop looked. The Falcon galleon was behind them, its port side facing. It was turning away. Mist swirled, and the galleon disappeared. Icy rain soaked Scoop's hair. They had escaped the Red Hawk threat, but she couldn't shake what Rufina had said about the stone. She pictured a pebble sinking down through the sea, finally coming to rest on the bed of the ocean. A terrible dread gripped her, a dread she was too scared to name.

Chapter 15

The Cloud

The ribbons of cloud that twisted around the ship thickened, until slowly, the Black Horizon was consumed by fog. Rain churned the ocean. Despite this, the air was unnaturally quiet. The wind had died down and the sea was flat. The ship cut, almost noiselessly, through the water, its creaks and groans eerie in the stillness. The crew drifted to the sides of the vessel, staring into the murk. Nobody spoke. Each stood alone, looking for something, anything, a landmark, a gap in the cloud, a sign of life. But there was none. Scoop shivered. This place was deathly.

They sailed on for a while, exactly how long was hard to tell.

There was a knot in Scoop's gut. She was so alert, so focused, she hardly noticed the rain soaking her clothes and running through her hair. For a moment, she thought she caught sight of a shape in the mist – a darker patch in the gloom. She leaned forward, peering out, but the shape vanished. She squinted, trying to pierce the fog. It felt as though the cloud was watching, biding its time, toying with them.

Then, through the rain, there was a noise. A gentle sloshing drifted across the water. Without taking her eyes off the sea, Scoop moved across to Fletcher, who was standing nearby.

'I heard something out there,' she whispered. 'Listen.'

Fletcher turned his ear to the sea.

After a moment, the sloshing came again.

'See? Did you hear that?'

'I did.'

'What was it?'

'I'm not sure. I think, perhaps…it sounded like an oar moving through the water.'

'Do you think there's another boat out there?'

'I don't know. I'll go and get the Boatswain.'

Fletcher disappeared into the gloom, leaving Scoop alone.

She listened again. For a moment there was nothing, just the constant thrum of rain.

Just as she was wondering if she'd imagined the noise, a thin, reedy sound floated through the mist. It was ghostly.

What's that?

The sound died away.

Scoop strained to listen, her breath swirling in the mist.

After a moment, the noise came again, fragile and broken.

It's a voice. Somebody's calling. She tried to make out the words.

'Hel...' she heard it say. 'Help.'

Somebody's in trouble.

'Help. Have mercy. Somebody help.' The voice faded into the darkness.

There was movement behind Scoop, and she spun round. Fletcher and the Boatswain stood behind her, pallid in the gloom.

'What did you hear?' asked the Boatswain.

Scoop steadied her breathing. 'Someone's out there...I think it's another boat. We heard an oar. And...' She paused, nervous to name what she'd heard.

'And what?' the Boatswain prompted.

'And...I heard a voice, calling.'

The Boatswain glanced apprehensively at Fletcher. 'What did it say?'

'Help,' Scoop replied. 'Someone was calling for help.'

The Boatswain and Fletcher moved to the side of the ship and stared out. The fog swirled, twisting around them, shapes forming and dissolving. Scoop had lost all sense of direction. She couldn't tell where they'd come from, and it was impossible to get a sense of where they were headed. The world had lost its boundaries.

'I can't see anything out there,' said the Boatswain.

'There's someone there. I know it.'

'I can only hear rain on the—'

The Boatswain stopped. Out of the dark, a sound like the ragged whine of a sea creature, drifted across the water. It was definitely a voice.

'Help,' it called. 'Please help. Don't leave me here.'

The Boatswain turned to Fletcher. 'Get the pirate.' Fletcher nodded and disappeared.

There was a wary look in the Boatswain's eye. 'What's out there?' he muttered.

Scoop pointed. 'Look.' In the cloud, a dark shape was forming.

The Boatswain gazed into the fog. 'It's a boat.'

Sure enough, out of the mist, a small skiff emerged. It drifted towards the Black Horizon, one moment visible, then obscured by cloud. It drew closer, its sail hanging limply from its mast. Scoop could make out a figure standing at its prow, holding an oar, every so often paddling to keep the skiff moving.

'Help,' the figure called again. 'Please, help. Don't leave me to perish.'

By now, the pirate and a few of the others had gathered, news of the sighting having spread.

'Who is it?' asked Freddo.

'I have no idea,' replied the Boatswain.

The pirate stepped forward. 'Keep your wits about you.'

The skiff was only a mast's length away now. Scoop could see the figure more clearly. They were hunched over, dressed in grey robes, a hood concealing their face.

'Who goes there?' called the pirate.

The figure stopped paddling and looked up. 'Just a poor, old man,' he croaked. 'The Storyteller bless you, sir. I thought I was going to die out here.'

'It is just an old man,' said Pierre. 'We should help him aboard.'

'Wait,' growled the pirate. He eyed the stranger, suspiciously.

'What are you doing out here, alone in the Southern Ocean?'

'If you please, sir, I was abandoned. They left me to the cruelty of the sea.'

'Who? Who abandoned you? And why?'

Nib laid a hand on the pirate's back. 'Why don't we question him when he's aboard? He's drenched. He doesn't look well.'

'Let him answer.'

'Whatever his answer, we can't leave him. He'll die.'

'If he answers this, we'll bring him aboard.'

Nib nodded.

'I ask again, who abandoned you in these waters?'

Scoop was torn. Nib was right. They couldn't leave the old man to face the elements. And yet, there was something about the stranger she didn't trust.

'If you please, sir, I was aboard the Red Hawk galleon, the one pursuing your ship. But they didn't appreciate my...my honesty.'

'Honesty? What do you mean?'

'I told them they shouldn't enter the Southern Ocean. I said as how it's accursed. The commander accused me of stirring up sedition, provoking rebellion. But I had to speak, sir. It was my duty. And I was right. We never should have entered these waters.'

'Why were you aboard the Red Hawk vessel?'

'I was the ship's doctor, sir. Just a poor old man, wanting to help those around him.'

'There you are,' said Pierre, 'he was trying to help. It sounds as though he was trying to help us too.'

The pirate grunted. 'Very well. Roll down the ladder and help the man aboard. Tie his skiff to the stern. When he's aboard, bring him to my quarters. I have more questions.'

'Yes, sir,' replied the Boatswain as the pirate strode away.

Turning to Freddo, the Boatswain gave the order to lower the ladder.

Once the skiff was secured, the old man climbed up. He moved slowly, painfully. As the Boatswain grabbed his hand to pull him aboard, he flinched and stepped back. The stranger collapsed onto the deck.

Nib moved forward to help. 'Thank you, my boy,' said the stranger, softly.

Taking the old man's arm, Nib shuddered. 'You're cold to the bone.'

As the old man straightened up, Scoop glimpsed his face. She stepped away. His skin was wrinkled, his eyes almost hollow in his skull. For a moment, she thought she recognised him. But how? From where? Quickly, he pulled his hood down again. Scoop realised she was shaking.

'We need to take you to the pirate,' said Nib. 'This is his ship.'

'Of course,' said the old man. 'But first, I have something to tell you.' He stared out across the water. The cloud had thickened. In the darkness, there was a dim flicker of lightning.

Nib reached out to take his arm again. 'I really think we should—'

'You *will* want to hear this,' interrupted the stranger.

Scoop's chest tightened.

'What? What will we want to hear?'

'While aboard the Red Hawk galleon, I overheard a conversation.'

The Boatswain, Nib, Pierre, Freddo and Fletcher edged closer. Scoop felt a tug of intrigue. She wanted to hear what the old man had to say. But something fought that desire. She froze, torn between the two impulses. Who was this man? What news did he bring?

'What?' Nib stammered. 'What did you hear?'

Below his hood, the old man smiled. 'I heard their plan,' he whispered.

'Then tell us!' the Boatswain cried. 'By gods, man, tell us what you know!'

The old man leaned forward, his voice like ice. 'Their plan was to deceive you, to lay a trap.'

Scoop's heart was thudding.

'How?' Freddo hissed. 'What do they plan to do!'

'Their plan was to make it look as though they had turned away, but really...'

'Really what?' The Boatswain's voice was hoarse.

'But really, they have continued to track you. They are in the cloud.'

'No!'

'They plan to ambush the Black Horizon when you are least expecting it. They will come upon you, cloaked by fog.' The old man spun round and pointed into the gloom. 'There! Look! They come!'

There was another flicker of lightning. In the dimness, Scoop thought she saw the outline of a galleon. It was ghostly, its flags like fire. It disappeared into the fog again.

Instantly, panic fell upon the crew.

'Curses!' the Boatswain yelled.

Freddo thumped the rail. 'How can it be!'

Nib was trembling. 'Did you see the size of that ship?'

'Get the pirate,' the Boatswain barked. 'Now!'

Fletcher turned and pelted across the deck.

'What will we do?' Nib cried.

'What can you do?' the old man whispered. 'See, there are the cannon!'

The galleon appeared again. It was alongside now, a row of black barrels trained on them like caged creatures, watching, ready to pounce.

Scoop screamed. Nib backed away. Freddo and the Boatswain drew their weapons.

The pirate strode across the deck. 'What's the meaning of this commotion?'

'Behold your downfall!' cried the old man.

The pirate froze. 'By thunder! They're upon us!'

'They are! Your end has come! See, there are an army of soldiers, too many to overcome.'

Scoop *could* see. There were hundreds of Red Hawks aboard the galleon. They manned the cannon, swung from the rigging, lined the decks, muskets in hand. Their coats smoked in the fog.

The old man didn't leave time to think. 'Behold their arsenal. Their fire torches are ablaze.'

They were. Vast piles of shot were ready to smash through the Black Horizon. Torches flared to life in the hands of the Red Hawks manning the guns.

'The Storyteller save us!' Pierre hissed.

'No!' roared the pirate. 'I will not allow this ship to go down without a fight. To your stations! Nib, Rufina, clear the decks; Alfa, Sparks, close the quarters; Knot, Fletcher, Scoop, lower the Storyteller, Princess and Yarnbard into the skiff – keep them safe at all costs; Freddo, Pierre, Boatswain, with me – defend the ship!'

Scoop fled towards the captain's cabin. Behind her, Freddo and the Boatswain roared as they ran to the higher deck.

Scoop's mind was racing. *We must get out of here! How has this happened?*

She flew into the cabin. Fletcher and Knot were already there untying the bodies.

Outside, the old man yelled, 'Look! A warning shot!'

'Brace yourselves!' the pirate barked.

Scoop gripped the wooden bunk. She found herself face to face with the Storyteller. *Help! Help us, won't you?*

'See, the cannon is lit!'

BOOM! The blast rumbled across the waves.

'Behold – a direct hit!'

The Black Horizon quaked with the impact. Scoop stumbled, scraping her knee.

'Quick!' Fletcher shouted. 'We need to get them out of here!

Now!'

Knot grabbed the Princess, sweeping her under one of his arms. He picked up the trolleys in the other hand. Fletcher and Scoop struggled to lift the Storyteller.

Together, they dragged the bodies out of the cabin. Scoop's ears were ringing. There was a crater in the centre of the deck where the cannon ball had hit. They headed towards the stern, where the skiff was secured.

Scoop glanced up.

What on earth... She froze.

'What are you doing?' yelled Fletcher.

There was no galleon there, just sea wreathed in cloud.

The old man's voice cut through the mist. 'Watch! The galleon will show no mercy.'

There it was again, fearsome on a war footing.

'Come on!' yelled Fletcher.

Scoop stumbled on, trying to keep up. Her hands were sweating. The Storyteller almost slipped from her grip. She pulled him up, straining with all her might.

'See,' the old man cried, 'the battle begins. Ten cannons are lit. Twenty!'

No!

Reaching the stern, Knot grabbed a rope, tied it around the Princess and began to lower her. The air was thick with the whizz and crack of cannon. Great plumes of water exploded around them.

'Someone down there in the skiff,' Knot panted. Fletcher jumped onto the rail and began to scale down. Leaping onto the little boat, he grabbed the Princess and guided her aboard. Knot passed the trolleys down after her.

'Behold, the mast is struck!'

BOOM! The ship shuddered again, listing dangerously. Wood whined under stress.

'See, it splinters!'

CRACK! The ship reeled like a whale struck by a harpoon. Scoop clung on as the Horizon plunged. The hull slapped the water, sending a vast wave crashing across the deck.

There were shouts of horror as the mast moaned. It was still upright, but it wavered like a dying man already shot. Scoop felt the Black Horizon tremble.

'Behold the mast fall!'

It toppled, mighty as a tree. The air whirred, ropes snapping like threads. The mast hit the deck with a terrible boom. Beneath Scoop's feet, the deck buckled. She lurched backwards, falling against the ship's rail. A splinter of yardarm crashed down, narrowly missing her. There was a scream from below. She looked down to see Fletcher, his hand impaled by the wood.

'Argh!' he yelled, yanking it from his flesh. He was bleeding profusely. 'Come on,' he yelled. 'We need to get out of here!'

Scoop turned back. Knot was struggling to tie the rope around the Storyteller's body. He stumbled as the deck tilted, the stern lifting. She pushed herself across to him and together, they looped the rope around the Storyteller's body.

'See, the hull is breached!' The old man was standing by a gash in the core of the vessel. Seawater was gushing in. He stood with his arms outstretched, as if summoning a demon, the hem of his robes wet, as water rose about him.

Knot looked at Scoop, his eyes wide. 'Yarnbard!' he said.

The old man was still in the captain's cabin.

'Oh no! Go!'

Knot scrambled back across the quarterdeck, disappearing below.

'Behold, the ship is snapped in two!'

The Black Horizon shook as water flooded its main deck. The hull cracked, wood snapping, rivets exploding, beams crumpling. The pirate bounded across the deck, leaping over the gash in its centre and scrambled up the steps towards the quarterdeck.

He was just in time. The stairs broke loose, swinging from their fastening. The pirate launched himself up, his feet swimming through the air. He landed on the deck. Clinging to it, he pulled himself towards Scoop.

'Quickly!' Fletcher yelled from below. Scoop looked down. The bow of the little skiff was being lifted as the Black Horizon's stern rose from the water.

As the pirate reached her, they began to lower the Storyteller. His body knocked into the side of the ship. When he reached the skiff, Fletcher untied him.

It was hard to stand now, the angle of the deck steep. Below, the sea raged as the vessel plunged into the water.

'See, the Black Horizon is wrecked!' yelled the old man. 'She sinks! She sinks!'

He was right. The ship was sinking. It was in two pieces. At the bow, Freddo, Pierre and the Boatswain were fighting for their lives. In the chaos, Scoop couldn't make out who they were battling. Was it Red Hawks? Or was it the cloud itself? And where was the Red Hawk galleon? She couldn't see it. The cloud swirled around the Black Horizon, twisting everything. There was a crack of thunder. Through the gloom, Scoop could see Nib, Rufina, Alfa and Sparks running to join the Boatswain. Scoop watched as they lashed out, hollering and shrieking. A wave of horror hit her. Mr Snooze was already in the sea, clinging to a small piece of wreckage. He kicked, trying to stay afloat, but the current was strong and he kept disappearing below the waves.

Behind him, the mist parted. Two sheer rock faces appeared, rising from the water. They framed the sinking ship.

The South Bookend Isles.

There was a strong current. It swept everything towards the gap between the rocks. Lightning flashed and thunder cracked around them.

Knot emerged onto the main deck again, carrying the

Yarnbard. He tried to scramble up to the quarterdeck but the steps had been washed away. He slipped, his great body lurching as the sea leapt up to grab him.

'Get into the skiff!' the pirate yelled.

'But Knot! The Yarnbard! We can't—'

'Get into the skiff!'

'I can't hold on much longer!' Fletcher yelled. 'Quickly, or the Horizon will take us down with her!'

Knot staggered, slipping.

'No!' Scoop cried as he toppled into the churning waves.

She watched him grab a piece of fallen mast and heave himself onto it, pulling the Yarnbard up with him. He looked directly at Scoop.

'Go!' he called, the storm swallowing his voice.

She hesitated.

'Go!' he cried again.

She climbed onto the rail. It was nearly horizontal now. Grabbing the rope, she clambered down, tears stinging her eyes.

Scoop leapt onto the skiff, the pirate behind her. The little boat was straining as the Black Horizon pulled it from the water.

'Untie us,' bellowed the pirate. Fletcher picked up an axe, his hand bloody. He swung it at the rope that fastened the skiff to the ship. Half the twine snapped, groaning under the pressure. Fletcher brought down the axe again. This time, the rope snapped. The skiff plunged down, hitting the sea. Icy water poured over its sides. Juddering, the boat rose back up.

The pirate threw Scoop a bandage. 'Bind his wound!' He waved at Fletcher's hand. Then, picking up a coil of rope with a small anchor attached, he swung it around his head. Releasing it, the anchor flew across the sea.

'Help us!' the pirate roared. 'By the Storyteller, help us!'

CLANG! The anchor hit something solid. Was it rock? Scoop couldn't see through the storm. The skiff lurched, but the anchor held tight.

The wreckage of the Black Horizon moved away, flowing towards the gap between the South Bookend Isles. Pieces of broken hull rose on monstrous waves, vanishing again into dark valleys of water. A strong wind had picked up, blowing everything towards the rocks. But the skiff held firm, anchored to whatever rock the pirate had found.

Scoop looked on helplessly as her friends struggled. The Boatswain, Freddo, Rufina, Alpha, Sparks and Pierre, were all clinging to the same piece of broken mast. They had managed to pull themselves across to Knot and the Yarnbard. Nib, however, floated on his own, struggling to swim to them.

'We have to help them!' cried Scoop.

'There's nothing we can do,' yelled the pirate.

'But we can't leave them. They'll die.'

'If we let go our anchor, we'll be pulled down with the wreckage too.'

Scoop watched her friends battle the waves, calling out, trying to help each other. Knot was holding the Yarnbard's head above water. Alfa was struggling to pull Sparks onto the mast.

The old man was in the water too, clinging to a piece of broken hull. Scoop looked at him with hatred. This was his doing, she knew it.

The old man pointed at Nib. He was still alone, fighting the current. 'Look!' he gasped. Sharks!'

'No!' screamed Scoop, reaching out.

Nib's eyes darted, wide and fearful, searching the water around him. He tried to scramble higher onto the piece of wood he was clutching. But his body jerked. Scoop watched in horror as he was yanked down. The sea around him churned. His arm appeared, thrashing, then vanished.

'No!'

Scoop willed him to emerge, to leap back onto the wreckage and pull himself to safety. She scanned the water, looking for a glimpse of an arm or knee.

Anything.

Any sign of hope.

But there was nothing.

And then she saw it – blood. The surf was stained red.

'No,' she whispered. 'Nib!'

There was one more violent swirl, and then the ocean fell still.

She leaned forward, looking for a sign of life, searching for her friend. But there was no movement.

Nib had gone.

Rain pelted Scoop.

'No,' she whispered, again. 'No, no, no!' Her words became a wail.

A sudden rush of wind swept everything towards the gap between the Bookend Isles. It was irresistible. Even the cloud couldn't fight the current. The ocean seemed to swirl into a ball of wind and cloud, a vortex that hung directly between the rocks. The air roared. Scoop watched as the battered remains of the Black Horizon were dragged between the islands.

Through the maelstrom, she thought she saw the old man transform into a large, black bird. It fought the wind, its wings pounding, but it wasn't strong enough. There was a rushing, sucking, slurping noise and with a jolt, everything disappeared between the rocks.

It was as if Scoop had jumped from a cliff. The roaring stopped. A silence, as violent as any bomb blast, engulfed her.

'What?'

The sea was empty. Everything had vanished – the remnants of the ship, the crew, the cloud, and the black bird – all had been swept through the gap between the Bookend Isles. All had vanished to nothing.

'What?' she said again.

With sickening speed, the water fell still. Ahead, the South Bookend Isles rose, a granite doorway in a clear ocean.

The picture of a sinking stone filled Scoop's mind. It sank

down through the sea, down through jade-green waters, until it disappeared into darkness.

She and Fletcher, the pirate and the skiff, were left alone. The others had vanished.

Chapter 16

Interlude

A hand reaches into a hollow.

'Letters?'

The floor thuds.

'Help her. She's fallen!'

The scene shifts to a chair by a patio door.

'Why didn't you tell me?

You didn't want to worry me?'

Disbelief. Anger.

Cherry blossom falls.

Spring snatched. Short. Too short.

Machine's beep.

The church is cold.

And then...nothing.

Libby wakes, a cold sweat pouring from her.

She rolls onto her side and closes her eyes again.

Chapter 17

The Merking

'Where are they?' yelled Scoop, leaning over the side of the skiff, frantically scanning the ocean. 'What's happened?'

The pirate stared at the South Bookend Isles, his face ashen.

'What have you done with them?' Scoop thumped his arm. 'Where have they gone?' The pirate was so fixed on the rocks, he didn't seem to notice. Scoop pounded his arm and then dissolved into tears, her head slumping onto his shoulder.

The sea lapped the boat gently, as if mocking them.

'Where are they?' she sobbed.

Fletcher pulled her away and she collapsed into his arms. He held her for a moment. He couldn't take in what had happened. All around, the sea was flat, grey and empty. 'What on earth's happened,' he asked, quietly.

The softness of Fletcher's voice seemed to stir the pirate. 'They've gone through.'

'Gone through? Gone through where? What do you mean?'

'Gone through the doorway.'

'What doorway?'

'Look.' The pirate pointed at the South Bookend Isles. 'What do you see?'

'Two rocks. Nothing else. We're in the middle of the ocean.'

'And beyond the rocks?'

'More sea. What do you mean?'

'You're telling me what you see with your eyes, but look with your whole being.'

Fletcher studied the rocks. They jutted from the ocean, rising to craggy points, their flat sides creating a passageway through the water. All he could see through the passageway and beyond, was ocean.

But then he saw a faint shimmer, somewhere between the rocks. He softened his gaze, allowing his other senses to work. The air in the passageway seemed to bend or blur. There was a softness to it, barely visible.

'There's something different about the air between the rocks,' he said, tentatively.

'Yes. There is. Remember what I told you? These islands mark the southern border of this realm.' Fletcher nodded. 'That's what you can see. It's a doorway – a doorway leading beyond this domain.'

Scoop looked up, her eyes puffy. 'A doorway? Is that where Rufina and the others have gone?'

'I believe so. They've been swept through the southern gate of the world.'

'And Nib?'

The pirate shook his head. 'I don't know. I couldn't see if he made it through.'

Scoop's shoulders dropped and she nodded.

After a moment, her expression changed. 'Where does it lead?'

'What?'

'The doorway – what's on the other side?'

'I don't know. Nobody knows.'

'You don't know, but...' Scoop's eyes widened. 'We have to follow them. We *have* to go after them.'

'No.'

'No? What do you mean? We have to! They're our friends. We can't just leave them!'

The pirate shook his head. 'You must let them go.'

'Let them go? I won't. I can't!'

'You must!' said the pirate, raising his voice. Realising how harsh he sounded, he softened. 'You must let them go, Scoop.'

'But, we can't just—'

'You've been given a job by the Storyteller.'

'I don't care!'

'You should. It's more important now than ever.'

'But Alfa, Sparks, Mr Snooze, Knot…'

'You have to let them go, Scoop. We have to trust that even in this loss, there's hope.' Scoop shook her head. '*You* have a different doorway to cross.' He pointed at the South Bookend Isles. 'That's not your journey.'

'But perhaps they lead to the same place?' said Fletcher.

'Perhaps.' The pirate looked sceptical. 'But we've no way of knowing. All we know is that you were told to cross the Threshold. You were not instructed to go through the South Bookend Isles. The Storyteller asked me to make sure you got there – that is what I intend to do.'

Scoop sank onto the skiff's bench, her head in her hands.

The pirate looked at the two apprentices. 'I know it's hard, painful. But if you trust me at all, I'm asking you to trust me now. We must reach the Threshold. You *must* cross it. I don't know how, but you will reverse this sickness and wake the Storyteller. That's the best chance you have of saving your friends, of saving all of us.'

Fletcher scuffed his foot along the skiff's boards. 'But what if we can't? What if we fail?'

The pirate sighed. 'We live with the possibility of failure every day. We all fail, many times and in many ways. But it's my belief that, even in this darkest of moments, our failure can be turned to success – if we only hold tight to our trust in the Storyteller. Things *can* be turned around. The only real failure will be if we're dissuaded to try at all.'

Fletcher couldn't believe what he was hearing. Could this darkness become light? It seemed unlikely. But he wanted to believe it. He longed to. He looked at the Storyteller and Princess asleep in the boat, oblivious to all that was happening.

'But he's asleep,' said Fletcher.

The pirate rubbed his eyes. 'He is. I can't pretend to understand. But I've trusted him my whole life. I won't turn away now, as much as I might want to.'

'You want to?'

The pirate snorted. 'Of course! I live with that temptation every day. I question whether it's been worth it, whether the sacrifices I've made have been for nothing. I want to go after the others too – they're my friends as well!' He paused. 'But I still have an irrational hope that they –' he pointed at the Storyteller and Princess – 'will bring us through this. I believe there *will be* resolution at the end, even though I see him there asleep.'

Fletcher stared at the Storyteller. He shared that hope too. He couldn't recall how or when it had taken root in him but he knew he couldn't turn his back on it, even now. He nodded.

The pirate turned to Scoop. 'This is exactly the sort of time we need to hold fast.' He pointed back across the sea. 'What's behind us can give us confidence to...' His voice trailed away. 'Oh...'

Seeing the pirate's expression, Fletcher turned too.

He gasped.

Behind them, rising from the ocean was a remarkable sight. A lone rock had been sculpted into a majestic figure – a statue, as tall as the Black Horizon had been.

How did we not see that? Fletcher wondered. The statue must have been hidden by the cloud as they'd passed. Ever since, they'd been focused on the Bookend Isles, ahead. It was only now they looked back they saw it. It was an extraordinary sight.

The statue rose from the ocean, water lapping around its waist, as if it were swimming, the rest of its body submerged. The rock was weathered and worn. The statue's features were noble, its eyes piercing and wise. It wore a crown, peaks cresting like waves. Seaweed hair tumbled down the figure's body, clothing it. In an enormous hand, it held a trident, the skiff's anchor caught between its prongs.

As they took in the sight, stone crumbled from the statue's

beard, bouncing down the monument, showering the water.

'What is it?' asked Fletcher.

'It's the Merking,' said the pirate. 'I've heard tales, but...' He shook his head.

'A mermaid?'

'Merman,' the pirate corrected. 'The most powerful in the Oceans of Rhyme.'

Fletcher could imagine its tail snaking below the sea, mighty as a whale. 'Who put it there? It must have taken an army to sculpt!'

'If it was sculpted.'

'What do you mean? How else could it have got here?'

'The mermaids of the North Bookend Isles say the Merking is alive. In the beginning, the merpeople were charged with guarding the doorways of the Bookend Isles, north and south, dwelling as they do between the realms of sea and air. They believe the Merking kept his watch so well, remaining so still, so alert, that gradually he turned to stone. And here he is, still guarding this doorway, keeper of the southern border of the world.'

There was a splintering and another flurry of stones tumbled down, splashing into the sea.

'Look.' Scoop pointed at the anchor. One of the trident's prongs had cracked and was balanced precariously.

Picking up an oar, the pirate rowed towards the statue, taking the strain from the rope. As the little boat drew alongside, he touched the rock. It crumbled in his fingers. He shook his head. 'The boundaries are collapsing. We don't have long.' He turned to the apprentices. 'We need to free our anchor.'

Fletcher looked up. 'If we pull hard enough, that prong will break and we can pull it down.'

'No,' answered the pirate. 'The Merking has stood here for generations. I won't be party to pulling him down, even if he is already crumbling,'

Scoop looked up. 'I'll climb it.'

Fletcher frowned, unsure.

'I'm the lightest,' she reassured him.

'You are,' agreed the pirate.

Reluctantly, Fletcher nodded.

Holding the boat close to the rock, the pirate helped Scoop climb onto the Merking's hand. She steadied herself at the base of his trident. Fletcher watched, nervously, as she began to scale the statue, slowly testing each rock before moving up. Gradually, she made her way up the twists of the Merking's hair.

'Careful,' Fletcher hissed, as she dislodged a section of beard. It crashed down, narrowly missing the boat. Scoop withdrew her foot, searching out a firmer place to stand.

Slowly, she moved higher, up the Merking's chest, until she was standing on his shoulder, her face level with the top of the trident. Reaching forward to free the anchor, she stopped.

'What are you doing?' Fletcher shouted up. 'Quickly, before the whole thing collapses!'

Another chunk of stone broke free and crashed into the sea.

Scoop looked down. 'There's something written here.'

'Where?' called the pirate, suddenly alert.

'On the trident. One word on each of the prongs.'

'Really?'

'Yes.' Scoop leaned forward to brush down the stone.

Fletcher's heart was thudding. 'Be careful up there!'

The pirate seemed agitated. 'The stories say the Merking carries a message, a message for the end of the age—'

'Let's hope it's not the end of my sister!' Fletcher interrupted. 'She doesn't look safe up there!'

'I'm fine!' Scoop called down. 'Stop fussing.'

'I thought the message would long since have been lost. What does it say? Can you read it?'

Scoop stretched out to clear some debris.

'I can't watch,' Fletcher muttered.

'SEEK,' Scoop called down. 'The word on the first prong is

SEEK.'

'SEEK what?' called the pirate.

Scoop clutched the Merking's crown, swinging further out. 'THE,' she called down. 'SEEK THE...'

'SEEK THE what? What's the third word?'

Scoop leaned further, her body swaying dangerously.

'Oh, come on, come on,' Fletcher hissed.

'It's worn away. If I can just...' Scoop reached out to try to brush more debris away but her foot slipped. A chunk of the Merking's shoulder came crashing down.

Fletcher ducked.

Scoop grabbed the prong, scrambling higher, her body bridged between the Merking's face and his trident.

'She needs to come down,' Fletcher snapped. 'It's dangerous up there!'

'No,' replied the pirate. 'We need to know what it says. Can you see?' he called up. 'What's the third word?'

'There's an S. I think that's the first letter. Yes, S,' Scoop confirmed.

'And?'

'I can't see.'

CRACK! A big portion of the Merking's arm fell away.

Fletcher's face flushed. 'Do we really need to know? Haven't we lost enough people today?'

'ACE,' Scoop called. 'The final three letters are A–C–E.'

'Seek the S...A-C-E,' the pirate repeated, ignoring Fletcher.

'No, hang on...It's an R not an A.'

'Seek the S...R-C-E.'

'Source,' Fletcher said. 'It must be. Now come down!'

'Is it? Can you see?'

There was a loud snap and the first prong of the trident broke away, bouncing down the Merking. It smashed against the side of the skiff. The anchor came loose and clattered down, making the boat tip.

Fletcher stumbled. 'Get her down from there!'

'Okay, okay,' said the pirate. 'Is the word SOURCE?'

'Now! Come down, Scoop! It's not safe up there!'

Scoop squinted at the third prong and then pushed herself away. Quickly, she began to scale down the statue. The disturbance was taking its toll. With a shudder, half the Merking's face split, scarring him from the top of his crown to his cheek. Scoop ducked as the creature's nose and one of its eyes rolled past, smashing into the ocean, the impact sending icy water across the skiff.

'Quickly!' pleaded Fletcher.

The statue was starting to quake now. Cracks appeared across its body.

Scoop scrambled down the last few stones and leapt onto the skiff.

'Let's get out of here,' called Fletcher. 'The whole thing's about to come down!'

The pirate caught Scoop's arm. 'Is it SOURCE?' he said. 'Is the last word SOURCE?'

'We can talk about that later, when we're safely away!' Fletcher picked up an oar and began to row.

'Is it?' the pirate demanded, not letting go.

'Yes,' Scoop panted. 'It is.'

'SEEK THE SOURCE.' The pirate grinned. 'Good.' Then, grabbing the second oar, he joined Fletcher and they rowed away from the great statue.

They cleared the rock just in time. A deep grinding rumbled through the ocean. With an almighty crack, the majestic figure of the Merking shattered. The statue crumbled, tumbling into the sea. The ocean churned, as great chunks of rock disappeared below the waves. The remains of the Merking's face descended slowly, still upright, like the captain of a sinking ship, until its crown disappeared into the depths. Scoop willed the Merking to leap back up, to explode from of the ocean. But he never did.

The sea fell still and the noise abated. It was as if the Merking had never been.

They stared at the empty ocean. After a moment, the pirate broke the silence. 'Take this.' He was holding out two pieces of stone – remnants of the statue that had fallen into the skiff. They each took a piece.

'Put it in your pocket. It will keep you safe.'

'What do you mean?' asked Fletcher.

'These stones still carry the power of the Merking.'

'Power?'

'Yes. As Keeper of the Doorway, The Merking protected these border seas. That power will still cover us while we have these stones. It will protect us. We're going to need it. The Threshold is surrounded by the Sea of Tears. These stones will save us from its heartbreak. It's the Merking's parting gift to us. You see, even loss can become a gift.'

Scoop put the stone into her pocket, aware she was carrying something precious, a remnant of an ancient life. She felt its protection surrounding her.

SEEK THE SOURCE, she thought. What did that mean? She had the strange feeling the message was meant for her and Fletcher and that the Merking had held it, waiting for the moment he could pass it to them. Having done that, he had crumbled away, returning to the sea.

She touched the stone. It was warm.

Fletcher raised the skiff's sail and the pirate sat at the tiller. A light breeze had picked up and Scoop felt the tug, as wind caught the sail. The skiff moved away, heading west.

Looking back, Scoop watched the barren rocks of the South Bookend Isles shrink into the distance. She thought of her friends – Alfa, Sparks, Rufina, Knot, Mr Snooze, the Yarnbard, Pierre, Freddo and the Boatswain. It was lonely without them.

Goodbye, she thought. *Thank you for being such fine company. I hope we'll meet again before long.*

With a pang of sadness, she realised she hadn't included Nib with the others. Deep in her heart, she knew why. She pictured him disappearing below the waves, the sea stained red with blood. Nib had gone. She touched the stone in her pocket again, but it didn't make her feel any better. There were some things the Merking couldn't protect her from.

As the South Bookend Isles disappeared across the horizon, she sat down, closed her eyes, and remembered her friend.

Chapter 18

Goodbye

The skiff drifted past the decaying hull of a ship, half submerged, like the skeleton of a whale, its bones picked clean. They had been sailing the Sea of Tears for days now. The water was eerily still. A low mist clung to the sea, insipid sunlight barely piercing the clouds. Even with the Merking's stone, Fletcher could feel sadness threatening to breach the skiff. He looked out, nervously. The quiet was disturbing.

They sat in silence, each lost in their own thoughts. Fletcher imagined Pierre's gruel, longingly, but then pushed the thought from his mind. He hadn't eaten since their last meal aboard the Black Horizon, but the bouts of hunger had lessened now, dissolving into a strange sort of clarity. He ran his fingers over the back of his hand. The wound he'd received was beginning to heal. He'd taken the bandage off. Underneath, a scar was developing. He felt the ridged skin. It was a strange sensation.

I recognise you, he thought, staring at the scar.

It wasn't the only thing he recognised. He glanced at Scoop. Her face was older, her skin weathered and tanned, but the changes looked somehow familiar. Fletcher wondered where he'd seen her like this before. Scoop caught his eye and they both looked quickly away. Was she thinking the same thing? Had she seen him older too?

And then it clicked. He recalled the night they'd spent in the camp of the Hermits of Hush, the night they'd faced the Nemesis Charm. It had shown them their future. He remembered the vision clearly: standing in front of a wide, black cave – the Threshold – staring into the blackness. He remembered being inside his older self, looking down and seeing the scar on the back of his hand and thinking he didn't have a scar. He remembered watching Scoop turn to say goodbye, before they stepped into the darkness, knowing there would be no return. He glanced at her again. That was where he'd seen her like this before.

That night, in the camp of the Hermits of Hush, they'd accepted the future the Nemesis Charm had shown them; they'd accepted the quest to cross the Threshold. He ran his finger over the rough skin of his scar again. That future was upon them. They were no longer the children who'd set out on the quest. They were on the verge of becoming adults.

'Look,' the pirate said, breaking the silence. Ahead, a dark island broke the horizon.

Fletcher met Scoop's gaze. His skin tingled with something between excitement and fear. It was Skull Rock. They were finally here.

* * *

It was hard work hoisting the Storyteller and Princess up the volcanic ledges of Skull Rock. They worked in silence, smoke from the ashy rocks rising around them. Inwardly, Scoop thanked Knot for remembering the trolleys amid the chaos, as the Black Horizon sank – they certainly made it easier to lift the bodies up the crag. Every time she touched the wood, she remembered Nib. Although it made her ache inside, it made her smile too. It was like having a little piece of him there with them.

As they worked, Scoop couldn't help but picture the giant skull in the cliff. As they sailed towards the island, it hadn't been visible at first. But rounding the eastern shore, it had taken shape – the dark fissures that made its eyes, the ridges that formed the bridge of its nose, and finally the cave – that wide, black cave that became the skull's mouth. Scoop shuddered. That was the destination they'd been moving towards ever since they'd accepted the quest. It filled her with dread.

'Scoop,' the pirate called down. He was peering over a ledge above, a rope in his hand.

'Sorry,' she said, shaking herself. The Storyteller's trolley was caught on a rock. She freed it and the pirate pulled it up, huffing with the effort. It disappeared over the ledge. A moment later, the pirate reached down. Scoop grabbed his hand and scrambled up the rock, onto a plateau. Fletcher was already there, the Princess and Storyteller next to him. There was an odd expression on his face. Scoop followed his gaze. Beside her was a sight she'd both longed for and dreaded. It was the cave. She swallowed. They were here.

The pirate rubbed his eyes. They were red from the smoke and he looked as though he were about to cry. 'Well...' he said, his words faltering. Scoop's throat tightened. She knew what he was about to say.

'Well...' he repeated.

'No,' Scoop whispered.

'I'm afraid this is where I have to say goodbye.'

'What?' said Fletcher. 'You're not coming?'

Of course he's not, Scoop realised. *He can't. He didn't face the Nemesis Charm. Only we underwent the preparation. Only we can cross the Threshold. Why didn't I think of it before? I always assumed he'd be with us.*

'I can't cross the Threshold,' the pirate confirmed.

Fletcher's eyes widened. 'We have to go alone?'

'You'll have the Princess and Storyteller with you.'

'But they haven't undergone the preparation either,' said Scoop.

'They already exist on both sides of the Boundary,' the pirate answered. 'They'll be alright.' He stepped forward. 'I've fulfilled my promise to the Storyteller. I've brought you this far. This is *your* journey now.'

They stood, fixed to the spot. Then, with a sob, Scoop ran forward and flung her arms around the pirate. He looked thrown, but then closed his arms around her and hugged her tightly.

'Thank you,' she whispered. 'We would never have made it

without you.'

The pirate looked embarrassed. He prized himself from Scoop's arms. 'Well, I was never one for long goodbyes. I wish you all the luck in the world. Not that you need it. You were chosen for this task. You *can* do it.' He looked from Scoop to Fletcher and then, with a nod, turned to leave.

'Where will you go?' asked Fletcher.

The Dark Pirate looked back. 'I'll return to the South Bookend Isles. I plan to follow our friends through to the other side. If I can be of assistance to them, I will.' Before Fletcher could say anything else, the pirate spun round and leapt over the ledge, his cape billowing as he disappeared.

Fletcher and Scoop were left alone. They stared at where the pirate had vanished, the rumble of breaking waves echoing up.

There was an ache deep in Scoop's chest. She turned to Fletcher and gave a small smile. 'Come on then, brother. There's no point in delaying it any longer. We have a job to do.'

Fletcher nodded.

Picking up the trolley ropes, the two apprentices dragged their mother and the Storyteller to the mouth of the cave and stared into the darkness.

Scoop glanced at Fletcher. 'This is it,' she said. 'This is the Threshold. We made a choice long ago. And now it's time.'

Fletcher's heart was racing.

Scoop turned and looked out, back across the sea, back across the Oceans of Rhyme, to the world that was her home. Fullstop Island, Bardbridge, Blotting's Academy, her room at Scribbler's House, the desk at which she'd studied, the bed in which she'd slept – they were all out there somewhere, beyond that endless sea. They had travelled so far to get here.

'Goodbye,' she said, simply.

Turning back, she held Fletcher's gaze for a moment. He gave a small nod of encouragement and then, together, they stepped into the darkness.

PART TWO

Chapter 19

Lost

I'm standing in a small room, my feet on a wooden floor. It's dark and damp. The smell of rancid food hangs in the air. Thin beams of light pass through slatted shutters, making the dust glow.

I'm in an entirely different world.

It's too big. I can't take it in. But I feel it, in the core of my being. This *is* a different world.

Outside, I can hear the sea. Not the fierce roar of waves crashing against Skull Rock, but the gentle rhythm of water sweeping a sandy beach.

It's quiet. Too quiet. I've not experienced stillness like this before. I feel a gap, an absence. It makes me dizzy.

'Can you feel it?' I ask Fletcher. He's standing beside me. We're both completely still, as if scared to move.

'Feel what?' he replies, quietly.

'Time.'

He looks at me and I know he understands.

The present moment seems to stretch. It's uncomfortable.

Back in my world (it seems strange to say that), back at Blotting's Academy, we were told about the Well Whisper, the voice of the island, stirred by the Storyteller, guiding its stories to completion. Words. Words drove my world, pushed it forward, gave it energy. Words made the sea sparkle with Fable Fish, built the golden domes of the Basillica Isles, made time fly like an arrow, words guided our steps, sank our ship, brought life, and ended it.

Here, there's nothing driving me forward.

I feel lost.

I shift my foot a little and stop. Then I move it the other way.

Here, I can choose.

And it's terrifying.

I'm aware of another feeling too, the sense I'm trespassing. My chest tightens.

'We shouldn't be here,' I say. My voice is louder than I'm used to.

'No,' Fletcher replies. 'But we are.'

Still, neither of us move.

Outside, the gulls cry. It sounds like they're trying to shriek over one another, desperately seeking attention. They sound confused. I understand how they feel.

All of a sudden, Fletcher walks forward. His footsteps make me flinch. He reaches the window shutters and pushes them open, dust showering down. They creak as daylight floods in. I squint. When my eyes adjust, I see Fletcher staring at me. He looks shaken, as if that small act of moving was the bravest thing he's ever done.

He turns to look at the room. We're standing in a small wooden hut – a cabin. It's a single room with a low ceiling. There's a kitchen area to one side. One corner has been partitioned with curtains. Through a gap, I can see an unmade bed. The room is simply furnished. A round table stands in the centre, a chair pushed under it. A gas lamp hangs above. The table is cluttered with paintbrushes, tubes and a stack of paper piled high. The only other furniture is an armchair, pushed into the corner, opposite the bed. There are dirty plates next to the sink and a pile of washing thrown against the wall.

On a small shelf next to the armchair, something draws my attention. It's a picture – a photograph. It's faded. I'm not sure if I should go to look at it. It's not mine, after all.

Fletcher sees me staring. 'Go on,' he says. 'Pick it up.'

I glance at him, unsure.

'It's up to us now. We have to choose our own story.'

Choose our own story? The thought horrifies me.

'But it's not ours.'

'This room isn't ours. This world isn't ours. But we're here for a reason.'

A reason, yes. I can already feel it slipping.

The Storyteller sent us, I remind myself. I look at him. He's lying on the trolley next to me, still asleep. He looks older here and somehow thinner, less substantial.

The Storyteller sent us, I repeat.

I look behind, a thought occurring.

'Where's the door we came through?'

There's nothing there, just the back wall of the cabin.

I want to go back. I don't like it here. I feel myself beginning to panic.

'Where is it? The…what's it called? The Threshold.'

Fletcher's face hardens. 'There's no door. There's no going back, remember?'

Remember? Yes, I do. But the reality of our situation is only just dawning on me. I thought I knew what I was getting into. I thought I was choosing. But I had no idea. Now, it's real. I'm stuck in a foreign world, nothing familiar, nobody to help me, and I have this slippery feeling like I can't hold on. I realise my hands are trembling.

'I'll look at it then.' Fletcher marches across and grabs the photo frame. He brushes away a layer of grime and stares at it. I see him frown.

'What is it?'

'Come and see.' I know he's challenging me. I still haven't moved. I've been fixed to this spot since we got here.

I step forward – my first step in this new world. The movement has its own momentum. One step leads to the next, the initial direction flowing into others, almost naturally.

I take the picture.

A girl stands on a beach. She's smiling, holding a red spade. She's young, maybe three or four years old. There's a woman behind her, arms outstretched, ready to catch the child if she falls. They're standing in front of a white beach hut with blue window shutters. I recognise the girl instantly, despite her age.

'Libby,' I whisper.

'Yes,' replies Fletcher.

I glance at the Storyteller.

This isn't the first time Fletcher and I have been to this world. We were brought here when we first started at Blotting's Academy. But it was different then. Back then, we were whisked here unexpectedly and only stayed a matter of minutes. To be honest, it seemed like a dream. Afterwards, I doubted it had happened at all.

While we were here, we met a girl named Libby. She was seventeen then. The girl in the photo has the same eyes, the same wispy hair. It's her.

When we met her, Libby told us she could leap into our world. When she did, she said, she became the Storyteller – that she *was* the Storyteller.

'Do you remember what she told us?' I ask Fletcher.

'I do. She said her mother had gone missing, that she didn't know where she was – that nobody did.'

'Yes.'

That's her, I think, looking at the woman in the picture, standing behind Libby.

'This is where she is,' I whisper. 'I know it. This is where she's hiding.'

Fletcher nods.

It seems little wonder this is where the doorway opened. There's a heavy sadness here, a sense of something torn, something that could rip worlds apart. And I feel darkness too.

I shudder. 'We have to get out of here,' I say. 'I don't like it.'

Fletcher walks to the table in the middle of the room and starts to thumb through the stack of papers. 'In a moment,' he mutters. Stopping, he pulls some scraps of paper from the pile.

Spreading them out, he starts to rearrange them, fitting them together like a jigsaw.

'This piece has been ripped,' he says.

He stops, a strange look on his face.

'What is it? What's wrong?'

Peering at the scraps, Fletcher begins to read.

'Grizelda stooped down and ran her hands through the hay. She hit something solid and stopped. Burying both hands into the box she stood up. In her grasp was a large glass jar.'

As Fletcher reads, I see the air in the corner of the room stir.

'She held it up to the light. It was filled with cloudy liquid. In the centre, suspended by the liquid, a heart glistened.'

Something is forming in the darkness: black cloth, a figure.

''What is that?' the captain said, his voice low.

'This, my dear, is a heart stolen from the Tombs of the Undead.''

As he speaks, I see her. 'Stop,' I whisper.

Fletcher ignores me.

'There was a commotion as the crew stepped away from the jar, muttering protective hexes.'

I step back, my heart pounding. It's Grizelda! She's here! Somehow Fletcher is summoning her. Terror grips me. But it's mixed with a sense of relief, perhaps at seeing another Mortale in this foreign world. Grizelda might be deadly but at least she's familiar: a reminder of home. The old woman glares at me, still not fully formed.

Fletcher continues to read:

'Grizelda's beady eyes flickered as she examined the heart. 'It's a thing of beauty, isn't it?''

Suddenly, the old woman flies at me, her arms outstretched, her mouth open wide.

'The limp muscle was still red with blood.'

I scream.

Fletcher spins round, dropping the paper.

As he does, Grizelda vanishes.

I'm pressed against the wall, my skin cold but sweat pouring from me.

'What is it?'

'We have to get out of here! There's power here – a darkness.'

'Alright, but can we just—'

'No, Fletcher! No, we can't! We need to go – now!'

Not waiting for a reply, I pick up one of the trolley ropes.

'But we don't know what to do. If we could just look round a bit...' Crossing the room, he picks up the photo. I must have dropped it.

'She was here, Fletcher!'

'Who?'

'Grizelda! As you read, she was here in the room. She flew at me!'

Fletcher's eyes widen. 'She was here?'

'Yes. We should go. Now!'

I start to drag the trolley towards the door. It scrapes over the wooden floor. Fletcher doesn't argue. He puts the picture in his pocket and follows, pulling the Storyteller after him.

Outside, we find ourselves on a deserted beach. It's cold. After the gloom of the cabin, the pale winter light hurts my eyes. Fletcher drags the Storyteller onto the sand. I glance back. We've come from a beach hut. It has blue shutters and peeling white paint. It's the beach hut from the photo. With a start, I realise we're standing where Libby played as a child, where she dug with that red spade.

There are other huts too, lining the sand, bright yellows and blues. But they're boarded up for the winter. I drag the Princess on, looking for somewhere to hide, somewhere to shelter.

I notice an upturned boat pushed back into one of the alleyways between the beach huts. It's tipped onto its side, grass growing around it and through the wood. It can't have been used for years. Panting, I pull the Princess across to it and push her underneath. Fletcher shoves the Storyteller next to her. Then, grabbing a tarpaulin from some crabbing nets, he stretches it over the top of the boat, creating a tent-like shelter. He moves around it, weighing it down with stones. When he's finished, both of us squeeze under the shelter and sit on the rough sand.

We listen to the tarpaulin flapping in the wind. 'So, what now?' I ask. Fletcher shrugs. I pull my knees to my chest and hug them to keep out the cold. We're on the other side of the Boundary but we have no idea what to do. We're on our own, utterly lost.

Chapter 20

Welcome to DREAM

Rufina's head was pounding.

'Welcome.'

Someone was speaking.

She opened her eyes, her vision swimming. There was a face in front of her. It was blurry, wreathed in a halo. Behind, she thought she caught sight of a large, black bird, but then it was gone and her vision lightened.

'Welcome,' the voice said again. Rufina recognised it.

Her whole body ached. She tried to speak. 'Where am I?' Her voice was croaky, barely audible.

She closed her eyes again. Instantly, a memory crashed over her: She was being dragged under. Around, great waves rose like mountains. The water was bone chilling. Fierce. She was struggling, fighting to stay afloat, debris crashing into her. A fragment of the crow's nest was tossed past, a remnant of the sinking ship.

She could feel Alfa gripping her hand. The irresistible current dragged her on. She fought. It pulled her towards the rocks ahead, jagged and deadly. And the roaring. Such roaring. It made Rufina's whole being tremble.

'Nib,' she whispered, opening her eyes.

'Rufina.' The face was there again. It was closer now, peering at her, concerned.

That face. She recognised it.

'Yarnbard?'

* * *

The old man peered at his friend. Her eyes darted erratically.

Her lips were moving but he couldn't make out what she was saying. He laid the back of his hand on her forehead. Her skin was icy cold.

'Rufina,' he said again, leaning closer. He turned his ear, trying to hear what she was saying.

She began to whisper, a breathy sound like punctured bellows. The wheeze gradually took shape. 'Yarn...' he thought he heard her say. 'Yarnbard?'

She was awake. She could see him.

'Don't move,' he said, laying a hand on her shoulder. 'Stay still. You've been through an ordeal. You need to rest.'

She focused on him, her eyes wide and fearful. He could see her grit. She was one of the strongest Mortales he knew.

'Yarnbard?' she mouthed again. 'But you're—'

'Asleep,' he interrupted. 'Yes.' He didn't want her to speak. She needed to conserve her energy. But as he looked into her eyes, he knew he would have to explain something or she would never rest.

She took another breath, ready to question him.

'Lie still,' he said. 'Lie still and I'll explain.'

Rufina released her breath.

'Yes, it's me. And yes, I am asleep.'

* * *

Rufina peered past the old man. Other things were beginning to take shape – blurry outlines. She was in a large, circular hall. Several camp beds were arranged in untidy clusters. A handful of figures moved between them. In a couple of the beds, Rufina could make out other people, blankets pulled over them. The figures all had a strange, shadow-like quality. They glowed, halos surrounding them, as if silhouetted by a brighter light. She could hear trickling in the background, a gentle, restful sound. The air in the hall also seemed to glow, giving everything a hazy, not-quite-real quality. Tiny sparks of light drifted, suspended in the air, making the whole scene feel...

'Welcome to DREAM,' the Yarnbard said, interrupting her thoughts.

DREAM? Rufina had heard of such a place in legends, but it was too much effort to try to recall them.

'DREAM,' said the Yarnbard, 'is the world beyond our world, or beneath it. It's a foundational place, the deepest level of our reality. DREAM is a reflection of what is. It is the other side of the mirror.'

Rufina scanned the hall again. She recognised this place. It was familiar and yet somehow it wasn't exactly the place she knew.

She breathed in, wanting to voice what she saw, but it hurt. 'Alethea?' she managed to wheeze.

The Yarnbard laid a hand on her shoulder. 'Don't talk. You need to rest.'

This was the Great Hall of Alethea, the castle of the Storyteller, Rufina knew it. Or at least it looked like it. But something was different, though she couldn't quite put her finger on what.

Another face appeared beside the Yarnbard, also dark and wreathed in the same bright glow.

Despite the pain, Rufina smiled. 'Mr Snooze?' she mouthed.

'Yes, it's me, dear.' The moon-faced man smiled back. 'Did I hear you talking of DREAM?' he asked the Yarnbard.

'You did. Your speciality subject, of course.'

'Indeed.' Mr Snooze knelt beside Rufina. 'DREAM is an echo of the Fullstop Island we know. DREAM's FULLSTOP ISLAND is almost indistinguishable, existing alongside it, but not precisely the same place.'

'How did we get here?' Rufina managed to ask.

'That's a mystery, my dear. None of us can be sure why we've been gathered here...although I might hazard a guess, if I may?'

'Of course. We are your students,' replied the Yarnbard.

Mr Snooze jiggled his head. 'Well, perhaps it's because ALETHEA is the heart of this world, its deepest centre. As such, it will be the last place to…' He trailed off, glancing at the Yarnbard, unsure whether to continue. The Yarnbard gave him a little nod. 'It will be the last place to disappear,' Mr Snooze finished. 'This place is lodged deep in the UNCONSCIOUS REALM. Because of that, it's our best stronghold.'

The Yarnbard nodded, thoughtfully.

The last place to disappear? Rufina repeated.

Mr Snooze continued: 'I believe ALETHEA itself has called us here as the ultimate act of self-protection. We may have arrived through different doorways – the Venus Flower, the South Bookend Isles – but the heart of the island has gathered us to itself. This is the last great bastion of our shared existence.'

The Yarnbard nodded. 'I've been here quite some time, you know – ever since I lost consciousness while fleeing the Red Hawks. I've been holding vigil, while my body lay safe aboard the Black Horizon. I greeted the Green Guardian, Christopher and Lady Wisdom here, many days ago. Now, I welcome you and the rest of the crew from the Black Horizon – Knot, Freddo, Pierre, the Boatswain, Alfa and Sparks…'

'They're all here?' asked Mr Snooze.

'They are.'

Rufina noticed the Yarnbard's voice had quietened. She felt uneasy. There was an absence, a name left from the list.

'And Nib?'

The Yarnbard laid a hand on her shoulder again. 'Nib didn't make it, I'm afraid. He—'

Rufina howled. 'No!' Her cry rang through the hall, her body convulsing with the effort. She had known it in her gut, but hearing it aloud sent the reality crashing through her. The other figures stopped and stared. For a moment, there was complete stillness in the Great Hall of ALETHEA.

'No,' Rufina said again, quietly. Her muscles shook

uncontrollably as she dissolved into tears. Sobs wrenched from the depth of her being.

'Shh,' the Yarnbard said, trying to comfort her. 'Shh, it's alright, it's alright.'

No, it isn't, Rufina wanted to shout. *It's not alright. It never will be. Nothing will ever be alright again.* But she couldn't speak through the sobs that rose in great bursts.

'Nib was a brave, brave boy,' the Yarnbard said. 'I don't think we would have made it here without him. And no ending is ever really final. There are stories beyond stories, dimensions we know nothing of. It is no coincidence this hall is circular, a never-ending wall.'

Despite the Yarnbard's attempts, Rufina couldn't stop sobbing. Her body rocked with lament. Nib was gone. She would never see him again. She rolled onto her side, curling into a tight ball. How could she handle such pain? How could she live with such grief? It would never end. She would have to carry this wound the rest of her days.

Behind, she heard the Yarnbard whisper, 'She needs rest.'

'I'll sit with her,' said a woman.

'Thank you, Felda.'

Rufina felt the presence of the Green Guardian beside her, a hand resting on her side. She allowed Felda's warmth to seep into her. It didn't ease the pain, but somehow it helped her to hold it. As Felda stroked her back, Rufina closed her eyes and wept.

* * *

Mr Snooze stared into the silver pool in the centre of the ALETHEAN hall. It was a sorry sight. A few straggling threads writhed sluggishly at the bottom of the basin. The head of the Department of Dreams could see a faint water mark where the liquid used to lap.

'It's drying up,' he said to the Yarnbard, the two men having retreated from Rufina's bedside.

'Yes,' replied the old man. 'The River Word is drying too. It will be gone altogether before long.'

Beside the pool, two candles burned, pools of wax spilling onto the floor around them.

'Your vigil?' asked Mr Snooze.

'Yes.'

'The Princess and the Storyteller – these are their lights, aren't they?'

'They are.'

Mr Snooze looked grave. 'Time is running out.'

'It is. We must protect these flames, keep them alight long enough.'

The candles were low. They flickered, sparking yellow and orange. 'Long enough for what, my friend? We're fading. This world is almost gone.'

The fire reflected from the Yarnbard's eyes. 'I still hold firm. I will not accept the end before it comes. We must protect these flames at all cost.'

Mr Snooze looked at him, his skin drooping, waxen as the candles that teetered, ready to collapse into themselves. He nodded. 'I will stand with you.'

'Thank you, my friend.'

'What of the other sleepers? Why are they not with us? Why are so few remaining?'

'Most of the island has been drawn into a place of stasis. They are unconscious.' The Yarnbard paused. 'Would you like to see?'

Mr Snooze nodded.

'Come then, follow me.'

Without a word, the two men wended their way through the hall toward the door to the castle's tallest tower.

'I warn you, it's a sorry sight,' said the Yarnbard, disappearing into the turret.

I'm getting used to that, thought Mr Snooze as he followed.

Chapter 21

Watching

I shuffle along the beach, my mind wandering. The sand crunches beneath my feet. I feel aware of every grain, every stone.

There's a pool of water next to one of the wooden partitions that divides the beach. I crouch, running my fingers through the icy liquid. The cold wakes my senses.

I'm supposed to be doing something. There's a reason I'm here.

Exploring.

Yes, that's it. I'm supposed to be exploring. I suggested it to…

I shake my head, irritated. I know the name. It's at the back of my mind, but I can't quite reach it.

Fletcher.

Yes. I said to Fletcher I'd explore. I'd see if I could find something to help us.

I straighten up. The beach is deserted, apart from a flock of seagulls circling someone in an old camping chair a little way down the beach. The birds wheel and dive around them, flapping chaotically.

I move closer, my head down. I don't want to be seen. A bitter wind surges from the sea, blowing straight through me. I watch my feet move across the sand. For a moment, they seem to fade. I blink and they become solid again.

I must be tired.

Reaching the next partition, I stop, a little way from the water. The person in the camping chair is staring out to sea, oblivious to me. There's another rock pool around one of the decaying beams. I crouch again, pretending to explore, but really peering over the wooden fence, spying.

The person in the camping chair is wearing a faded, red

puffer jacket. They have an old blanket thrown over their legs. They're feeding the seagulls, throwing scraps of meat and fish from a plastic box. The birds scream, fighting for the scraps. One of the bigger birds dives, viciously. The person waves a hand, trying to shoo it away. As they do, they turn to the side and I see their face.

It's a woman. I recognise her.

I rack my brains trying to remember where I've seen her before.

After a few moments, I realise I've zoned out and am staring at the barnacles clinging to the wood.

I shake myself and look up, examining the figure again.

It's the mother – yes, of course.

Whose mother?

I scrunch my face, trying to remember.

Libby's mother!

My senses flood back. I'm suddenly alert. This is important.

That's Libby's mother. She's is the reason Fletcher and I are here.

I inch closer, listening. She's talking to the birds.

'Get away with yer!' she shouts. 'Share! I've told yer before – there's enough for all of yer!' She kicks out at one of the gulls. It flaps away, screeching. 'You've had enough, you have!'

Throwing another scrap, she watches the birds leap on it. 'Have yer found it yet? Have yer?' She pauses, waiting for a reply. 'No? I bet yer haven't even looked, have yer? I don't know why I bother.' She waves both hands and the birds jump away in a swirl of feathers but are soon back, fighting over the scrap again. She points out to sea. 'It's out there somewhere, d'yer hear? I've told yer before! He made me throw it away! You've got to find it, bring it back! Go! Find my pen! It's out there somewhere under the water. Go! Go!'

She stands, knocking her blanket to the floor. The gulls screech, taking to the air. Libby's mum collapses back into the chair with a groan.

'What are you doing?' she asks herself. 'You don't even know why you want it back, do yer? Yer threw it away for a reason, remember? Yer can't live with all that noise in yer head – all those Mortales making yer life a misery. That's why yer came here, wasn't it, to get away, to escape!' She looks up. 'But when they're gone it's too damn quiet. I hate this quiet.' She glares at the gulls. 'Yeah, you keep on screeching, but go find it – go find my pen. I need it back! Maybe it is a source of noise, but it's a source of life too – my life – d'yer hear?' She rocks back in the chair. 'What am I doing, talking to birds? They don't care. They only care about this.' She tosses the rest of the scraps onto the sand and the gulls swoop in a savage whirl.

With a groan, Libby's mum grabs her blanket and stands up.

I step away, not wanting to be seen. Turning, I dash across the beach to find Fletcher. As I run, I glance back. Libby's mother has vanished. The beach is empty.

When I reach the boat, Fletcher's staring into the distance, a vague expression on his face.

'I've seen her,' I pant.

I don't think he registers who I am at first. His eyes focus. 'Who?' he says. 'Who have you seen?'

'Libby's mum. She's out there on the beach, talking to the seagulls.'

'Talking to birds?'

'Yes. But listen…'

I recount what I've heard.

When I finish, Fletcher pauses. 'The source? That's what she said – the source of life?'

'Yes.'

He reaches into his pocket and pulls out a stone. I know what it is, although the memory feels distant. It's the rock from the Merking's statue. I run my hand over my pocket and feel a stone there too.

'SEEK THE SOURCE,' Fletcher says. 'That's what was written on the...on the...'

'Merking's trident,' I prompt. I feel childish saying it. Merking? Trident? It seems so far-fetched. But there's the stone in Fletcher's hand. I can't deny that.

'Yes,' he replies, looking frustrated. 'So...' he pauses. 'So, the pen's the source? Is that what you're saying? That's what we're seeking – a pen?'

'I don't know. But if it is, we're done for. Her pen's lost. I heard her say it. The stupid woman threw it in the sea. She was telling the gulls to go and find it.'

I feel hopeless. Are we relying on seagulls to get us out of this mess?

Fletcher closes his eyes. He looks weary.

'If that's the source, it's gone,' I repeat, almost wanting him to feel worse.

He opens his eyes and sighs. 'I've been thinking. This might sound weird, but just before we stepped through the Threshold, the pirate said something that stuck in my head. He said the Storyteller *and* Princess exist on both sides of the Boundary. That's why they could cross the Threshold.'

'So?'

'Well...if Libby is the Storyteller back in our world, perhaps...' he pauses.

'What?'

'Perhaps Libby's mum is the Princess?'

I stare at him.

'I've been thinking about it since I read that ripped paper in the beach hut. You know, when you saw Grizelda appear. Those words summoned her. And do you remember what Libby said when we met her all that time ago? She said the journal – the one with our stories in – it had been her mother's. She had started our stories and Libby was finishing them. So...' Fletcher pauses again. 'So, our world was created by Libby and her mother – the

Storyteller *and* Princess. It's a shared world. We're children of them both.'

I stare at him, trying to take in what he's saying. *Our world was created by Libby and her mother. It's a shared world.*

'And you know what that means?' Fletcher asks.

I shake my head.

'There must be *two pens* – *two sources*. Maybe Libby's mum's pen *is* lost, but perhaps we can find the other one.'

'A second source?'

'Yes. We could still find Libby's pen, couldn't we?'

I feel like Fletcher's clutching at straws. 'Even if that's true,' I ask, 'how would we find it? We've no idea where Libby is.'

Fletcher shrugs. 'There must be a clue in the beach hut. Her mum must have kept something, a reminder, a memento, something that will tell us where Libby is.'

It's a long shot, but it's possible. 'But even if there *is* a clue,' I say, 'how are we going to get it? It's not like we can just walk up and ask.'

Fletcher gives me an intense look. 'We need to break in.'

'What?'

'We need to break into the beach hut.'

'No. I don't like it there! And what if she catches us?'

'We wait until we're sure she's gone. This stretch of sand is like an island. I've been looking around. It's just a beach with a small shop and café. You have to catch a boat to get to the mainland. Libby's mum must have to do that at some point. She must have to go there to get food. So, we wait. We wait and watch. And when we're sure she's gone, we break in.'

I can't believe Fletcher's suggesting this. 'I don't know…'

'Do you have a better plan?'

I don't. I just feel hopeless. I shake my head.

'Well then. This is our best shot. And if you don't want to do it with me, I'll do it alone.'

My cheeks flush. Why does he have to speak to me like that

– even here where we have nobody but each other? 'No,' I snap. 'We'll break in together!'

'Right then,' Fletcher replies. 'We'd better start keeping watch then, hadn't we?' He turns away and stares at the beach hut. 'I'll take the first shift.'

Chapter 22

The NIGHTMARE Army

From the tallest tower of ALETHEA, Mr Snooze looked out across FULLSTOP ISLAND. He had no words for what he saw. As far as the eye could see, the island was covered in cobwebs. A thick, white webbing criss-crossed everything, shimmering with DREAM-like intensity, sleep sparkles suspended around it. The web covered the foothills of the mountains; it clung to the pillars of WISDOM'S HOUSE; it crept down the dirty, brown banks of the river; and it drew BARDBRIDGE into a sticky, bulbous clump. Even the ships at the PORT OF BEGINNINGS AND ENDINGS were bound by the fibrous mesh.

The island was eerily still, but every so often, Mr Snooze caught sight of a shape lurking beneath the web.

'Are they...?'

'Gigan Ticks, yes,' the Yarnbard finished.

Mr Snooze could see one of the giant spiders hiding in the shallows of the PUDDLES OF PLOT. It was enormous – a great, hairy, arachnid. He shivered as he watched it burrow into the web, disappearing into its twisted labyrinth.

'They're the only things fully alive out there now,' said the Yarnbard. 'Look.' He pointed at a bulging, white cocoon that hung from the top of one of the THREE TOWERS. Mr Snooze could see others secreted in the sprawling web. 'The Gigan Ticks are guarding them.'

'What are they?'

'They are the other villagers. You asked where they were. Now you can see with your own eyes. We are the only ones left, the only ones who have not been captured and stored.'

Mr Snooze took in the eerie scene. He frowned. 'I'm not sure you're right,' he said.

'What do you mean?'

'I sense something else out there, something other than the Gigan Ticks.' He sniffed the air. 'There's a disturbance in DREAM.'

'What? What do you sense?'

Mr Snooze turned to the Yarnbard. 'Did *she* make it through with us?'

'Who?'

'Grizelda. Did her crow form make it through the Bookend doorway?'

The Yarnbard hadn't seen it, but it was possible. Everything had happened so quickly. One moment, he and the other Guardians had been silently keeping vigil, the next, a pile of bodies were writhing on the floor, coughing and spewing water, wriggling like fish caught in a net. In the chaos, the old woman may have made it through. 'I don't know,' he said. 'It is possible.'

'She's out there. I feel it. There's a disturbance in the fabric of DREAM. A doorway is being unlocked...'

'A doorway? What doorway?'

'NIGHTMARE,' the moon-faced man whispered. 'The doorway to the dark side of DREAM.' He began to edge away, back towards the turret that led to the Great Hall. 'We need to return,' he said. 'NIGHTMARE is coming, and when it arrives, we need to be ready.'

* * *

Grizelda peered into the darkness, her lips twisting into a wicked grin. Strips of dark cloud twined around her, as if caressing the old woman. On returning to FULLSTOP ISLAND, she had located her old ally, Melusine, and summoned her to DREAM. The tall Shapeshifter stood beside her now at the opening to the CENTRAL CHASM, her skin pale as ivory, her lips red as blood. Only pallid light filtered through the web above them, forcing Melusine to open her snake eyes wide to pierce the gloom.

'How sure are you thiss will be a success?' she said.

The old woman spat into the chasm. 'What d'yer take me for, snake brain? D'yer think I'd come up with a half-baked plan at a time like this? We're nearly at the end, ain't we? It's time for us to tighten our grip around the neck of this good-for-nothing world and to choke the life right out of it. I ain't plannin' to ease up on its windpipe until it's beggin' for mercy.'

Melusine hissed, a long tongue flicking from her mouth. The strips of cloud slithered around her shoulders too, binding the women in darkness.

'Now, let's get on with it, shall we, before one of those hairy monstrosities turns up to spoil the party. It's time to open the ancient doorway that separates the ABYSS from the CENTRAL CHASM. It's time to let darkness off its leash. You ready?'

'Yess.'

'Right then, get on with it, make the sacrifice. I didn't bring you 'ere for nothin', did I?'

Melusine pulled a knife from her dress and in one swift movement lowered it to her palm, slicing her flesh. She bared her teeth as she squeezed her hand into a fist. Blood dripped into the CENTRAL CHASM.

Grizelda heard it sprinkle the rocks below. 'Good. And now the words.'

The women raised their voices.

'*Come Vampire and Werewolf,*
Gorgan and Jinn.'
'*Banshee,*' Grizelda crowed.
'*Succubus and Incubus,*' Melusine hissed. The words echoed through the chambers below.
'*Manticore and Zombie,*' they recited together.
'*Cupacabra, Poltergeist, Mummy and Ghoul.*
Come Changeling, Cyclops, Golum and Troll.
Sirens sing.

Cerberus bark.
Demons shriek.
Behemoth roar.
We call the Headless Horsemen to ride once more.'

As they spoke, ribbons of cloud threaded down into the hole.

'Great Craken rise from Davey Jones's jail,' Grizelda wailed.
'Witch things fly. Giants hail!

Night army, be loosed, be loosed at last.
Night army, rise up, take arms, look fast.
Night army, fall in, advance, close ranks.
NIGHTMARE awake, breach daytimes banks.
The clock strikes twelve!
The clock strikes twelve!
Night is here!'

The two women fell still.

At first nothing stirred. But then, from deep below there was a faint boom. A low rumble echoed through the chasm. Melusine glanced at Grizelda, her tongue flicking. The old woman's chest heaved. 'Shh,' she breathed. 'I hear them.'

Melusine turned back. Deep in the earth there was a buzz. It was the scratching and clawing of creatures scurrying across rock. Dim thumps punctuated the hiss. They were joined by an eerie, discordant wail that echoed up, making Melusine's skin crawl. The noise grew louder, as if a storm were approaching. Yelps and unnatural harmonies joined the clamour, shrieks, hoots and growls. The ground was pounding. It trembled beneath Melusine's feet. A great roar burst from the hole. Melusine stepped back, but Grizelda stood, unflinching, searching the darkness.

She could see movement below. Cadaverous shapes leapt

from rock to rock, swarming up. Monstrous figures emerged. There were bats and serpents, headless men and snake-haired women. Shadow creatures drifted up, flaming Demons, Shades and Wraiths. Trolls burst out of the darkness, clubs in hand. Vampires, their teeth bared, scrambled over the edge of the hole, ahead of the Mummies, their decaying cloth catching the rocks.

Out they swarmed, pouring onto the earth, a frantic horde that surrounded Grizelda and Melusine. They bayed and stomped, hollered with rage, spears raised, clubs held aloft, scythes at the ready.

The last to emerge was the hulking figure of the Behemoth. It clambered out of the hole, the earth shuddering as it moved. Its skin was thick as rhinoceros hide, its hands cankerous and hairy; two great tusks protruded from its bulbous head, a long trunk hanging between them. When it finally reached the ground, it tore through the web above and stood, its head poking out from the canopy.

Silently, the cloud threaded its way back out of the hole and circled Grizelda again, becoming her cloak. She raised her hand and the horde fell still. 'Behold, the NIGHTMARE army,' she cried. 'This night we will extinguish the last light of this wretched world. I claim it as ours. Prepare for war!' A bloodcurdling cry rose as the NIGHTMARE army hollered and jeered.

In ALETHEA, the Guardians and the crew of the Black Horizon froze.

'What was that?' whispered Sparks.

'Come, my friends,' the Yarnbard said, his hands outstretched. He stood by the candles in the centre of the hall. 'It is time to for us to gather, to stand together, for I fear that, before long, the last great battle will begin and the NIGHTMARE army will be upon us.'

Chapter 23

Provisions

I grab the packet and slip out of the shop, running back across the beach, the plastic crinkling in my hand. My heart's thumping. I'm starting to get used to this snatch and run life. I don't want to lose the rush it gives me. It's the only thing keeping me alive at the moment.

I rip the packet open and push the pastry out of its wrapping. I'm still running as I stuff it into my mouth. It tastes so satisfying. I've developed quite a craving for the sausage rolls they sell at the beach shop. I want to eat it all. So much. But I won't. I'll save some for Scoop. She's not been looking well. And she's becoming forgetful. It's worrying me. She's thin. It's almost as if she's starting to...

I stop the thought. It's an illusion.

All of a sudden, my foot hits something and I trip, falling forward. I reach out to break my fall and the sausage roll tumbles from my hand. Before I have time to scramble up, a seagull swoops down and grabs it, jamming its beak into the pastry.

'Get off!' I yell. 'That's mine!' I push myself up and run at the bird, but it leaps into the air. If I wasn't so angry, it would look comical, the sausage roll hanging from its beak.

I shake my fist at it. 'That's mine!'

It settles on top of one of the beach huts and watches me with greedy triumph. Then it plunges its beak into my food.

I groan with frustration.

We can't go on like this. It must be nearly two weeks since we decided to break into the beach hut – I've lost track of time. Libby's mum rarely goes out. When she does, it's just to sit on the beach and talk to the gulls. She must have a pile of provisions in there. I just hope they're not going to last much longer.

The weather's changing. It's getting colder. When it rains, the air is left bitter. There was even a flurry of snow yesterday. Scoop and I huddle under our boat, trying to keep warm, but the tarpaulin is no real protection.

We've managed to scavenge the odd thing from bins. It's amazing what people throw away – an old blanket, a jumper, packets of barely touched food. We're learning not to be fussy. We can't be. We have to take whatever we can – or steal it. I've been slipping into the shop, coming out with crisps, chocolate bars…and the odd sausage roll. I haven't been caught yet and I'm getting braver, taking risks, almost as if I want somebody to see me. But they don't. It's like I'm not there at all.

When I get back to Scoop, she's sitting just down from the boat, staring at the beach hut. Her face is drawn. She's wearing an old blue jumper that's far too big for her. It's torn at one elbow. Underneath, I can see her red tunic, dirty and worn now. I wonder if her badge is still fastened to it – the book with the quill in the centre and "Blotting's Academy" stitched in fancy lettering. That all feels like a lifetime ago now.

I glance back at the boat. The two trolleys are still there, tucked away. I think I see two bodies on them. I might not want to admit that sometimes I see Scoop fading, but with our mother and the Storyteller, it's undeniable. Sometimes when I look, they're not there at all. Other times, I see the barest outline of a face or leg.

I can't look. It breaks my heart.

I turn back to Scoop. 'We can't go on like this.'

'Hmm?'

'We can't carry on like this.'

She ignores me. 'Did you get food?'

'I did.'

Her face brightens.

'But one of the gulls stole it.'

She turns away, clearly angry.

'It's not my fault,' I snap. 'I'm doing my best!'

I wish I didn't speak to her that way. But I can't help it. I'm so tired.

'Whatever.'

I take a breath. 'We can't carry on like this,' I say again. 'We need food.'

'You had food, but you lost it.'

'I mean real food, not something just snatched from the shop – something actually filling.'

'Well, what do you suggest, Fletcher?'

I hate the way she spits my name.

'I thought maybe I'd try to get across to the mainland, see if I can find something there. What do you think?'

She glares at me. 'Oh, right. And leave me here on my own?'

'Well, one of us needs to stay and keep watch.'

'And you've chosen yourself to have that adventure, have you?'

'You go then! I don't care! I'm just hungry. One of us needs to do something!'

'No, I'll stay here. You go and have a good time.'

I start to say something but think better of it. Instead, I turn and walk away, my face hot with anger. I wasn't planning to leave straight away, but my temper gives me energy. I stomp towards the jetty. It's about a quarter of a mile away, through the maze of beach huts. Before long, I'm there.

Half an hour later, I'm on a simple, wooden ferry crossing the lagoon behind the spit. It's a natural harbour sheltered from the sea. I'm still fuming. The wind is blustery as the boat pushes out. I huddle in a corner at the back, my coat thrown over me. I'm going to take advantage of the fact I seem to be invisible. Sure enough, a ferryman with a cigarette hanging from the corner of his mouth, passes me without so much as a glance, as he collects money from the other passengers. I look back at the thin strip of sand, lined with beach huts, as we move away from it. Slowly, my anger begins to drain into weariness. I hope I'm going to be able to find provisions on the mainland. I'm not sure what to expect when I get there. I don't know anything of this world, apart from the few hundred meters of beach we've been inhabiting. But I'm too tired to be scared. I just need something to go right for a change. I need to feel like someone or something's on our side.

The journey through the estuary takes about half an hour. We pass the remnants of a submerged tree, its dead branches sticking out of the water. I watch a gull with a fish hanging from its beak being chased by another bird. Slowly, the lagoon narrows into a river, its banks lined with tall grass. The boat bumps through the water. For a moment, the memory of an older, larger ship fills my mind, but it fades quickly, leaving only emptiness.

Behind the tall grass, I see a tower appear, castle-like, shining in the winter sun. As we round a bend, it comes into view more clearly. A few moments later, we're chugging past moored sailing boats. I study their names, *The Wild Goose*, *Serenity* and *The Robin*. Then, the ferry pulls up at a little jetty, and the ferryman throws a rope to his colleague.

I stumble onto the riverbank, my head swimming. I try to take in where I am. A neat green runs along the edge of the water. There's a bandstand, riverside cafés and the tower still visible above the houses. Not knowing where else to go, I wander towards it. I cross through a car park past a sign that reads, "Christchurch Priory". A moment later, I'm heading through its grounds, the tower gleaming above me. I walk on, my legs carrying me forward without thought. Once through the grounds, I emerge onto what must be the town's high street. It's busy with shoppers. I stop. Ahead of me, a blue banner runs along the top of a shop. It reads, "Bookends: The Store with a Difference".

Bookends, I say to myself. The name feels familiar.

And then I'm walking again, moving up the high street, passing card shops and patisseries, estate agents and clothing stores.

People push past me, heading in the other direction. They don't look at me; don't acknowledge me in any way. The shoppers, the noise, the traffic – it's overwhelming.

Another sign catches my eye: "The Ship Inn" and, across the road, an optician named "Scriven."

Scriven.

I keep walking, I don't know what else to do. I find myself passing through an underpass. As I emerge, I see another shop: "Dream Doors: New Kitchens for Old".

A dream shop, I say to myself.

My mind is churning. There's something strange about this place, something almost familiar. I pass "Castle Home Hardware" and then "Starlight: Classic Bengali and Indian Cuisine".

*Dream, Castle, Starlight, Bookend, Scriven, Ship...*I turn the names over in my head.

They stir something in me, the uncomfortable feeling that this place is a reflection of something I knew long ago.

Or perhaps I'm the reflection. Perhaps I'm just an echo, an image, a shadow.

The thought unsettles me and I stop. I find myself beside another inn: "The Railway". A picture of a green steam engine spews smoke on the sign above. Curious, I turn the corner. A little further along I find a wide, red brick building. "Don't smoke. Don't ride bikes. Don't skateboard or rollerblade. Don't loiter on the platform", a sign on the gate next to it reads.

A high whine catches my ear. Moments later a huge metal engine snakes into view. I've never seen anything like it, so long, so sleek, so powerful. It pulls to a stop and its doors slide open. A crowd pours onto the platform.

This is a port, a land port.

A boy whips past on a skateboard, nearly knocking me from my feet. Then the crowd streams through the little gate. I'm swept along and find myself walking again, retracing my steps, back past the Railway Inn, back through the underpass, back down the high street.

Nobody sees me. Nobody speaks to me. I'm a figment, non-existent.

And then it happens.

A hand grabs my leg.

I pull away, spinning round.

'Get off,' I hiss.

A man with a cracked tooth is staring at me from where he lies on the floor, pressed into the corner of an arch, surrounded by plastic bags. His legs are covered with an old sleeping bag. He looks at me, his eyes wild.

'I see you!' he spits. He jerks his head into a nod. 'I see you!'

'What?' I back away, my heart thudding. 'Who are you? What do you want?'

'Me? I'm nothing. Nobody.' Spittle flies from his mouth.

'Leave me alone,' I say. But as the words leave my mouth I know I only half mean them.

This man sees me.

He's the first person who's not looked straight through me since we arrived in this forsaken world. I'd forgotten what it feels like to be seen. It scares me. I've got used to hiding. But I can't turn away.

The man nods again, slower this time. 'Yes, I see you.' He points. 'I see you go up the street and I see you come back.' Suddenly, he scrambles towards me. I step back. 'We have to stick together, we do – us invisible ones.' He points from himself to me.

I'm not like you! I think. *I'm a hero, an adventurer, son of the Storyteller! You're a stinking down and out.*

But he sees me.

'Here, wait,' he says, scrambling back to his plastic bags. He rummages through them, his movement twitchy. Pulling something out, he turns back, a broad grin on his face.

'Take it!' he says, thrusting a slip of paper towards me.

'What is it?'

'Food. Take it.'

Food?

'You need it,' he says, seeing my hesitation. 'I know. I see the signs. We're the same. We're – unseen, forgotten. But I see.'

'How's it food?'

'Voucher. I'm not s'pposed to give it you. S'pposed to be a "designated provider", but I don't mind! Take it to this place.' He turns it over and jabs the back. There's a leaflet stapled to it with a map. 'You get food there.'

He holds out the voucher.

I reach forward and grab it. It reads, "Christchurch Food Bank".

'Good,' he says, looking pleased with himself. 'You need it. I can get more. Now go, get food! Go! Go!' He waves me away, nodding again.

My stomach grumbles and I nod.

Invisible? Unseen? Perhaps we aren't so different after all, I think, as I turn away and head along the street in the direction of the food bank.

* * *

I follow the map until I arrive at a tall, red brick building with a pointed roof. There's a large wooden door to its front but it's locked. I venture round the side and find a smaller door that's ajar. Fastened to the wall next to it, an inconspicuous little notice reads, "Christchurch Food Bank: Opening Times". Nervously, I push the door open and edge in. I find myself in a high-ceilinged room, lined with tall shelves, stacked with green crates. Through the gaps in the crates I see boxes and tins of food. My belly grumbles again.

Ahead, a young woman stands at a counter that separates the shelves from the entrance. She rocks a baby in buggy a little too forcefully. The child is asleep though, her head to one side, a thread-bear teddy clutched in her hand. An older lady stands behind the counter, wearing a baggy orange jumper, a green tabard over it with a badge labelled "Hilary" pinned to it. She's packing food from one of the green crates, every so often stopping to brush straggly, silver hair from her eyes. Through a door behind her, I glimpse other people in green tabards busying themselves with crates of food. The two women are talking. I edge closer to listen.

'How much do you get paid for doing this then?' asks the young woman. She bites her fingernail.

Hilary smiles. 'Paid? Oh no, we don't get paid. This is voluntary.'

The young woman's eyes widen.

'We've got some good stuff today,' Hilary says. 'Cereal, tea, pasta, tinned potatoes and biscuits.' She leans over the counter and smiles at the child. 'How's the little one doing?'

'Okay, yeah...okay,' replies the young woman, defensively.

Hilary smiles and then finishes packing the bag. She holds it out and the young woman grabs it, stuffing it under the buggy. She stops for a moment and glances up. 'But, why – why would you do that?'

'Give of my time you mean?'

'Yeah, you know...to people like...you know...' She looks away and fusses with the bag.

'I'm no different to you, dear. I've had my share of hard times too – we all have.' Hilary pauses. 'I do this because I believe in more than just words. I mean don't get me wrong, words are important, but they need to be made *real*, they need to be made *flesh*.' The young woman frowns. 'I just believe you have to do something, you know?' Hilary adds with a shrug. 'I'm a practical person.'

'Oh,' the young woman says. 'Well, thanks anyway.' She gives a curt smile and takes the brake off the buggy. 'Come on, let's get you home,' she says to her sleeping child.

Hilary stares at the door as the woman disappears. Her smile melts into a faraway look.

I'm left standing in the middle of the room, feeling awkward.

Just as Hilary's turning back to the shelves, she hesitates and stares in my direction. Her eyes focus. 'Oh,' she says, blinking. 'I didn't see you there.' She frowns at me. 'Have you been there long? Have you come for food, dear?'

I nod.

'Come here, then. Don't be timid. Have you got a voucher?'

I nod again. Approaching the counter, I give her the slip of paper. She studies it and then looks at me. 'How old are you, dear?'

I shrug.

'Quiet one, eh? That's okay. A lot of people are shy when they first come here. Now, let me see, I'm guessing you're no more than fourteen or fifteen.' She waits for me to respond. I give a little nod. 'Okay, well you're in luck. They've just changed the rules. I can give food to under sixteen's now.' She stares at me. 'But we're supposed to have a little chat, you know? I'm supposed to find out if there's anything else you need, anything we can help with.'

'There isn't,' I say, bluntly.

'Yes, well...next time, perhaps?'

'Yes,' I lie.

Hilary looks unsure, but pulls a pen from her tabard pocket and ticks some of the boxes on the voucher. 'I've filled it in as best as I can. But next time we must have that little chat, okay? Anyway,' she says, her face brightening, 'let's see what we've got.' She ducks behind the counter and pulls out another green crate. 'Beautiful day out there, isn't it?'

Is it? I hadn't noticed. 'It's cold,' I say.

'Yes, not long until Christmas. Are you looking forward to it, dear?'

I shrug, not sure what to say. I watch her packs fruit, vegetables, some tins and a box of cereal. My mouth is already watering. I want to grab the bag and get out. I need to eat!

Hilary glances up as she packs. I feel the same tightness in my gut as when the homeless man looked at me.

She sees me.

Finishing packing, she holds out the bag. I take it, impatient to leave, but as I do, she lays her hand on mine, holding me there. Her skin is cold.

'If you need any help,' she says, 'you just come here and ask for Hilary, okay?'

I nod, feeling uncomfortable.

'Good,' she says, releasing my hand.

I pull away, shaken by the intensity of her gaze.

She sees me. She sees who I am.

'I've put an extra bar of chocolate in there.' She winks. 'A little treat for the winter.'

'Thanks.'

As I leave, I glance over my shoulder. Hilary's watching me. She turns away, obviously not wanting to be caught staring.

As I walk away from the food bank, I replay what I heard Hilary say to the young woman. *I believe in more than just words… words are important, but they need to be made real, they need to be made flesh.*

I'm not exactly sure what that means, but it sticks in my head and I can't shake it. As I walk back to the ferry, I repeat it over and over: *words are important, but they need to be made real, they need to be made flesh.*

Chapter 24

The First Assault

The Yarnbard gathered the crew of the Black Horizon and the remaining Guardians around the candles by the silver pool. They waited in an uneasy cluster. Even Rufina was among them, although she hadn't spoken since being told about Nib's death.

Sparks sat on the cold, stone floor. She fidgeted, fiddling with her fingers, trying not to think about the spine-chilling cry that had just echoed across the island.

She squinted at the candles. They sparked and flared. They looked dangerously low, as if the slightest gust of wind would extinguish them.

Freddo had climbed the stairs in the wall next to the Great East Window and was staring out along the valley, through one of the clear panes of glass. He looked tiny under the huge, curved arch.

'What do you see?' the Boatswain called.

He leant against the glass, shielding his eyes from the moonlight's glare. Shadows from the window's tracery fell across his face. He didn't look well. 'They're coming,' he said, 'along the river path from the village.'

'Who?' asked Pierre.

Freddo shook his head. 'I don't know. A mob of some kind... but not like any mob I've seen before. There are...' he said, and paused, trying to find the words, 'half-animals...beasts of different kinds...giant folk...and riders, I can see riders – riders without heads.' Sparks shuddered. 'Leading them is a huge beast. I've never seen anything like it. It's as tall as the Scythe and it's ripping through the web as if it's nothing more than tissue.'

Sparks thought she could feel the floor trembling. 'What are they?' she asked.

'They are the NIGHTMARE army,' said Mr Snooze. 'They've been loosed from their prison deep below the earth, and now they seek vengeance.'

'Vengeance? But what have we ever done to them?'

Wisdom spoke, her voice quiet and clear: 'Like all darkness, their cause is driven by blindness. They don't perceive the goodness that surrounds us, that lives in each of us. To them, this world is cold. It's heartless. So, that's what they reflect. They don't know love. They're burdened with many ills: fear, self-loathing, rejection and pain of all types. All they desire, is to see an end to their misery, to finally extinguish the lights of a world, which for them holds no joy.'

Sparks shook her head. 'Then what are we to do?'

'We must keep the lights alive,' said the Yarnbard. He pointed at the candles. 'These are the lights of the Storyteller and Princess. While they burn, there is still hope.'

'But there are so many of them,' Freddo called, beginning to descend the stairs, 'and so few of us. How can we ever defeat them?'

Wisdom spoke again: 'We have more help than you realise. Their belief that this world is nothing but darkness is a lie. It will show itself as such. And remember, darkness cannot cross into ALETHEA of its own choosing. That law is deeply sown and clearly written. They will not breach these walls while we stand strong.'

'Should we not go out to meet them,' the Boatswain asked. 'Surely that's the hero's way?'

'No, that's vanity. We won't defeat the NIGHTMARE army on its own terms. They *are* too strong for us. We won't overcome strength with strength; instead we must overcome blindness with light.'

'Come, we must form a circle around the flames,' said the Yarnbard, 'a circle that must not be broken. Circles are strong, my friends. They have no beginnings or endings, making all equal. It is from this place of togetherness that we'll make our final stand. From here, we'll keep darkness at bay and magnify the light.'

'How?' asked Sparks.

The Yarnbard looked at her, his eyes glistening. 'By telling stories – the stories of our world. By keeping them alive. They are our light, our strength. You are apprentices at Blotting's Academy, even here, even now. How else did you imagine we would take our stand? The stories we tell will shine brighter than any weapon darkness can turn upon us. Come now, sit with me.' Slowly, the Yarnbard lowered himself to the ground and settling, reached out his hands. One by one, the rest of the company joined him. Sparks took Christopher's hand. His skin was rough and warm. To her other side, Knot reached out. She placed her hand in his. He closed his fingers and she felt his grip comfort her. Gradually, the circle formed, an unbroken chain surrounding the flames. When all were settled, the Yarnbard spoke. 'So, who will begin? Who will tell the first story?'

'I'll do it,' a deep voice replied from beside Sparks.

'Good,' the Yarnbard said, turning to Knot. 'Then, if we're all sitting comfortably, it's time to begin.'

* * *

Grizelda surveyed the jagged rocks of the GREAT WHITE CLIFF. The golden dome of ALETHEA perched on top like a jewel waiting to be plucked from a crown. 'Mine,' she whispered. 'Finally, mine.'

She turned to face her troops. Melusine had organised them into regiments. An army of Headless Horsemen made up the right flank, their black, skeletal steeds pawing the ground. Next to them, the Vampires stood in disciplined rows, resplendent in long, ebony cloaks and blood red breastplates. The Zombies were next. They were a much less ordered bunch. They scratched their peeling skin and twitched, shuffling and staggering. Frozen, beside them, were the Mummies, like ancient statues, arms outstretched, faces concealed beneath soiled bandages. An army of Medusas, hair writhing, perched on the rocks to the side of what once had been the SILVER LAKE (now just a puddle in the centre of a muddy ditch). They averted their eyes so as not to turn other parts of the army to stone. In front of them, a wailing, keening gaggle of Banshees swung their tangled hair, proclaiming the deaths of all in the castle. Trying to stay out of the way, a group of Trolls and Giants played knucklebones with the rocks. Behind them all, the Behemoth towered, its body swaying in the moonlight.

'Right,' Grizelda said to Melusine. 'Let's get on with this, shall we? We've waited long enough. Get that useless, fat beast to signal the start of the battle.'

Melusine looked up at the Behemoth and waved. It didn't see. She hissed and waved again, jumping slightly. Seeing her, the Behemoth straightened up. Its head reached nearly half way up the GREAT WHITE CLIFF. As it took a breath, the air around the NIGHTMARE army swirled, and the Vampires' cloaks billowed. The creature raised its trunk and let out an ear-splitting trumpet. The noise echoed down the valley, sending rocks toppling from the top of the gorge. It was heard as far as TALL TALE TREE FOREST, where the trees bent backwards in alarm. Across the island, the Gigan Ticks retreated into the safety of their web. Some of the NIGHTMARE army shrank in terror, others joined the blast with hollers and shrieks. Only Grizelda stood, unmoving, her eyes fixed on ALETHEA, high on the top of the cliff.

'Send the Vampires,' she whispered.

Melusine took a breath. 'Vampires advance.'

The blood-starved soldiers moved forward in perfect unison, the clicks of their boots ricocheting from the hills. As they approached the base of the cliff, they mutated. A wave of half-bat, half-lizard creatures leapt onto the rocks, clinging to them. They darted up. Grizelda watched the band of dark bodies move higher, but as they neared the top of the cliff, they sprang away, leaping into the air, becoming a cloud of bats. They descended again and transformed back to their human forms. One of the Vampires brushed himself down and shook his head at Melusine.

Grizelda tutted. 'Alright. Let's see if you can do any better, shall we? See that?' She pointed to a cave in the base of the cliff. 'That used to be hidden behind the waterfall, that did.' Only a pitiful dribble now trickled down the rocks, making the opening clear to see. 'That's the underground entrance to ALETHEA. In there, you'll find a door to the castle. Take some of yer Shapeshifters and see if they can shift 'emselves past it. Some of 'em are so thin in the brain, they might just be able to slip through the cracks; not namin' any names o' course.'

Melusine beckoned a small group of Shapeshifters. One by one, they slipped into their animal forms. A troop of rats, termites and bugs moved towards the tunnel. Melusine was the last to transform. With an angry flick of the tongue, her snake form slithered to join its faction.

Grizelda watched as the creatures crawled and scuttled into the tunnel. She tapped her foot, irritably. It wasn't long before a rat scuttled back out, followed by the other creatures. One by one, they transformed back into their human shapes.

'I thought as much,' Grizelda muttered.

Melusine began to speak. 'We couldn't—'

'Shut it.' Grizelda cut her off. 'I don't have time. My patience is wearing thin. Send the Giants.'

Melusine glared. 'Giants! Advance!'

The bare-chested goliaths dropped their Jacks and lumbered forward, sploshing through the muddy lake. Muck flew through the air, splattering the regiments. Reaching the cliff, the Giants lifted Thor-like fists and began to pound the rock.

Chapter 25

Invasion

I shake Fletcher's shoulder. I'm not gentle. His eyes spring open and he scrambles to his feet, looking disorientated. The bags of food he brought back a few days ago are empty, thrown into the corner of the boat.

'What—' he begins.

'She's leaving.'

'Who?'

'Libby's mum. Who do you think?' I can see his eyes focusing as he drags himself from whatever dream world he's been occupying. I jab him in the arm.

'Ouch!'

'Are you going to stand there all day or are you going to do something useful?'

He blinks. 'She's leaving?'

'Yes!'

'Not just to feed the gulls?'

'No. She's carrying empty shopping bags and she doesn't have her chair with her.'

He takes in what I've said and grins. 'Then what are we waiting for?'

It's been a while since he spoke to me with that dry, sarcastic tone. My heart lifts. I'd almost forgotten what a good team we make…how much I love my brother.

'I was waiting for you, Fletch,' I reply. 'I still am…'

He strides towards the beach hut. 'Then how come I'm still in the lead?' I hear him say.

Catching up with him, we peek around the corner of the alley beside Libby's mum's beach hut. She's already part way along the beach, leaning heavily on her stick.

'We'd better get on with this, hadn't we?'

'Wait. Not yet. Let's make sure she's definitely leaving.'

I nod. 'Okay. Good idea.'

We follow her to the jetty, always staying a few metres behind, sneaking through the warren of alleyways. She walks determinedly, ignoring those she passes. Nobody pays her any attention. I feel like a spy. We're on an adventure again. It makes me feel alive.

Sure enough, we watch as Libby's mum boards the ferry and sets off across the lagoon. 'We probably only have an hour,' I say. 'The ferry runs every twenty minutes, and I don't think she'll want to hang around on the mainland any longer than she has to.'

'No,' Fletcher agrees. 'We'd better get on with it then. So... how are we actually going to get into the hut?'

I smile. 'I've been thinking about that, Fletcher. Follow me.'

* * *

Back at the beach hut, I lead us to the far corner of the cabin. There's a narrow gap that cuts into the dune. We squeeze down it. The cabin is dilapidated, its paint flaking. The smell of mould is pungent. I stop by a small window in the centre of the back wall and slip my fingers under its shutters. Running them along the rough wood, I find a catch.

'The lock on this window is faulty,' I say, keeping my voice low. I don't know why I feel the need to be quiet; there's nobody around.

'You've been doing your homework.'

'I have, Fletcher. I'm not just a pretty face, you know.'

He smirks. 'No, that's my role.'

The lock gives, and I tug the window open. 'Right then, don't just stand there looking pretty, give me a hand.'

Leaning on Fletcher's shoulder, I clamber up to the window.

He mumbles complaints as I use his hands as a foothold. I push the top half of my body into the cabin, and the sound of the sea deadens. It's dismal inside. The air is musty and stale. I scramble up, pushing my feet over the lip of the window. Tumbling down inside, I scuff my shin. The cutlery in the kitchen jangles as I hit the floor. I pause for a moment, waiting for my eyes to adjust.

'Come on,' Fletcher hisses. 'Open the door. Quick.'

'Give me a chance!'

'We don't have long.'

'I know!'

I glance at a little clock standing on the kitchen surface. It's slow but still ticks. I guess it must have been ten minutes since Libby's mum left.

'Take your time,' Fletcher snaps, as he pushes into the cabin. I close the door behind him and the beach hut falls into a tense hush.

'Where should we start?'

'Let's split up. I'll search the main section around the table. You look through the kitchen and around the bed.'

I nod and head straight to the kitchen units. There are still unwashed plates in the sink, one of them furry with mould. *How does she live like this?* I open the first cupboard and inspect the tins and jars. 'Remember to put everything back exactly as you find it.'

'I know!' Fletcher's already thumbing through the papers on the table.

Slowly, I begin my search, starting at the top, right-hand cupboard and working methodically through each in turn, looking for something, anything, that might give us a clue as to Libby's whereabouts. The cabin is simply furnished. It doesn't feel like a home, doesn't feel lived in. I open the next cupboard. There's not much there – a couple of plates, a chipped cup, a single saucepan and a battered frying pan. The cupboard is thick with dust. Carefully, I move each item, putting them back exactly as I find them. The wooden units creak, despite my efforts to move quietly. It feels as though the cabin is watching, wary of the intrusion. Fletcher is riffling through the little drawer in the table. I glance at the clock. Another ten minutes has passed. I'm trying not to panic, not to speed up the search. I need to be meticulous. But my hands are clammy and my stomach's clenched.

There's nothing here, I think, lifting a basket of broken pens and used batteries. The thought buzzes through my mind like a persistent fly. *We're not going to find anything.* I run my fingers under the kitchen surface and then stand on an upturned bucket to examine the top of the cupboards. With each passing moment, my anxiety rises. What if there really isn't anything here, no clue to be found? What then? We'll be stuck in this accursed half-life.

The clock ticks on – twenty-five minutes, thirty-five, forty.

There's a loud creak outside. Fletcher and I freeze and look at each other. We listen intently. Wind buffets the little cabin. Shoes shuffle across the decking of the front porch. I hold my breath. Fletcher's gripping a moth-eaten winter coat. He's been searching its pockets. Careful not to make a sound, he hangs it back on its peg and signals for us to move to the far side of the hut, away from the door. I tiptoe towards the wall, aware of every squeak, every scrape of my shoe. I don't know what we think it will achieve. The hut's tiny. There's nowhere to hide. If Libby's mum comes in now, we'll be caught. But somehow it feels safer pressed up against the wall.

'She can't be back yet, can she?' I whisper, looking at the clock. It's been forty-five minutes since she boarded the ferry. Time's running out, yes, but she shouldn't be back yet.

Fletcher shrugs.

We wait, barely daring to breathe. The decking reverberates with a footstep again. But there's no key in the lock, no movement of the latch.

Fletcher edges towards one of the windows.

'What are you doing?'

He waves for me to be quiet.

Reaching the window, he peeks through one of the slats in the shutters.

I wait for what seems like an age, the shuffling growing louder. Suddenly, Fletcher spins away from the window, ducking out of sight.

'What's happening?' I mouth.

'It's okay,' he whispers. 'It's not her.'

'Who is it?'

'I don't know. Just a nosy tourist. False alarm.'

I breathe out, but I'm still tense.

Sure enough, a moment later, we hear the unwanted visitor descend the steps and disappear.

'That was close.'

Fletcher crosses back to the coat he was examining. 'Come on, we don't have long. She could be back in—'

'Ten minutes,' I finish. We glance at each other, nervously. I need to voice my fear. 'There's nothing here, Fletch. We're not going to find anything.'

'We have to!' There's determination in his eyes.

His conviction gives me a boost. I nod and turn to the bedroom area, pulling back the curtain that separates it from the rest of the hut. It's a mess. The sheets are bundled at the bottom of the bed. I run my hands through them. They're damp. I shudder, knowing I'm intruding on someone's personal space. It's a strange sort of intimacy that makes me feel queasy. There's nothing there. Dropping to my knees, I explore the space beneath the bed, running my hands along the metal frame and peering under it. I hold back a sneeze. There's so much dust. I'm panicking now, moving frantically. There's nothing here either, nothing on the floor around the bed, only a half-empty glass of water, green with algae.

CRACK! Glass shatters. I spin round, my nerves shot. My hands are trembling. Fletcher's staring down at the shards of a broken vase.

'What are you doing!'

His face flushes. 'Do you think I meant to knock it over?' His fists are clenched.

I take a breath, trying to calm myself. We can't afford to get into an argument.

'It's okay.' I raise my hands in a reconciliatory gesture. 'We just need to get it cleared away.'

He nods and begins to pick up the pieces.

I glance at the clock again. There are just a few minutes left before Libby's mum might return. This is a disaster.

I go to help, but as I do, something gives beneath my feet. I look down, moving my weight back onto the floorboard behind me. It squeaks, sinking a little. It's loose.

My heart skips. Kneeling, I run my fingers around the join in the wood. One of the boards juts up. Pushing down on the other end, the board rises. I slip my fingers under it. It's stiff, but with a crack, the wood flips up. There's a space underneath, a secret compartment, and in it...

'Letters!'

'What?' Fletcher looks round, pieces of broken vase in his hand.

The letters are yellowing, bound with a faded, lace ribbon. I pick them up. It's like holding treasure.

'Libby!' I say, holding them out. 'Letters to Libby! Fletch, this is it! We've found it!'

He rushes over, his hands still laden with pieces of broken vase. 'There's an address,' he says, examining them.

'Her address! Fletch, we've got it!'

'Yes! I knew we'd find it. Right then, let's get out of here!'

I look at the clock – two minutes until the hour is up.

I point at the broken vase. 'What are you going to do with that?'

'I'll get rid of it outside. Hopefully she won't notice it's gone.'

Fletcher bounds to the door.

I scan the room. Have we left everything as it should be? The window's still ajar, and the loose floorboard's propped against the wall. Setting them right, I dash after Fletcher.

We sneak back around the corner to our boat. We're just in time. Libby's mum appears, limping along the beach, laden with shopping.

Diving back under the tarpaulin, we pull it down to hide us. Fletcher grabs the letters from me, and we stare at them. The top one reads:

Libby Joyner
25b De Lacey Mount
Kirkstall
Leeds
LS6

'I'm going to go.' Fletcher says, scrambling to his feet.

'What?'

'I'm going to go there.' He jabs the address. 'To find her.'

'What do you mean? Now?'

'Yes.'

'But Fletcher—'

'There's no time like the present, is there?' He signals to the Storyteller and our mother, their outline faint. 'We can't wait any longer.'

'But...but how are you going to get there?' After weeks of waiting, this is happening too quickly.

'There's a place in town – a station. It's like a port but on land. I think I can get there.'

'But what about me?'

'You need to stay here, with the Storyteller and Princess.'

I shake my head. I don't want to be left alone.

'I'll be as quick as I can,' he says, seeing the look on my face.

'But we need to do this, Scoop. We can't wait any longer. We have no choice.'

I rack my brains for an alternative, but deep inside I know he's right. Now we have the address, we need to find Libby. What else can we do? And there's every reason to hurry and no reason to wait. Who knows how long it will be before the Storyteller and Princess vanish altogether. And one of us does need to stay with them.

'Okay,' I say, my mind grappling to keep up. I feel sick.

'Good.' He nods.

Before I know it, he's ducking under the tarpaulin. I've always been jealous of Fletcher's ability to act quickly. I dither. I struggle to make choices. Sometimes his decisiveness seems brusque, rude even, but sometimes it's exactly what's needed and, although I feel suddenly bereft, I can't help but think this is one of those times.

I lift the tarpaulin and call after him. 'Be careful!'

He glances back, nodding.

I'm alone. Outside, it begins to snow again. I hope Fletcher finds Libby. I hope he stays safe. I watch him disappear into one of the alleyways. That might be the last memory I have of him. I hug my knees to my chest, trying not to let fear overwhelm me. I'm scared of being alone, scared I'll never see my brother again. I slump to the side and close my eyes, trying to block the world out, the letters still clutched in my hand. I wish I could wake up from this nightmare. I wish we could go home.

Chapter 26

Stories of Light

The noise of the Giant's attack thundered up the cliff to ALE-THEA. Knot paused, midway through his story. He glanced at the Great East Window. It was shaking.

'Do continue,' said the Yarnbard, apparently unaffected by the tumult. 'We must tell our stories, keep them alive. We must remember! Do not be distracted.'

'Oh yeah, course,' replied Knot, looking back to the circle. 'Where was I? Oh yeah.' He tried to ignore the booms from below. 'Well, I don't remember much of my childhood, just a few things. Climbing Great Furnace with Da to carry rocks down in the stone barra. I remember the smoke and the heat, Da's face being red and dirty, bits of ash in his beard. I remember being pleased when he gave me rocks to carry. It made me feel useful, part of the clan. I was one of the Rock People, see. I remember sorting through rocks with Ma, in a big, old kitchen with stone walls, all the pieces laid out on a big, wooden table. Some of 'em had minerals in, yer see. Others, 'specially the lava, were good for fertilizin' soil – brought a pretty penny at the Market of Miracles, I remember Ma sayin'.'

Knot paused and looked down. 'I remember raiders comin' – princes and their armies in big, posh ships. I remember Ma pushing me into the cellar. I remember being scared. We weren't supposed to be scared, Rock People. They said we was made of rock. I think that's why they saw us as monsters, why they came every summer to kill us. But we *weren't* monsters.

Every autumn, when the raiders left, there would be funeral pyres. The flames went high. I remember the stars in the sky, brighter than anything yer see here. We'd stand and watch the bodies burn. That autumn, Da was one of 'em.'

The Giants' pounding stopped, and the hall fell still.

'I remember Ma packin' a bag for me. There weren't much in it, just a coat and me Jack rocks. She took me to a boat filled with people I didn't know and put me on it. I remember her tellin' me the boat was gonna take me to a better place.

But it didn't.

Halfway across the sea there was a storm. The boat hit a rock. It sank. I don't know if anyone else survived.

I remember being dragged out of the water by an old woman. She was sprawled on the beach, her feet dug into the sand to stop her being pulled into the waves. I remember her cursing as she pulled me from the water.

She saved me that day.' Knot looked down, embarrassed. 'Grizelda. Grizelda saved me that day.'

'But after that, she made my life a misery. I was her slave. Rock People aren't slaves, they're free people. She used to say me and her had somethink in common. She said we'd both been spat out, puked up by life – that we weren't worth nothing we didn't take for ourselves.

I believed her, I did. There was princes and posh soldiers, and then there was us, less than rock, less than rubbish.

I didn't think I was worth saving back then. I didn't care she made me her slave, that she got me to do things that would make me ashamed now. I went from the rock of the Furnace Islands to the rock of the Story Caves. Rock was all I knew.

That's where we kept Master Fletcher and Miss Scoop, back when they were little'ns, in that rock prison. Anyways...'

Sparks stared at the candles, her mind drifting.

She saved me that day – Grizelda.

The woman trying to breach the castle, trying to kill them, had saved one of their company. She'd saved Knot. He wouldn't be here without her.

Only because she wanted a slave, Sparks told herself.

But that felt too easy, and Knot's words kept churning in her mind.

She saved me that day – Grizelda.

One of the candles sputtered, orange light flaring up. The wax was almost gone.

Stories of light, Sparks said to herself as the flame settled. *We must tell stories of light.*

* * *

Grizelda kicked a stone. It landed in the mud of the SILVER LAKE and sank. So far, nothing had worked. The Giants had only managed to dislodge some scree; the Manticores had flown up on their scaly wings, only to return, roaring and snarling, enraged at not being able to pass through the enchantment; the Sirens had sung, only to lure a Cyclops to stab its eye on a tree branch; and the Headless Horsemen, well they were utterly useless when faced by a cliff.

'Call this a NIGHTMARE army?' she said. 'They could barely scare a baby in a pit of vipers! They're useless, utterly useless, the lot of 'em.'

Melusine didn't reply.

'This is your fault, yer know!'

'We need access to the castle,' Melusine hissed, 'and then the army can do its work.'

'Oh yes,' Grizelda mocked. 'O' course. Why didn't I think of that? Well done. Such intellect, such insight. We have to gain access to the castle. Whatever would I do without your tiny little snake brain?'

Melusine's tongue flicked angrily. 'You know the enchantment—'

'I do!' snapped Grizelda. 'Darkness cannot cross the boundary to ALETHEA without being invited. Yada, yada, yada. I thought that stupid rule might have fallen away by now. But no. How tiresome. Well luckily for you, I have a contingency plan.

What yer got to say about that?'

Melusine was silent.

'Cat got yer tongue?'

Melusine started to reply but Grizelda interrupted. 'Oh, never mind. I don't care, anyway. I'll tell you what's gonna happen. I have somewhere to go, someone to meet. You stay here and look after this bunch of morons. Set up camp and don't let 'em kill one another. Do you think you can do that?'

'Of courssse!'

'Good. Well, I'd better get goin' then. I don't have time to waste stood 'ere swapping pleasantries. I'll be back before dawn, got it?'

Not waiting for an answer, Grizelda walked away. The NIGHTMARE army parted for her as she headed through its ranks. Black cloud billowed behind her, leaving a trail of darkness in her wake. Melusine watched the old woman disappear along the path back towards BARDBRIDGE. Turning to the Chimera, she ordered bonfires be lit and gave word that the NIGHTMARE army prepare to move to a siege footing.

Chapter 27

Separated

I watch the world fly past: snowy fields, cables and pylons, barns, bridges and trees that block my view. A town whistles by, its houses squashed together, and then it's gone. I've never known such speed. It makes me feel small.

This land, this world, it's huge.

There are cars waiting at a crossing. They look like models. Signals and spires, factories and flooded rivers flash by. All the while, my reflection stares back at me from the train window. A bird hovers at the edge of a field, searching for prey. It only knows that little patch of land. It's so small, so insignificant.

I'm no different, I think.

My reflection flickers as we enter a forest, becoming solid as the train goes into a tunnel. My eyes are deep, my nose sharp. I've thrown my coat over me, pulling it up to my mouth to try to hide my face from the guard. I don't know why I bothered. He walks straight past without asking to see a ticket, just like the ferryman.

Good, I think. Although part of me wishes he saw me.

On the table in front of me is a train map. I've studied it. The corners are now dirty and bent. I've plotted my course.

Christchurch to Waterloo.

Waterloo to King's Cross.

King's Cross to Leeds.

Three steps. Easy.

I look back out of the window as the sun blares, and my reflection fades.

Easy, I tell myself again, but it's hard to trust when the world seems so vast.

* * *

I wake up, my cheek still pressed against the letters. The ribbon has left a mark on my skin. I feel disorientated. I'm not sure how long it's been since Fletcher left. I wish he was here. I wish he hadn't gone.

I look at the letters to distract myself, staring at the handwritten address. Why write letters if you're not going to send them? I run the end of the ribbon through my fingers, enjoying the feel of the lace, and find myself tugging the loose end a little. The bow shortens.

They're not mine, I tell myself. *It'd be wrong to open them.*

I tug a little more.

Almost without noticing, the bow slips open and the letters tumble onto my lap. There must be about ten of them, each neatly sealed, each addressed by the same hand, each dated. I spread them out.

They're not mine, I tell myself again. *It would be wrong to open them.*

Fletcher would open them, I think.

I find the earliest letter. It can't have been written long after Libby's mum went missing. I turn it over in my fingers. It has the same musty scent as the beach hut. I run my finger along the line of the seal.

It would be wrong to open it.

And then I'm slipping my finger under the fragile paper. It's brittle and dry. The seal is loose. It opens almost without me realising. Before I know it, I'm pulling the letter out and unfolding it. I know I shouldn't read it, but I need something to do, something to distract me, and now it's open...

Dear Libby...

* * *

It's been three hours since I left Christchurch. I picture Scoop huddled under the boat. Thinking of her alone makes me uncomfortable.

I'm leaning against a river fence, the iron railings cold on my legs. A boat passes, a crowd of partygoers on its deck, its music loud. Lights dance on the water.

My head is swimming. Around me, the air buzzes with noise: a busker's saxophone, the whirl of fairground music and the constant babble of conversation. I'm surrounded by a village of wooden cabins – a market. They look like gingerbread houses, lined with lights, piled high with chocolates, candles, decorations and little glowing snowmen. I can smell roasting chestnuts. It all seems a bit...fake.

I'm in London, on the South Bank of the River Thames, so a sign hanging from a tree made of teddy bears tells me. This is the Christmas market.

It's packed. A boy on a skateboard tries to push through the crowd but soon gives up. Flipping up the board, he disappears into the sea of people. Above me, blue and white lights hang across the market, spilling into the trees, causing star-like explosions in their branches. Beyond, a giant wheel rises, its glass carriages carrying people through the night sky.

I can't take it in.

So many people.

I walked here in a daze, searching for a tower I glimpsed from the train as it pulled into Waterloo – a giant, twisted spike of glass and metal. It reminded me of something deep in my memory...or imagination – another tower, another three towers, but made of rock. I don't know where the memory comes from or how it found its way into my mind. It's like a cuckoo's egg – a memory of a different home. It feels like a dream. But somehow that tower awoke the memory, and I had to try to find it.

It's somewhere behind me now, I think. I lost direction amid the corridors of buildings and queues of traffic. Instead, I found myself here by the river. On the other side, a building spreads beyond the big wheel. It looks like a matchstick model of a toy palace. From its tallest tower, a clock shows the time. A bell sounds, echoing across the water with a deep boom. I count each strike in my head. One...Two...Three...Four. These winter nights begin early. The sound wakes me. I need to find my way across this city. I begin to move back towards the station, threading through the crowd. I've seen entrances that lead underground. There are trains in the tunnels under this city. They'll carry me on.

Waterloo to King's Cross. Step two.

As I enter a doorway and begin my descent, images of a portly man dressed in red flash on screens that line the walls. 'Season's Greetings,' he says, winking. 'What will you wish for this Christmas?'

* * *

I stare at the letter, a secret message from mother to daughter.

Dear Libby,

I wish I could see you. I wish I could tell you how much I love you.

I'm writing this because I need you to understand. I need to explain. And yet, at the same time, I know I will never send this. It's funny, I hadn't realised, but I already have a hiding place for it in my head – under the old floorboard, where I used to keep my treasures as a child – my shells and stones. That says it all. That shows the deep conflict that runs through my life. I am like this letter, full of words never to be spoken.

I don't know how I got here, and I can't excuse it. I remember leaving your breakfast on the table that morning, not even stopping to put my coat on. My legs had a momentum of their own. I don't know exactly what prompted me to walk out the door. I was aware of the cloud I've been living under these past months, of course. But, although that may have been the trigger, it wasn't the cause. Rather, it was an amalgamation of everything, of what my life had become.

I want to justify it, but I can't.

As I've grappled with that cloud, I've become aware of something else: another me, another self, lurking in the shadows – a past self. She was there that morning, under the surface, silent and un-named. For so long, I tried to ignore her, to push her away. I tried to be what everybody expected of me. I did as my father told me, Libby. I put my pen away, the source of my life. I did as my husband told me, to shelve my dreams, to focus on what mattered – being a good wife, a good mother, a good woman, while there was still time. But she was always there, living alongside me, quietly in the darkness – the girl I tried to hide, tried to kill.

I used to write Libby, all the time. I'd scribble on the corners of my schoolbooks, on the backs of envelopes, on my hands when there was no paper to be found. I marked my skin. And I used to draw – nothing special, just doodles, useless smudges of ink. I wore pretty dresses and loved to dance. I loved to listen to music. Where did that child go?

I know full well.

She never left. She was always there in the shadows, growing in bitterness, biding her time.

That morning, she quietly inhabited me, led me away and brought me here.

But what am I supposed to do? Hide? Wait? For what? For my life to expire? I'm not her anymore. But I'm not me, either. I don't know who I am. I'm lost, incapacitated, a useless cripple. This disease seeps into my body. My legs are getting worse. I must lean on that wretched stick even to move. I'm slowly decaying.

You're better off without me, Libby, without this war that rips through me. I hide it well. You may not have heard the bomb blasts, but it has torn me. I cannot be known as a Joyner any longer – joiner – that always made me laugh. I've gone back to using my maiden name, Speller.

I'm torn, Libby. And I'm scared I'll tear you.

I needed you to know.

Your loving, unworthy, mother.

I put down the letter. How can someone live feeling so divided? I can't tell if I'm sad or angry. The letter's heartbreaking. Libby's mum's hurting. But it also feels selfish, self-obsessed even. I picture Libby, the girl caught by the bomb blast of her mother's life. This isn't fair. It's an injustice that needs righting, a chasm that needs bridging.

Chapter 28

The BLACK LAKE

Grizelda stood at the top of the CENTRAL CHASM, her toes flexing over the edge, a sheer drop below. Ribbons of black cloud slid from her shoulders and threaded into the hole. A moment later, they looped back up, circling down again, as though beckoning the old woman.

'Yes, yes,' she said, impatiently. 'I'm getting too old for this, ya know.'

A thick band of cloud hovered in front of her, swaying like a cobra eyeing its prey.

'Alright, alright, keep yer hair on.'

Grizelda slipped off her shoes. She'd done it a hundred times at that other hole, the Abyss, but it was different here at the heart of THE ACADEMY. It made her uneasy.

'Get a grip,' she muttered.

Pulling a coil of rope from her cloak, she found a rock to fix it around. Once it was secure, she tied the other end around her waist and returned to the hole.

'Well, 'ere goes nothin'.'

Leaning back over the chasm, she let the rope take her weight. The black cloud slithered into the darkness. With a huff, the old woman pushed herself out and began to abseil down, descending into the caves below.

* * *

Slowly, carefully, Grizelda moved through the STORY CAVES. The cloud slithered ahead like Ariadne's thread, guiding her through the labyrinth. Every so often, it doubled back, slipping around the old woman's waist before continuing onwards.

'I'm goin' as fast as I can,' Grizelda muttered. 'I'm not gettin' any younger, yer know. Yer don't want me havin' a fall and bashin' me head open, do yer? What good would that do yer? All yer pretty plans would go up in smoke.'

The old woman followed the cloud through the maze. She prided herself on knowing the STORY CAVES as well as anyone. She'd spent long enough in them, after all. But she didn't recognise this part of the network. The tunnels seemed to be narrower, darker than she was used to.

Just as the caverns were becoming impassable, the old woman pushed through a crack and found herself in a vast chamber, its ceiling disappearing into the darkness. It was bigger than any chamber Grizelda had seen before. She couldn't see the far side. How did such a place exist so deep underground? She was standing on a small, stony bank. Apart from that, the whole cave was covered with water, but it was black water, thick and lifeless. Sleep sparkles hovered in the air, but they cast no reflection on the lake.

The old woman stopped at the edge of the water. 'Now what?' she asked. There was no further to go.

The cloud slithered forward, brushing the surface of the water. When it neared the centre, it snaked down, piercing the lake's skin and disappeared below.

Grizelda was left alone.

She fidgeted, stones shifting beneath her feet. She didn't like it here. It gave her the heebie-jeebies. And it made her feel…vulnerable. That wasn't a word Grizelda cared for. If the cloud left her, she had no idea how she'd find her way out. The thought of wandering the darkness until she collapsed didn't appeal at all.

'Pull yerself together,' she muttered. 'You haven't come all this way to lose yer nerve now, have yer?'

She tapped her foot, waiting. 'Come on, come on, what's keepin' yer?'

Just as she was about to call out, something shifted in the

middle of the chamber. A shape emerged from the lake. She peered through the gloom. A black boat was rising silently from the water. The vessel was simple, with a high, arced prow. The cloud circled the boat as it floated towards her. There was a figure aboard – a tall man, draped in black, standing at its helm. He didn't seem to be rowing or guiding the boat in any way. He was just standing as it drifted towards her. Grizelda had the unnerving feeling he was watching her.

The Ferryman. She shivered. There weren't many things that scared her, but the Ferryman was one of them. She'd always hated stories of him as a child and demanded they not be told. The Ferryman was tasked with carrying souls to the world of the dead. If there was one thing Grizelda didn't like, it was the thought of death itself; her death, her life being snuffed out, ended, full stop.

The boat reached the bank and stopped. The Ferryman didn't move.

'Well, ain't yer gonna invite me aboard?'

He didn't reply.

'Talkative down here, ain't yer? Right then. Well, there ain't no point standin' around.'

Grizelda waded into the BLACK LAKE, the bottom of her cloak becoming sodden and heavy. She clambered awkwardly up the ferry, pushing her legs over the side, until she toppled into it, landing like a sack of potatoes.

Standing, she brushed herself down. 'Don't help or anythin',' she muttered.

'Right then. I'm ready. Cast off, or whatever it is yer do.'

The hull of the boat scraped against the stones as it moved away from the shore.

Grizelda twisted her cloak nervously. Where were they going? She still couldn't see the other side of the cave. 'I can't breathe underwater, yer know?' she blurted.

Again, she was met with silence.

As the boat drifted towards the centre of the lake, the cloud began to wrap itself around Grizelda. It encircled her, until she was completely hidden, held in a black cocoon. Then, slowly, the boat sank down into the BLACK LAKE and disappeared.

Chapter 29

Source

The train rocks me gently, lulling me into a fitful sleep, and before I know it, another two hours have passed.

The landscape is dark now, although I can still see its outline against the navy sky. Every so often, I glimpse snow in the twilight. Red brick cities have replaced sleepy villages, and the horizon seems to have gathered into hills, although maybe it's just low hanging cloud. London feels far away. I've been dreaming about rumbling through the tunnels of the big city, emerging into King's Cross, its girders like phoenix wings. I keep replaying the moment I walked past a crowd gathered around a trolley, half-buried in the wall, "Platform 9 3/4s" written above. This is a strange world.

The train's beginning to slow now. Warehouses and crowded streets close in. We're pulling into a station.

LEEDS

I sit up, suddenly awake. I'm here, here in Libby's city. I spring up and join the queue of people waiting to leave the train. I jig from foot to foot, unable to keep still. I'm here. I've made it.

But what now?

* * *

I read each of the letters in turn – January, February, April, August, December, then almost one a month throughout the following year.

The conflict is clear throughout. Sometimes the letters are poetic. Libby's mum talks of the sea, of the debris on the beach, of the gulls – painting pictures with her words. Other times, the letters descend into a sort of madness. She repeats the same phrases again and again: that she loves Libby, that she's sorry, that she can't explain or excuse her behaviour, that she's a burden, that Libby is better off without her. And the pen, her silver pen, the one she used to write her stories – our stories – she returns to it often. She calls it her source – a source of life but also of conflict.

At one point, she tells of how she's locked the pen away. She's never going to use it again, she says; she can't control what it releases. Mortales spring into her imagination, threatening and accusing her. One name keeps coming up – Falk. It seems familiar, although I can't place where I've heard it before.

A few letters on, it's clear she's taken the pen out again and is writing. There's an uncontrolled quality to her words.

I read on, gripped, not sure how much time has passed.

I pick up the next letter and stop. It's the last one. It's dated January of this year. Why did she stop writing in January? That's almost a year ago. It gives me an odd sensation; like perhaps I'm drawing closer to the woman we've been watching these past weeks. I pause a moment longer and then rip open the envelope and begin to read.

* * *

I hold the map book close to my nose. It's hard to see it in the dim street light. I bend the cover back to make it easier to read, but the road I'm looking for is right on the fold. Typical. De Lacey Mount, there it is. I trace my finger over it and look up, trying to work out where I am. The bus stopped opposite Norman Row. All the roads here have the same name: Norman Row, Norman View, Norman Grove, Norman Mount. It seems someone had a severe lack of imagination. I scan the red brick wall ahead, looking for a street sign.

Back Norman Mount. There it is, hiding below a satellite dish. At least I know I'm heading in the right direction.

Rows of red brick houses run down the hill. Coloured lights

flash in some of the windows. One of them has a large reindeer in its garden, an inflatable Santa stuck to the wall.

I walk through the slush, water soaking into my shoes. I don't notice it really. I'm too preoccupied thinking about what I'm going to do when I reach Libby's house. Will I knock? Will I wait outside until I see her? I have no idea.

As it is, my questions are answered as I turn onto De Lacey Mount. A teenage girl stands at one of the yard gates, halfway down the road. She's yelling at a man in the doorway. I freeze, my heart almost stopping. It's her. It's Libby!

I dive behind a parked van and peek out, my back pressed against the metal.

She's a couple of years older than when I last saw her, but it's definitely her.

I've found her!

Libby's yelling, but I can't take in what she's saying. My mind's racing. I peek out from behind the van again, trying to focus.

'You can't make me go!'

'Don't make a scene,' replies the man in the doorway. It's her dad, it must be. I can see the resemblance.

'I don't care who hears! You can't make me!'

'It's Christmas Eve tomorrow, Libby. We're going to see your aunt and that's final.'

'But I hate her!'

'Libby!' Her dad looks shaken.

'It's not what Mum would have—'

'Your mum,' her dad interrupts, raising his voice. He stops himself and takes a breath. 'I'm not going to talk about this now, not in the middle of the street.'

'Fine!'

'But we're going. It's arranged.'

'Whatever!'

Libby stomps away. She doesn't look back. I watch her dad

take a breath to call after her, but he changes his mind. His shoulders drop, and he disappears back into the house.

I dart after Libby, ducking behind the cars.

She vanishes around the corner at the bottom of the street. When I reach the junction, I see she's crossed the main road and is heading towards a broken, grey tower, set back among some trees.

Kirkstall Abbey, I think, remembering the name from the map.

I follow as she heads into the abbey grounds. The tower is lit garish yellow, pools of electric light breaking the shadows. I notice Libby's carrying a pile of papers.

What's she up to? What are they?

There's a river at the edge of the grounds, and a weir. Reaching the water, Libby stops. I come to a halt a little behind, hiding behind a tree, the hiss from the weir masking my noise.

She's not going to see me, I tell myself. *She's too focused on whatever she's doing.*

Moving around the tree, I edge a little closer. Libby's face is red and blotchy. I can't tell if she's angry or upset. Perhaps both. She takes out a sheet of paper, crumples it into a ball and flings it into the river.

There's a jolt in my gut.

It hits the water and drifts towards the weir. In the distance, a freight train rumbles past.

Pausing only momentarily to watch, Libby pulls out another sheet, screws it up and tosses it after the first.

No!

'I'm done!' she says.

The paper moves slowly with the current.

I know what she's doing. This is her writing. She's throwing it away.

Throwing our world away! I think.

I move closer. She can't do this! She mustn't!

Libby throws another crumpled ball into the water. She's

talking to it. She reminds me of her mum, speaking to the gulls.

'What's the point?' she spits. 'There is no point! I won't do it anymore! I can't, anyway, even if I wanted to. This is where I threw it – my pen – into the river. I can't leap without it. No other pen will do. It has to be that one. It's under there somewhere, gone. Now, you have to join it.' She pulls out the next sheet of paper, crumples it, and throws it into the river.

What did she just say? She's thrown her pen away – the one I've come all this way to find? The second source, it's also lost?

I feel like I've been punched in the gut. Libby's mum threw her pen into the sea. And now this?

Like mother like daughter!

But if both pens have gone...

This is over.

I feel numb. My journey's been for nothing. SEEK THE SOURCE – that's what we were told. But the source is gone! Lost! Thrown away!

How dare she! This is my life! How can she treat us with such contempt? Do we mean nothing to her?

She throws another ball of paper into the water. It slams through my gut.

This is it, our world being discarded.

I picture the Storyteller and my mother, their bodies fading. I picture Scoop. I won't let her do this. I can't.

'Stop!' I yell, running across to her. 'Stop this *now*!'

But she doesn't look round. She doesn't even flinch.

She can't hear me.

I've been aware of being invisible to others, but to Libby? Surely she must see me. She *has* to!

But she doesn't. She doesn't respond in any way. I really have become nothing.

Libby throws another sheet of paper into the water. The pile is thinning now.

I move in front of her.

'Listen!' I scream. 'Why won't you listen?' I wave my hands in front of her face. I need her to hear me! I'm close to her; we're almost nose to nose.

For the briefest moment, Libby pauses.

'You can hear me,' I whisper. 'I know you can.'

Her eyes dart. She's aware of something, I'm sure of it. But she gazes beyond me to the paper floating silently away.

I'm a ghost, a figment.

She steps forward. Before I can move, she pushes right into me. But we don't bump into one another. Instead, she steps right through me, as if my body is just air.

But I feel her. As she passes through me, I feel her touch. It jolts like electricity. She feels it too and cries out, stumbling back, tripping on the root of a tree. Falling, she drops her papers. They scatter like leaves. I move forward to help, electricity snapping as I touch her again, making me stumble too.

'Ouch!' She scrambles away, terrified.

'It's me! It's Fletcher!'

Her eyes don't focus on me. Darting forward, she snatches the rest of the papers, gathering them in her arms. She's about to push herself to her feet when she freezes, looking at the ground in front of me.

I glance down. On the grass is the photo we picked up at the beach hut – the picture of the girl holding the red spade. It must have fallen out of my pocket when I stumbled.

Libby picks it up.

'How…?' she whispers. She shakes her head. 'It can't be. I haven't seen this since… How did it get here?' She glances around, but there's nobody here. Other than us, the abbey grounds are empty. She examines the photo, holding it gently, almost reverently. She runs her finger over the image of the girl, her childhood self. Then, I see her focus on the face behind, her mother, waiting, ready to catch the child.

'Mum,' she whispers. 'This is a sign. I know it. I don't know how it got here, but I know it is. And I know what I need to do.'

Spinning round, she begins to run back across the abbey grounds, back through the gate, back along the street in the direction of her house. My heart thumps as I give chase; barely daring to hope I've got through to her, that I brought something here, even without knowing, that may reach Libby, and in doing so, save our world.

* * *

The last letter is shorter. It's simpler in tone. But I think it's the letter that makes the most sense. It gives the impression of a woman beginning to heal, slowly moving on...

Dear Libby,

I've thrown it away, my silver pen. I've finally done it. I tossed it into the sea, into the depths.

Since then, my head has quietened. I struggled with the still-ness at first, but now I feel more ordered, as though I've thrown away a part of myself, finally allowed it to die.

With that death has come a realisation. It almost makes me laugh to see how simple it is.

The pen is not important. It's just an instrument, it's not the song. The pen is not my source, not even the words that flow through it. They're the notes, yes, but they're not the music.

Words on their own mean nothing, they're just marks on the page. Only when words are received, when they're shared, do they bring life. It's that connection that's important.

Relationship is the source! Words must be made real; they must become flesh – that is the end of their quest.

Do you remember when you were young, too little to even feed yourself, I used to sing to you? I used to tell you stories. I remember those moments as being the happiest in my life, the most complete I've felt. That contentment came from something being

179

shared, something pure – our relationship, mother and daughter. I realise now, I became a storyteller to join our worlds together. I don't know how I've not seen it before!

I needed time to accept the fate that awaits me. I'm sorry I had to leave to do that, but I needed space; space to reconcile to my past, space to confront this cloud I find myself in.

But I'm ready now. I will see you again soon.

Your loving, blinded, mother.

I look up. *We've got it wrong!* I need to tell Fletcher. *We've been searching for the wrong thing! The pen is not the source.* Libby and her mother, they are the source – their relationship. But it's broken, torn and separated.

I look around. The beach is empty. Fletcher is long gone.

Just like us, I think.

Chapter 30

The Night Figure

The BLACK LAKE waited underground, deathly quiet, perfectly still. Even the sleep sparkles around it had stopped moving. They hung, suspended, as if time itself had stopped.

In the darkness, the curved prow of the Ferryman's boat rose from the lake, its progress as smooth as the moon's course. The Ferryman stood at its helm. Around it, the sleep sparkles began to stir again. At the centre of the boat, the black cloud circled, forming a tight cocoon. Once clear of the water, it uncoiled to reveal Grizelda's stumpy body. Next to her was a second figure, dark as night. Icy coldness emanated from it, making the air around the boat freeze. It looked like one of the Mummies, wrapped in bandages, its face concealed. But its bandages were black. The figure stood, motionless as death.

The boat crept noiselessly to the shore. It drew to a stop, and the cloud slithered over its sides, oozing back towards the entrance to the chamber. Without a word, the old woman followed. The night figure moved silently after her. Together, they followed the cloud out of the chamber, beginning their journey back to the surface of the island and to ALETHEA.

* * *

The fires of the NIGHTMARE army illuminated the GREAT WHITE CLIFF. The troops were in disarray. The Trolls and Giants were fighting again, the Vampires were complaining about the Banshees' wailing, and nobody was happy with the Zombies. Melusine was at her wits end. She'd considered slithering away, leaving them to their petty squabbles, but she'd have to face Grizelda if she abandoned her post. Instead, she moved between the regiments, listening to their complaints and trying, as much as possible, to snuff out sparks of conflict before they erupted into full-force fires.

She was trying to explain to a Wraith that they had best keep out of the way of the Cyclops, since it was still half-blind from its run-in with the Sirens, when she felt it – an icy cold, creeping through the air. It made her breath swirl. She silenced the Wraith.

Melusine wasn't the only one who sensed the change. Gradually, the NIGHTMARE army fell still, leaving only the crackling of the fires.

As the temperature dropped, a thick frost spread through the camp, creating a long, white carpet. Around it, crystals began to cluster on the trees.

The army parted to reveal two dark figures, in sharp relief to the frosty path. The cloud twisted ahead of them. Melusine recognised the first. It was Grizelda. But who was the second, black as the night?

Slowly, they moved towards her, the ground crackling around them. As they approached, Melusine felt as though her blood was freezing.

'Who is thiss?' she asked, as Grizelda drew near. The night figure waited a little way from the women.

'You'll see,' croaked the old woman. There was something different about her voice. It was stripped of its brash rasp.

Melusine narrowed her eyes, but nodded.

Glancing at ALETHEA, Grizelda crossed to the night figure. Freeing the end of one of its bandages, she began to unwrap its head. She worked her way down its body to reveal messy brown hair, a grimy forehead, chestnut eyes and a strong nose. The bandages fell to the ground like shed skin. Melusine stepped back. What was this? She recognised the face. But, it couldn't be…

Grizelda continued to unwrap the night figure until he was freed from his bandages. When the last one fell to the floor, she stepped back.

The figure was a boy, little older than an academy apprentice. He was tall and gangly.

'But...but it can't be,' hissed Melusine.

* * *

In the Great Hall of ALETHEA, the circle sat around the candles, their hands joined. Alfa was telling of how her parents first realised she could shift the seasons. It had been a sunny winter's day and she'd melted a circle of ice with a song. She was about to sing it to the circle, when a voice interrupted, echoing up the cliff from outside. It was an ordinary voice, a friendly voice.

'Hello,' it called. 'Hello. Is anybody there? Could you let me in? It's cold out here.'

Everyone froze. Rufina, whose head had been bowed, looked up, alert.

'No!' stuttered the Yarnbard. 'Don't listen. It's a trick of the night.'

'Hello,' the voice called again. 'Please, let me in. I know you're all in there. I need to join you.'

'Don't break the circle!'

'Rufina! It's me. It's...'

Rufina leapt up.

'No!' cried the Yarnbard, stumbling to his feet. But it was too late. Rufina was sprinting towards the stairs that led to the castle's underground entrance.

'Stop her!' yelled the Yarnbard. 'Somebody stop her!'

Freddo, Pierre, Christopher and the Boatswain sprang to their feet, giving chase.

Mr Snooze held out his hands. 'With me,' he wheezed. Alfa, Sparks, Felda, Wisdom and Knot shuffled in, joining hands again, the circle tightening.

Footsteps rang from the stairway below. Sparks could hear

Freddo and the Boatswain shouting. The Yarnbard stared down the steps, his face stricken as the noise of a key in a heavy lock echoed up.

* * *

Melusine stared at the boy's face. She recognised him from the Wordsmith's Yard. He was the stable lad.

'Hello!' he called up again.

A slow, rumbling creak echoed from the tunnel. The door was being opened.

Grizelda's eyes narrowed. 'Call the advance,' she whispered.

'NIGHTMARE army!' Melusine cried. 'Attack!'

There was a roar as the night army rushed forward, pouring into the tunnel towards the entrance to ALETHEA.

* * *

Rufina stood, helpless, as the NIGHTMARE army swept past her. Trolls, Werewolves, Golems and Orc rushed up the steps towards the Great Hall. She gripped the door, searching for a face in the crowd.

As Grizelda pushed past, she winked. 'Thank you, me dear. Much obliged.' She disappeared up the stairs.

And then Rufina saw him.

'Nib,' she gasped. Stepping out, she blocked his path. 'Nib, you're here, you're alive.' Halting in front of her, Nib stared at Rufina. 'I'm sorry,' he whispered. Rufina reached out to him, but as she did, an icy gust burst from his body. Nib crumpled, collapsing inwards. He disintegrated into her hands. She was left clutching a strip of black bandage. Rufina sank to her knees and drew the cloth to her cheek. There in the doorway to ALETHEA, she nursed it, as the NIGHTMARE army surged past.

Chapter 31

Stealing

I follow Libby back to her house, slipping into the hallway just before she pushes the door closed. I notice she shuts it quietly, turning the handle so the lock doesn't click. She glances towards the lounge. The rhythmic bells of a Christmas song spill through it. Her dad's watching TV. She begins to creep up the stairs, tip-toeing, missing certain steps, moving from side to side.

She knows where they creak, I think, following. She pushes herself against the wall and slips up the last few. *She's obviously done this before.*

I glance through the banisters, into the lounge. A plastic Christmas tree stands to the side of the room, a few lonely presents beneath it, the light of the TV flickering on its branches.

I stop.

That wallpaper – I've seen it before. I recognise the faint shine of golden brown diamonds. I don't know why such a small detail leaps out, but it makes my skin tingle. I rack my brains, trying to remember where I've seen it before.

Of course! Not where, but when! The memory comes flooding back: the noise of the Great Hall; the smell of rich food; reaching out to take the Storyteller's hand, everyone's eyes on me; the hall vanishing and Libby appearing; the soft music from her iPod; the feel of the sofa; the journal, our lives written in black and white; and the revelation that Libby is the Storyteller. *That's where we met her, there in that room, the night we were swept here; the night of the Great Wedding Banquet.*

I'm surprised the memory's still there. I thought I'd forgotten all but the briefest glimmer of that world. But it's still intact, hiding in the shadows.

I hear Libby moving about on the landing above, and it shakes me from my trance.

Come on. Now's not the time for sentimentality. I need to focus.

Pulling myself away, I head upstairs to find Libby in her room, throwing clothes into a sports bag. She zips it shut.

Pulling out her phone, she begins to tap the screen. I feel awkward standing there, unseen.

It's okay, I tell myself. *I'm here to help.*

Cautiously, I edge closer, trying to see what she's looking at. I peer over her shoulder.

MY TRAVEL. Libby taps a train icon and the display changes. PLANNER. I watch as she begins to type. The word comes up quickly. LEEDS. I already know what she's going to put next. CHRISTCHURCH.

She's going there! She's going to the beach hut! She's going to find her mum!

I think of her dad, still watching TV, unaware of his daughter's plan. For a moment, I'm sad for him. He seems so disconnected from Libby.

But I don't have time to dwell on it. Libby taps GO and a list of train times and prices appear.

'One hundred and forty-six pounds!' She shakes her head.

Opening her bedside table drawer, she pulls out a floral, plastic purse and takes out a little bundle of notes. Sitting on her bed, she begins to count them. Twenty…thirty…forty…fifty. She lays each note out carefully. 'Not enough,' she says, running her hand through her hair.

She sits for a moment, frowning. 'Is it still there…?' she says to herself. 'It must be.' Scuttling to her bookcase, she fumbles at the back of the top shelf. 'Yes, here it is.' She pulls down a silver moneybox, covered in dust. Running her fingers around the rusted lid, she pulls it off. The coins jump noisily. Libby stills the tin and runs her fingers through the copper and silver inside. 'Good girl,' she whispers, 'I'd forgotten about hiding these.' With a grin, she pulls out three more notes, folded into neat squares.

Flattening them, she adds them to her pile. 'Ninety,' she whispers. 'Still not enough.'

She sits down again and taps her leg, distractedly. She glances at the door. 'No,' she whispers. 'I can't.' Turning away, she bites her lip, but then looks back again. 'It's for Mum.' Getting up, she sneaks onto the landing and leans over the banister to check for movement below. The TV's still blaring. Creeping up the hall, she slips into the room next to hers. I follow to find myself in a dim bedroom, the curtains closed. It smells of sweat and stale deodorant. There's a double bed in the centre, the duvet pulled up hastily. One wall is filled with mirrored wardrobes. This is her dad's room. I don't feel comfortable being here. Not turning on the light, Libby tiptoes around the bed and carefully opens his bedside drawer. Lifting a magazine, she riffles through it and pulls out a bulging leather wallet. Glancing at the door, she opens it. She stops, a strange expression on her face. I edge closer to see what the matter is. There's a photo of Libby in the front of the wallet. She flips it away and begins to thumb through the wodge of paper inside. 'Yes,' she hisses, pulling out a few crisp notes. Stashing the wallet back in the drawer, she slips out of her dad's room again and back into her own. Reaching her bed, she adds the new notes to the pile.

'One hundred and ninety pounds. Yes, that will do.'

Libby stuffs the money into her pocket and picks up her bag, throwing it over her shoulder.

Moments later, we're heading down the stairs again. She moves with urgency but still careful not to make them creak.

Then, we're out onto the street once more. The night is blacker now, colder. I gulp the cool air and realise I've been holding my breath.

We walk quickly towards the bus stop. I can't believe what's happening. We're going to Christchurch. We're heading back to Scoop, to Mother and the Storyteller. I can scarcely contain the thrill I feel. We're going back, and Libby is going to find her mother!

Chapter 32

Circles

The morning's bright. Too bright. It hurts my eyes. Flurries of snow swirl in the wind. The tarpaulin flaps, but I'm too tired to tighten it.

I'm drawing circles in the sand. I don't know how long I've been doing it. The motion is comforting. My fingers are red and there's sand lodged under my nails.

Round and round, round and round... I repeat to myself, trying not to think.

After a while, my arm begins to ache, and I stop. I hug my knees to my chest, and I stare at the deep grooves in the sand. I feel numb.

What am I doing here?

I push the question from my mind.

What am I doing here?

Every time I stop making the circles, the same question torments me.

What am I doing here?

It won't stop. It's relentless.

What am I doing here?

It makes it hard to breathe.

'I don't know!' I say aloud.

'I don't know.'

I hug my legs tighter.

What am I doing here?

I can't remember.

How did I get here, to this boat, to this beach?

No answer comes back.

I search the empty sand, my eyes darting.

What am I doing here?

My chest tightens. I'm too scared to move.

I'll wait. Somebody will come. They'll come for me.

Behind me are two empty trolleys. I know they're here for a reason. I'm sure they are. But when I try to remember, my head hurts.

I pinch the skin on my arm, needing to feel something. The pain wakes my senses. For a moment, I think I see a figure on one of the trolleys – a man, auburn hair trailing onto the sand, his skin sallow, his eyes sunken.

I recognise him. At least I think I do.

I stop pinching and the image fades.

I want the tarpaulin to stop flapping. I want there to be an end to this cold. *I* want to fade.

This is the end of the circle, I find myself thinking. *I started with nothing. Then, I think, I found something. But now, I'm back to having nothing. Round and round, round and round.*

I reach forward and start to run my fingers around the grooves in the sand again. It feels soothing.

Round and round, round and round...

No memory, just circles in the sand.

* * *

I'm groggy. The wind stings my skin, waking me. After a day and a half of travelling, I'm back on the ferry, heading across Christchurch Harbour to Mudeford Quay. The boat bounces on the water. It's late morning and the winter sun is bright. The ferryman wears a crown of tinsel around his woolly hat, although none of the merriment spills into his face. A cigarette still hangs from his mouth.

Libby sits on a bench in the corner of the ferry, her knees drawn to her chest. She stares across the water with a faraway expression. Lank hair blows across her face, making her look dishevelled. In the rush to leave, she forgot to pick up a warm coat, and her skin is red and rough with goose bumps. She looks exhausted. It's no wonder. The two of us spent the night wandering the streets of London, waiting for the first train to Christchurch.

We walked along rich shopping streets, hung with lights, stopping to stare at models of fairy tales in the shop windows.

We sat on the steps of a church, by a tall column and a huge Christmas tree, the sound of a choir spilling through its doors.

We passed the sparkling signs of theatres.

Libby seemed to be wandering without direction, walking just to keep warm.

We avoided revellers staggering along the riverbank.

We huddled in a doorway at the bottom of a grey, concrete bridge, until forced to flee by a drunken man, who seemed to be threatened by our presence.

We nursed a mug of coffee in an all-night café.

We waited on the concourse of Waterloo Station as the sun began to seep through the grey clouds.

I say we, but really Libby did these things alone. I was just a shadow.

On the train back to Christchurch, I dropped in and out of sleep. We were delayed by winter weather, but I barely noticed. By the time we reached Southampton, the train was packed with people heading to the coast for Christmas Eve.

Now I'm on the ferry again.

I've travelled hundreds of miles, and although I've only been away one night, it feels as though weeks have passed.

'Merry Christmas,' the ferryman grunts, as he takes Libby's ticket money. She doesn't reply. 'And Season's Greetings to you, too,' he mutters, moving to the next customer.

The ferry is busier than I'd expected. Couples sit with arms entwined, families huddle together with gloved hands and flushed cheeks. A little girl waves a sparkly wand at the birds, whispering Cinderella spells. An old lady in an elf hat hands out sweets. There's a festive atmosphere aboard. Only Libby and the ferryman look melancholy.

I don't know what to feel. I swing between excitement and doubt.

Gradually, we draw closer to the row of beach huts, their colours muted in the winter light. This place: the beach, the harbour, the mud flats, the ferry, they seem so peaceful after the bustle of the city and the heat of the train. I feel like I'm approaching the edge of the world, a bridge to another realm.

I wonder how Scoop's getting on.

I wonder if the Storyteller and our mother are safe.

I'll soon find out.

Chapter 33

Wisdom's Last Treasure

'The castle is breached,' the Yarnbard whispered.

He stumbled back to the circle to join the others. 'Whatever happens, we must hold this circle. Do you understand?' he said, his eyes fierce. The company nodded. '*Whatever happens,*' he repeated. 'Don't let me down.'

The sound of boots echoed upwards. Sparks shivered. She didn't know if she could do it, if she could hold the circle. *You will,* said a voice inside, *for the Yarnbard, for the Storyteller, for everything good in this world.* And despite her doubts, Sparks knew the voice was right, she would hold the circle for as long as there was breath in her.

As she found her resolve, Freddo, Pierre and the Boatswain tumbled back into the Great Hall, swinging the door shut behind them. They braced it. A moment later there was a sickening thump as the NIGHTMARE army slammed into it. Then the pounding began.

'We must carry on telling stories of the light,' said the Yarnbard. 'We must remember. Alfa could you continue—'

'If you don't mind,' interrupted Wisdom, 'I would like to speak.' The old man stared at her. There was sadness in his eyes. Slowly, he nodded. 'Thank you.'

Wisdom drew herself up straight. 'I think the time has come to tell *Wisdom's Last Treasure.*' She took a deep breath and began.

'I remember my childhood as though it were yesterday. It was idyllic. I played among the fruit trees, caught cherry blossom in the spring and kicked up showers of red and gold leaves in the autumn. Our orchard was full of song: the rich flute of the blackbird, the tinkling of goldfinch, the sweet melody of the nightingale.'

A hammer blow struck the door, sending a shock wave through the Great Hall.

Wisdom continued, undaunted. 'My sister and I spent our days chasing kingfishers along the riverbanks and feeding doves. We were twins.' She paused.

Freddo and the Boatswain were straining to hold the door, their faces purple. Pierre spun away as an axe head smashed through the wood.

'We *are* twins,' Wisdom corrected, 'born of the same flesh, made of the same substance.'

There was a cry as the door to the Great Hall exploded into splinters. Grey hands stretched through, waving wildly, ripping the wood. The Boatswain tried to hack them back, but it was too late. The door gave way, falling forward and, with a holler, the NIGHTMARE army spilled into the ALETHEAN hall.

Freddo tried to run, but a Troll seized him, picking him up by the scruff of his neck. He wriggled, but the creature lifted him high off the ground. It raised its club.

'No!' yelled Alfa.

'Don't break the circle!' the Yarnbard commanded, gripping her tightly.

There was a slurping sound, followed by a thump. Behind the Troll, a figure scrambled to his feet, appearing as if from nowhere. He was drenched, seaweed hanging from his hair.

Seeing Freddo dangling from the Troll's hand, he pulled a cutlass from his belt and threw it. The blade circled, flashing through the air. It struck the back of the Troll's head and the creature fell forward, crashing to the floor with a swoosh.

Freddo pulled himself free. Turning to the man who'd saved him, he said, 'What took you so long?'

The man grinned. 'My timing's impeccable.'

The Dark Pirate, Sparks thought, her heart leaping. *He's back!*

Freddo and the pirate dashed to the circle, skidding across the floor to join them. The Boatswain, Christopher and Pierre were already there. They linked hands.

'Thought you might need a little help,' the pirate said. 'Seems I was right.'

Slowly, the NIGHTMARE army spread around the edge of the hall, a sea of bared teeth, raised weapons and bulging eyes.

'Now, where was I?' asked Wisdom.

'You and your sister,' Alfa spluttered. 'But surely we can't—'

'Ah yes.'

Behind Wisdom, Grizelda stepped into the hall. Taking in the scene, she hissed, 'Attack!'

'Right on time,' said Wisdom, as the army of the night leapt towards them. 'I'm not usually one for flashy shows, but I think this is the time for a little magic.'

Wisdom let out a loud, clear call, something between an owl hoot and the cry of a stag.

Whoa! thought Sparks, as she watched a Vampire's face contort and a Banshee raise her hands to her ears.

The call ended with a deep click that bounced from the walls.

Outside the circle, time slowed. The onslaught of the NIGHT-MARE army continued: limbs flailing, lips twisting, creatures lunging forward, but all as if pushing though water. As the NIGHTMARE army slowed, the candles in the centre of the hall rose, floating in mid-air, their flames casting long shadows.

From the edge of the hall there was a slow clap. 'Oh, very good, very swish. I'm proud of yer.' It was Grizelda. She, like the circle, was unaffected by the slowing of time. 'I'll give yer one thing, you've got style. But you know yer only delayin' the inevitable, don't yer? Yer only drawin' out yer sad demise. We've won. Come on, admit it. Yer can't beat this lot. It's over.'

Wisdom sat up straight. 'I'm telling a story. And I intend to finish.'

Grizelda looked irritated. 'Oh, do yer? Stories.' She tutted. 'Always stories. So tiresome. Alright, I'll allow yer this one little indulgence – think of it as giving the condemned her last meal.

Don't say I ain't generous, though. But you won't stop us.'

Sparks looked around. Grizelda was right. The NIGHTMARE army was still advancing. Swords were being lowered, axes brandished and chains swung. A surge of violence was about to break over them.

Ignoring the onslaught, Wisdom continued.

'When we reached our twelfth birthdays, it was announced that my sister and I were to be given gifts. We put on our prettiest dresses, mine the greens and golds of spring, my sister's the rich reds of autumn. The gift was a bird each, two chicks for us to nurture and grow. I named mine Life. My sister named hers Knowledge.

'Life was a fragile creature with plumes of pink, yellow and corn. But my sister's bird had feathers of the deepest black. It was a crow.

'Over the years, we watched our gifts grow. We launched their first flights, we gave them twigs for their nests, we observed them feeding: Life drinking the nectars of the tall flowers, my sister's bird ripping carrion, its beak bloody...'

The NIGHTMARE army was uncomfortably close now. Sparks could smell the foul breath of an orc. What was this madness? Why were they listening to a story as their enemies closed in? This would soon be over. Sparks didn't want to die. She looked past Wisdom. On the other side of the circle, a black knight had pulled ahead of the pack. He was riding a jet-black charger, spit flying from the beast's mouth. Slowly, the knight was lowering a lance and he was aiming it straight at Wisdom.

Wisdom continued, unaware. 'We both cared for our birds. We loved them equally. As they grew, we grew, but our branches spread in different directions.

'Through the years, I've only ever had one bird, one love. She has been with me from the beginning. I've seen her take many forms, but it has always been her, always Life. But my sister's crow multiplied, becoming many, until a great flock followed her wherever she went. She watched her birds grow and die, grow and die, only the murder surviving. As she watched this dance of birth and loss, the thing my sister came to fear most was death itself. Through her gift, she saw only parts, only separateness and endings. And so she declared all things to be folly, a name she chose to take for herself...'

The lance was dangerously close now.

'The knowledge of separateness carries a dreadful curse, a burden my sister has always had to bear. She has learnt to fight, to survive, never to let go or give in, no matter the cost. She's become hardened to life like a crow tearing flesh.'

Wisdom needs to do something! Sparks thought. *She must move! We have to run!* She opened her mouth to warn Wisdom, but the Guardian of Hidden Treasure looked at her. For a moment, it was as though Sparks and Wisdom were the only the two in the hall. In Wisdom's eyes, Sparks saw her say, *I know. It's alright. Be still.*

Sparks closed her mouth.

'But I know that Life is not separate,' Wisdom continued. 'All parts, all pieces, all ends are temporary, but Life is one. She does not end. That is why today, I'm able to pass my Life to my sister. There's no loss. There's nothing to defend.'

Releasing the Boatswain's hand, Wisdom reached into her pocket and pulled out a tiny bird. She held it, cupped in the palm of her hand and ran her fingers through its bright feathers. The bird was small, not much more than a chick, its crest still downy. It stared at her with big eyes.

Wisdom opened her mouth, her eyes widening and her body tilting forward. Sparks gasped. The lance had struck. It moved, still in slow motion. It was piercing Wisdom right through her heart.

Wisdom took a sharp intake of breath. 'Today, I choose to put Life into the hands of Folly,' she panted, 'for Folly to choose to do with as she wills.'

Wisdom lifted her hand and the bird sprang from it, spreading its wings. It flew above the NIGHTMARE army towards Grizelda.

The tip of the lance appeared, pushing out through Wisdom's chest, a bright circle of crimson spreading around it.

'But as you take my Life, sister,' whispered Wisdom, 'know that once again you will bear our shared name. You will know that, from the beginning, you were meant to be the bearer of both Knowledge and Life – we heard it earlier, how you saved a boy from drowning. You may not see it, but you are a Life bearer too. This day, we close the circle. This day, I choose to share my Life with you. It will not end. It will continue in you.'

As she finished, the little bird landed in Grizelda's hand. Then, with a gasp, Wisdom slumped forward and did not breathe again.

Sparks gripped Knot's hand.

Grizelda looked at the little bird and blinked. It stared back with big, innocent eyes.

'Life?' the old woman whispered.

Chapter 34

Empty

As the ferry draws close to the jetty, music from a brass band floats across the water. Close to the café, I spot a group of musicians huddled together. Winter sunlight glints from their instruments, many of which have been wrapped in tinsel.

The children wait impatiently for the ferry to dock. When it does, they leap onto the jetty, shouting and giggling, and run towards the band and the crowd gathered around it.

I follow Libby. I'm finding it hard to think. I'm running through all the possibilities of what might happen now. This is it, our last shot. If we miss this…

It's not even worth thinking about, I tell myself, trying to quiet my mind.

As we step onto the beach, the brass band strikes up another tune. 'God Rest Ye Merry Gentlemen,' a choir sings out. They're wearing garish Christmas jumpers knitted with polar bears, snowmen, reindeer and Christmas trees. Libby and I skirt around them, avoiding the festivities. As we pass, I notice there's a table set out with colourfully wrapped presents. A group of silver-haired ladies are giving them to the children who've just arrived.

We slip between the beach huts as the choir sings, 'Oh, tidings of comfort and joy.' The sound deadens, and the wind drops.

Libby walks quickly, her fists clenched. She darts through the alleyways until we emerge further along the beach. It's quieter here. The crowd are staying close to the café.

Libby stops and glances one way and then the other.

She's trying to remember, I think. *She's trying to remember how to get to the beach hut. I wonder how long it's been since she was last here.* I picture the girl with the red spade. *Was that the last time?*

Deciding which way to go, Libby sets off.

Yes, that's the way. She heads towards Scoop and the upturned boat. I follow, trying to control my breathing.

We pass a hut with a red bird above the door, its wings spread, the name "Phoenix" written below.

She's going to find her! I speed up. *She's going to find her!*

We pass the tap where Scoop and I have been collecting water these past weeks.

She's going to find her!

And then, we're there, standing outside Libby's mum's beach hut. Libby pulls the photo from her pocket and checks it, looking up at the hut and then back to the picture. I can see the years that have passed since she stood here holding that red spade: the days at school, the violin practices, the nights eating pizza in front of the TV, the birthday parties, Christmases and holidays. And I see the disappointments too, the fallouts and broken friendships, teenage pressures and missed opportunities. And on top of it all, writ large, there's the heartbreak of her mum's disappearance.

Pushing the photo back into her pocket, Libby climbs the steps onto the decking. She stops at the door, shifting her weight from foot to foot. Reaching into her coat pocket, she searches for something. It's not there. She tries her other pocket, then pats her jeans. She's getting agitated.

What are you doing? Just knock!

The brass band is still playing in the distance. The music mingles with the noise of the waves. This feels like a dream.

Libby reaches out and tries the door. It doesn't open. She groans in frustration and then thumps it, loudly. The noise echoes through the hut.

I wait, barely daring to breathe. *I should get Scoop. She should be here.*

But there isn't time. I can't miss this.

I'm shifting my weight from foot to foot, just like Libby.

Where's her mum?

A gull swoops down and perches on top of the hut. It cries out, a loud, vicious call.

Where is she?

Libby tries the door again, rattling the handle. It doesn't shift. She bites her nails.

What's happening? Where's her mum? She must be here. She never leaves!

I move forward. Perhaps I can help. Perhaps I can call her.

Libby peers through the window. The shutters are closed. She bends down, trying to peek through one of the slats.

The hut looks empty.

Shaking her head, she runs her hand through her hair and crouches on the porch, resting on her haunches. She bites her nails again. She looks lost. 'Stupid,' I hear her whisper. 'Stupid, stupid, stupid.'

Wiping her eye with the edge of her sleeve, she stands. 'Waste of time! Stupid!'

No! What are you doing?

As if in a dream, Libby walks down the porch steps.

No! You can't go! This is it! This is the moment!

But she *is* going. She strides away across the beach. I look at the hut. It's empty.

This can't be happening.

'Stop!' I scream. 'She's here! You're in the right place! You haven't come all this way for nothing!' I'm shouting so loud my voice cracks. 'Stop!' But Libby doesn't look back. It starts to snow again, big drops settling on my coat and my eyelashes. As she walks away, Libby pulls something from her pocket and drops it. It's the photo. It lies crumpled on the beach, the spade like a blot of blood on the sand. Slowly, bright drops of white settle on it. I don't know what to do. I watch, paralysed, as Libby walks away. Gradually, the red spade disappears beneath the snow.

* * *

A hand grabs my shoulder. I jolt awake.

'Scoop!'

The voice is urgent, harsh. The grip hurts.

'Scoop! Wake up! It's going wrong! She's leaving!'

I pull away, scrambling into the corner of the boat. 'What?'

I think I recognise the red-faced boy staring at me, but I can't place him. He looks angry. It scares me.

'Come on!' he yells, his eyes bulging. 'We have to do something!'

I press myself back against the wood. 'What?'

'Why are you looking at me like that?' He eyeballs me. 'Pull yourself together – we need to do something!'

'Sorry...who...who are you?' As the words leave my mouth, I know they're wrong. I recognise this boy: his long, pointy face, his tight lips, the way his hair flops across his forehead.

He opens his eyes wide, his expression changing. He looks disorientated, vulnerable.

'Scoop, it's me. It's Fletcher. What are you talking about?'

'Fletcher?' I repeat, slowly.

But his vulnerability only lasts a moment. His face hardens. 'Look, we don't have time for this!' He grabs my hand and pulls me out of the boat. I struggle, but his grip is strong. 'Come on!' he yells. 'I'm sorry, but you need to pull yourself together. She's leaving!'

'Who's leaving? What are you talking about?'

'Libby!'

The name stirs something inside me.

'She was here. She found the photo...' he stops. 'Look, I don't have time to explain now. She's here, but she's leaving – that's all you need to know. And we have to stop her!'

He tugs my arm, pulling me along the snowy sand. I resist a little but let him drag me. There's music in the distance. I zone out, losing myself in the sound. I examine the boy again. I definitely recognise him. Perhaps he's the one I've been waiting for. We stumble on, our feet sinking into the snow. He's hurting my arm.

Where have I seen him before?

No answer. The blankness terrifies me even more than this unknown, angry boy. Somehow, I've lost myself. And despite the fact the boy looks so furious, something deep inside me trusts him.

'This can't be happening,' he mutters. 'We need to stop her!' He looks over his shoulder. 'Where's her mum?'

'Mum?'

'Yes. Libby went to the beach hut. She knocked. There was no answer. You were supposed to be watching.'

Was I? My cheeks flush.

The boy pulls me around a corner onto a wide throughway between the beach huts. As we head away from the sea, the sound of the waves fades and the band's music swells. I can see the musicians ahead, a crowd of people wearing woolly hats around them.

Suddenly, a lady in a penguin jumper steps in front of us. The boy almost crashes into her. 'What the—'

She beams, her straggly hair blowing in the wind. 'Hello again!'

The boy goes to move round her. 'Get out of the way!'

I tug his sleeve. 'Don't be rude!'

The lady looks thrown but continues to smile. 'Don't you recognise me? I met you the other day at the food bank.' The boy peers past her to a jetty beyond the band. There's a queue of people waiting for a ferry. The lady's smile wavers. 'Oh, I'm sorry,' she says, 'I know people don't like to talk about it. It's just I recognised you and I thought I should say hello. I'm Hilary, remember?' She holds her hand out. 'And you are…?'

The choir suddenly busts into a new song.

'Hark the herald angels sing...'

'I don't have time for this,' the boy says. 'She's going!'

Trying to salvage the conversation, Hilary turns to me. 'What about you, dear?'

'What?'

'What's your name?'

I stare at her, fixed to the spot, searching the blankness. There's nothing.

I don't know. I don't know my own name. How can somebody not know their own name? I glance at the boy. I need to say something. He's still staring at the people waiting for the ferry. What was it he called me earlier?

'Scoop!' I say.

'That's an unusual name, dear.'

My cheeks burn. *It is, isn't it? It's a stupid name.*

'We need to go,' says the boy.

'Of course, dear. I don't want to hold you up, but as it's Christmas, we're giving out a few treats – spiced wine, sweet bread, and we have a present for each of you, if you can wait a few moments.'

'We can't!'

The boy's rudeness embarrasses me. I don't know why. It's not like we're together. I don't even know who he is, really.

'I can!' I say.

Hilary smiles. 'Lovely.' Crouching, she picks up a little flask.

'What are you doing?' the boy hisses. 'We're going to lose her! Don't you realise how important this is? This is it!'

I shake my head, defiantly. For a moment, he looks hurt. Then he glares at me. 'Fine! I'll do it myself. I've always had to act alone when it mattered. I don't even know why I bothered to wake you. You're useless!'

His words sting.

Pushing past Hilary, he storms off.

'Oh dear,' Hilary says. 'I do hope I haven't—'

'It's fine,' I interrupt, grabbing the little flask. It's warm. A sweet smell drifts up.

'Spiced wine,' Hilary says. 'Non-alcoholic, of course. It represents the blood of Christ on this most holy night.'

I breathe in the fragrant scent. The music washes over me. My head feels fuzzy. The sound of the choir rises. 'Veiled in flesh the Godhead see, hail the incarnate deity...'

'There it is, right there,' says Hilary. 'That's what it's all about, isn't it – the mystery of Christmas. That's why we're giving out this wine.'

I don't understand what she's saying, but there's something in her eyes that stills me.

Putting the glass to my lips, I drink. The wine's hot, its aroma fills my nose.

I've tasted something like this before. A long time ago.

My heart leaps at the glimmer of a memory, and heat radiates through me.

I remember something!

'Word made flesh, you see,' Hilary says. 'That's what it's all about – the creative force that speaks life into everything becomes *real*, becomes *physical* – the vastness of the universe veiled in the flesh of a little child. And you know what that means? Nothing is left out, nothing is rejected; everything, from the biggest to the smallest is included – that's the good news.'

My heart leaps. *Noveltwist!* I remember the name! *That's where I've tasted something like this before – Noveltwist Cordial.* The wine gives me the same sensation, lifting me, clearing my head, waking me.

I'm Scoop, daughter of the Storyteller.

With a jolt, I remember the boy. *Fletcher! He's my brother.*

How could I forget?

I peer past Hilary, looking for him. The group is still standing in line by the jetty.

I remember it all: Fullstop Island, Blotting's Academy, The Black

Horizon, our journey here, crossing the boundary…

Hilary's still speaking. '*Everything* is in relationship, you see, from the tiniest baby to the furthest star. And you know what that means? It means it can all be made whole again – the rips can be mended. And we're part of it, me and you, joined together in one great community.'

And I remember Libby Joyner.

Libby's here! She's here!

Hilary hands me a chunk of bread. I take it without thinking, stuffing it into my mouth. It's sweet on my tongue.

'The body of Christ,' says Hilary. 'The word made flesh.'

Seek the source.

Libby's mum's letters come flooding back.

We are the source, our relationship. That is where life is to be found.

The choir swells. '…Risen with healing in his wings. Mild he lays his glory by. Born that man no more may die. Born to raise the sons of earth. Born to give them second birth…'

I must get to Fletcher. We must find Libby. We need to get her to turn back.

Hilary thrusts something into my hand. It's a long, thin box, wrapped in red and gold paper. 'Open it,' she says. 'It's for you.'

I tear the paper, distractedly, still looking for Fletcher ahead. I understand why he acted the way he did now. I understand his urgency.

Flipping up the lid of the box, I glance down.

'It's a pen.' Hilary grins. 'The Word made flesh, you see? It was Martin's idea. He's the theologian among us.'

A pen.

'It's your pen.'

And then it hits me.

My pen.

I stumble.

'And here's one for your friend, too.' Hilary thrusts another box into my hand. 'And a pad. What use is a pen without paper?'

I look up, meeting Hilary's gaze for the first time. For a moment, we see each other.

'He's my brother,' I say.

She nods. 'I could see it. Well, Merry Christmas to you both. And God bless.'

'Thank you,' I say. And I mean it.

I stumble forward, away from Hilary, my head spinning.

I have a pen – my pen.

The pen is not the source…

Seek the source…

I became a storyteller to join our worlds together. We are the source, our relationship.

Libby Joyner. It's there in her name.

I became a storyteller to join our worlds together.

In that moment, I know exactly what we need to do. I know what we're here for and what we must become.

Words must become flesh – that is the end of their quest.

* * *

'You can't get on the ferry! You can't!' I hear his voice before I see him. Fletcher's standing to the side of the jetty, yelling into the crowd. His face is blotched, his clothes ragged. But nobody pays him any attention.

The ferry has docked and people are beginning to filter onto it. With a start, I see her there in the queue – Libby. She looks cold, her eyes red.

'Fletcher,' I call. 'Fletcher. I know what we have to do!'

He turns to me, his eyes wild. 'We have to stop her!'

'I know! Take this.' Reaching him, I thrust the present into his hand.

'What? We don't have time. She's—'

'Just do as your told for once! Open the box.'

To my surprise, he does as I ask. He rips off the paper and

flips open the lid. He pulls out the pen.

'What am I supposed to do with—'

'Take this too.' I tear a wodge of paper and hand it to him.

'I don't understand.'

'*I became a storyteller to join our worlds together.* That's what Libby's mum wrote in her letters.'

'You read the letters?'

'Yes. And I understand now. *Words must become flesh – that is the end of their quest.*' Fletcher stares at me. 'We are words, Fletcher, characters in a story. But our challenge is to become storytellers in our own right. That's always been the end of our quest.'

'Become storytellers? But—'

'We have the power to write the future, to stop Libby getting on that ferry.' I point at the pen in Fletcher's hand.' There it is, right there. It's not magic. It's not the source. It's just a pen. The source is our relationship with Libby and her mother. We already have it. We need to stop pretending we're somehow different. This is where we are now, here in this world. This is where we belong. We must embrace it. We must become fully flesh. That's the only way we'll see what's broken joined together again.' I hold up my pen. 'So, will you join me?'

* * *

I stare at the pen in Scoop's hand.

Fully flesh.

I remember Hilary's conversation at the food bank: *Words are important, but they need to be made real, they need to be made flesh.*

I don't understand, not fully, but I know Scoop's right. I feel it as I hold the pen.

To my side, I see Libby boarding the ferry.

'Will you join me?' Scoop says again.

I think what I'm about to do is going to change me, change the world I know. It's a leap of faith, but what have I left to lose?

I look at Scoop and nod.

By the side of the jetty we kneel on the sand, lower the paper to the ground and begin to write.

Chapter 35

The Last Day of Advent

Out of the corner of her eye, Scoop caught sight of a sudden movement on the ferry. She looked up to see Libby bound off the boat and sprint down the jetty, back towards the beach.

'Look!' she said, grabbing Fletcher's sleeve. 'Fletch, look! She's coming back!' Scoop frowned. 'But something's wrong. Why's she running?'

Libby leapt off the jetty and dashed towards the warren of huts. Disembarking from the ferry was a tall man, his shoulders hunched, the collar of his black, winter coat turned up against the wind. 'What?' Fletcher said. 'No...it can't be.'

'What is it?'

Fletcher pointed. 'See that man? He's why she's running.'

'Why? Who is he?'

Scoop looked. The man had scruffy, black hair and his face was shadowed with stubble. He looked weary.

'That,' said Fletcher, 'is Libby's dad.'

'Libby's dad?' Scoop could see the resemblance. He had the same deep-set eyes. 'But...what's he doing here?'

Libby's dad began to stride along the jetty. 'I don't know,' said Fletcher, 'but I'm going to find out.' He turned to Scoop. 'You follow Libby. I'll follow her dad. I'll meet you back at the beach hut, okay?' He stared at her. 'Perhaps there's still a chance of turning this around, after all.'

Scoop wasn't sure she could allow herself to believe it. They'd been let down so many times, disappointed, tested to their limits. Was something finally going their way? Could the story finally be turning?

Fletcher scrambled to his feet and dashed after Libby's dad, heading towards the brass band. Pushing herself up, Scoop darted after Libby, careful not to slip on the ice.

When she reached the alley along which Libby had disappeared, there was a trail of footprints in the newly fallen snow. Following them, she made her way back towards Libby's mum's cabin. When she reached it, Libby was staring at the hut, still as a statue. She had a strange expression on her face, as if scared.

Not scared, Scoop thought. *She looks as though this place has wounded her in some way.*

Steeling herself, Libby stepped forward. But she didn't head to the door. Instead, she slipped around the side of the hut, making her way to the back of the cabin. Scoop followed to see Libby disappear down the narrow gap between the hut and the dune.

Pushing into the gap after her, Scoop recalled the last time she'd been there, only days before – they'd been looking for a clue as to Libby's whereabouts. Now Libby was here, right in front of her.

Libby made her way to the window in the middle of the back wall. Reaching up, she ran her fingers under the shutters. A moment later, Scoop heard the lock give. Libby pulled the window open and scrambled up the wall. She was breaking in to the beach hut, just as they had.

* * *

Fletcher followed Libby's dad past the brass band, past the café and through the group of ladies giving out gifts. He strode out across the snowy sand, towards the sea. When he reached the water, he stopped. The waves' foam lapped around his feet, but he didn't seem to notice. He stared across the choppy ocean, his coat crisp against the snow, the wind ruffling his hair. He stood like that for a few minutes, just staring. Then, bracing himself, he set off along the beach towards the upturned boat and Libby's mum's beach hut. Fletcher noticed a wodge of paper sticking out of his coat pocket.

I recognise that, he thought. *That's Libby's writing. What's he doing with it?*

* * *

Scoop gripped the windowsill, ready to follow Libby. As she began to pull herself up, there was a sharp cry from inside.

'No!' It was Libby. 'No!' The cry came again.

Scoop scrambled up, pushing her elbows onto the sill to take her weight, her legs dangling down outside. Her heart was thudding. What was wrong? She froze, hanging half-in and half-out of the cabin.

Libby was kneeling in the centre of the hut. Next to her, her mum was sprawled on the floor, her legs twisted awkwardly, her stick lying uselessly by her side. She was gripping a brush, a streak of red paint scrawled across the floor.

She's fallen, Scoop thought. *That's why she didn't answer the door!*

Libby grabbed her mum's hand. 'Mum! Mum!' She was breathing hard. 'Mum! It's me! It's Libby.' She leaned forward, turning her cheek to her mother's lips, checking for breath. 'Mum, it's okay. You're going to be alright. I'm here now.' She unbuttoned the top of her mum's blouse, her hands trembling. Then, half-hugging, half-pulling, she turned her onto her side. 'I've found you! I've finally found you! Why did you go? We'd have looked after you. We'd have helped. It's okay, I'm here now. I've found you...I've found you.' Libby straightened up. There was red paint on her top. She twisted round to pull a cushion from the chair by the table. Libby's mum's eyes flickered, opening. She tried to focus on the person next to her.

'Libby?'

Libby spun back, the cushion in her hand. 'Mum? You're awake! Yes, it's me. You're okay. I've found you.' Gently, she lifted her mum's head and slid the cushion underneath. Her mum searched her daughter's face, her eyes watery.

'Libby? Is that really you?'

'Yes, it's me.' Libby's voice cracked. She wrapped her arms around her mum. The two women held each other. Scoop heard Libby's mum whisper something, barely more than a breath. 'I love you too,' replied Libby, kissing her cheek. 'I love you too.' Kneeling in the centre of the cabin, she rocked her mum, gently.

* * *

CLICK.

The sharp sound of a key in a lock broke the moment.

Libby flinched, startled.

Scoop looked up to see the latch of the door lift. With a creek, it opened a little. Winter light spilled through, throwing a stark shadow across the floor. Someone peeked around the frame, silhouetted. It was Libby's dad. He scanned the room, taking in the scene, then stepped into the hut, his winter boots heavy on the floor.

'Dad!' Libby gasped. She tried to speak. 'I'm sorry...I was just...I just needed to...'

'It's okay,' her dad said, his voice low. 'Calm down. Breathe. I'm not angry.'

Gently, he closed the door.

Scoop looked back at Libby.

'What?' she said aloud. Her elbow slipped from the window and she almost fell. She scrambled back up, gripping the frame, her knuckles white.

But... How...?

The wooden boards next to Libby were empty.

Libby's mum had vanished.

What's happened?

Scoop scanned the room, searching for the body. Had Libby moved her? No. There hadn't been time.

There was no sign of a body, no stick, no paintbrush. Libby's mum had gone.

And then Scoop noticed it: a faint trace of red where, moments ago, the body had been. But it was barely visible, as if the floor had been scrubbed.

Libby's dad walked quietly across to his daughter and knelt beside her. She was shaking. He put his arm around her. The two of them knelt, staring at the place where Libby's mum had lain.

Outside the hut, Scoop felt something brush her leg. Flinching, she looked down. Fletcher was below.

'Don't do that to me!'

'Sorry,' he whispered. He was carrying a wooden crate. 'I thought this might help.' Standing it on its end, he slipped it under Scoop's feet. She stood on it, the box taking her weight. Fletcher climbed up next to her.

'Fletcher...' she began.

'I know. I saw it too. I was peeking through the front window. She was there...and then she vanished. She faded, just like...' He paused.

'Like what?'

'Like a Mortale,' Fletcher stared at Scoop. 'Just like the Storyteller and Princess.'

'But how?'

Fletcher shook his head. 'I don't know.'

Libby's dad was leading Libby to the armchair in the corner of the room. Her skin was pale. He guided her to sit. Once she'd settled, he pulled the chair from the table, drew it close and sat, facing her.

Scoop's mind was churning.

When she'd seen Libby's mum on the beach, she'd vanished.

As they'd followed her to the ferry, nobody had seen her.

She looked at the floor of the hut. It seemed so empty.

This whole place feels empty, as if it hasn't been lived in for months.
She glanced at the mouldy plates, remembering the dust on

the surfaces, the algae in the water glass.

Scoop frowned.

No. She didn't like that thought. She pushed it away.

Libby's dad gazed around the cabin. 'Do you remember when Mum made you that sand sculpture?' he asked. 'She tried to carry it in on a picnic blanket. She wanted to keep it. But it collapsed as she brought it through the door. There was sand everywhere.'

'It was a dolphin,' Libby replied, quietly.

'Ha yes, that was it. I'd forgotten.' He paused. 'We had some good times here, didn't we?'

Silence.

'I wasn't sure you'd notice,' muttered Libby.

'Hmm?'

'That I'd gone.'

Her dad rubbed his eyes. 'Of course I noticed, Libby. You're my daughter. You weren't in your bed this morning. It's Christmas Eve, for God's sake. I had your presents ready to show you. You know I like to give them to you early so you have time to guess what they are, just like...' His voice trailed away. 'Anyway...'

Libby glanced up. 'How did you know I'd be here, though?'

Her dad pulled the wodge of papers from his pocket. 'This. You left it on your bedroom floor.'

'Dad, you shouldn't have—'

'I've been reading it, Libby. I've read it all – on the train on the way here. It's good. Really good.'

Libby shook her head.

'It is. You have talent...just like your mum.'

'Don't.'

'It's true.' Her dad paused again. 'You wrote her into your story...'

She wrote her into the story? Scoop turned to Fletcher. 'She wrote her into her story,' she whispered. 'Then, she *is* a Mortale – like us.'

Fletcher shook his head. 'Part of her, perhaps. But not all of her. She's still Libby's mum, she's still flesh.'

'Yes. But even part of her...'

The thought was there again. Scoop shook her head. It couldn't be.

Libby's dad continued: 'And you wrote this place into the story too. When I read it, I knew this is where you'd be.' He stared at the floor. 'I'm in it too. A little.' He looked sad. Glancing up, he said, 'I'm sorry, Libby.'

'Dad, you don't have to—'

'I do, though. Reading this has made me realise how far we've drifted, how absent I've been. I'm sorry for that, I really am...'

'Dad, really it's—'

'Let me finish. I'm not very good at this.' Libby fell still. 'When your mother died—'

'Dad!'

Died? Did he just say died! But...

Scoop struggled to breathe. The thought she'd been trying to push away could no longer be ignored. What they'd seen earlier – Libby's mum on the floor – it was a memory, nothing more. Libby hadn't come here to find her mum, she'd come here to remember. This was a memorial. The faint trace of red that stained the floor was all that was left of the moment itself.

Libby's mum was dead.

Scoop's mind was reeling. If that was true, what had this all been about? The quest to the Threshold, crossing through it, life beyond the Uncrossable Boundary, what had it been for? They'd been sent to reunite mother and daughter. But that was impossible.

It had been a futile quest right from the start.

All this time, the beach hut had been empty. What they'd observed of Libby's mum was a collection of memories, ghosts, scraps of truth stitched together to make a story, a fantasy Libby wanted to believe – that her mum was still out there, waiting to be found.

She and Fletcher were part of that story. It was the only thing that made sense of their existence.

But it was a lie.

Libby's mum was dead.

Scoop couldn't speak, she couldn't move.

She stared at Libby. How could she do this to them?

Reaching forward, Libby's dad laid a hand on his daughter's knee. 'You need to accept it. You can't go on pretending. Mum's gone. You need to let her go.'

Libby turned away.

Her dad lifted the wodge of paper. 'In this,' he said, tentatively, 'you say I stopped her writing. That I was against it.'

'You were.'

Her dad's body tensed. 'Perhaps, towards the end. I thought it was confusing her, muddling her head. She became obsessed. She cut me out, cut everybody out. That's why she ran away, wasn't it, why she went missing. If she hadn't finally written to you, if you hadn't found her here, we'd never have had those last few months together. That damned writing book would have stolen—'

'Perhaps she left because she couldn't cope with being ill, Dad. Perhaps it was that simple. You can't blame a symptom and pretend it's the disease. I think her writing helped her make sense of it.'

Her dad's shoulders slumped. 'Yes, perhaps you're right. Perhaps I did get it wrong.' He held up Libby's writing again. 'But this is wrong too. It's not the whole story. When we were younger, your mum and me used to talk about her stories all the time. She'd share them with me. We came up with ideas together.' He shook the papers. 'We talked about this story, you know, these characters. I came up with an idea for how Fletcher and Scoop would finally graduate from Blotting's Academy.'

Libby looked up, her brow furrowed.

'I know. Hard to believe, isn't it?'

'What was the idea?'

Her dad gave a small smile. 'I suggested they should become human, become flesh. I thought that would make a good end to their quest, for them to become a real boy and girl – like in Pinocchio. I joked with your mum, saying that then *they'd* be able to write *our* story, they'd become our storytellers and we'd be characters in their tale. Your mum laughed, but I could tell she liked the idea.'

Fletcher was about to speak when he saw a movement by the door. The latch was lifting. Unnoticed by Libby and her dad, the door opened, and two figures slipped in. They were thin, insubstantial, almost ghosts, but Scoop recognised them.

'Storyteller?' she whispered.

Fletcher stared. 'Mother?'

'They're awake.'

The Princess closed the door behind her.

Libby's dad was still speaking. 'The thing is, when I was reading what you'd written, I couldn't help but see your mum in it. Not just in the parts you've written about her, but in all of it. She flows through this –' he tapped the pages – 'like…like the Thames through London. She's in all of it.'

Slowly, the Storyteller and Princess moved around the edge of the hut, towards Libby and her father. And as he spoke, their bodies started to become solid again.

'It helped. You know, I don't use words like this often – I'm a Yorkshireman after all – but reading this was…somehow healing. As I read, it was as though, even though she's gone, she was still with me. I don't know if that makes sense?'

Libby gave a little nod.

The Storyteller and Princess moved closer. Their skin, their hair, their clothes were becoming more real. By the time they reached the armchair, they looked more alive, more awake, than Fletcher had ever seen. The Storyteller's auburn hair shone, and the Princess's skin was radiant. They stood beside Libby and her father.

'I mean, in a way she is still here, isn't she? In this hut, in our memories. And she's in you. I see her in you so much. She's in this, too, in your writing.'

The Princess stepped forward and laid a hand on Libby's shoulder. Reaching out, she placed her other hand on her father's back. Then, looking up, she met Fletcher's eyes. A deep peace filled him. *This* was what their quest was about.

Seek the source.

Relationship is the source.

Here it was, right in front of him – being played out between Libby and her father.

The Princess smiled. *Now, you understand.* She seemed to glow. An intense, golden haze surrounded her. Fletcher had to shield his eyes. As he did, he heard the sound of a breath being released. It sighed through the hut. And when he looked back, the Princess had gone. Wisps of golden mist floated around Libby and her dad. Gradually, it seeped into them and disappeared.

Libby breathed in.

'She's inside them,' whispered Scoop.

Libby's dad continued. 'What I really wanted to say, Libby, is that you should keep doing this. Keep writing. You're good at it. I got it wrong with your mum. I won't get it wrong with you. I promise.'

Now the Storyteller stepped forward. Just as the Princess had done, he placed his hands on Libby and her dad.

'I promise to support you, Libby.' Her dad gave a bashful smile. 'I'll be your biggest fan. It might get embarrassing, you know.'

The Storyteller began to glow. The air was charged. This was a sacred moment.

'This is a fresh start, Libby. No more hiding. No more being separate. We're Joyners, after all.'

The Storyteller's body burned bright, glowing like a candle. His light filled the room. Just before Fletcher had to look away again, the Storyteller met his gaze.

Well done. You are no longer apprentices. On this last day of Advent, I name you fully fledged Adventurers, graduates of Blotting's Academy. Be alive!

Then, with a blinding flash of light, the Storyteller also vanished.

Libby breathed in deeply once again, her back straightening. She seemed to grow.

'Thanks, Dad,' she said. 'You don't know how much that means. Perhaps I can do this, after all.'

'You can,' her dad replied. 'And, I have something that might help. I found it with your mum's letters under the floorboards, after we found her here.' He lowered his head. 'But I couldn't deal with it at the time.'

Standing, he walked across to the loose floorboard, feeling for it with his feet. When the board gave, he knelt and prized it up. It sprang back with a crack. Reaching into the hollow, he pulled out a small, red book. Blowing the dust from it, he brought it to Libby. 'This was your mum's. It's her last piece of writing – the end of her story. Perhaps you can find a way to weave it into yours.'

Libby stared at it. This was her last opportunity to read, fresh, her mum's words.

'Go on,' her dad said. 'Read it to me.'

Libby took the book and ran her fingers over the waxy cover. She opened it. Her mum's handwriting was there, the ink blue, little smudges where the pen had run, sentences crossed out and amended, doodles at the edges of the page. She imagined the pen in her mum's fingers, moving across the page, creating a world that bubbled up from inside her, that carried her mum's spirit with it. The handwriting was familiar. But these words were new. Slowly, savouring them, Libby began to read.

Chapter 36

Life

Grizelda looked at the little bird and blinked. It stared back with big, innocent eyes.

'Life?' the old woman whispered.

She could feel its heart beating through its feathers, so small, so fragile. Its little body was warm. If she closed her fingers, she could squeeze the breath right out of it, as easy as squeezing juice from a raspberry. She could end it now.

Why had her sister done this? Why had she given her the choice? Why had she trusted her?

She's a fool, a bitter voice whispered. But despite all the lies Grizelda had told herself, and despite the black deeds she'd clothed herself in, she didn't believe it.

Grizelda had spent her life hating her sister. Since they'd been given their gifts all those years ago, she'd nursed a deep bitterness. She'd woken this bitterness each morning at first light and cradled it as the sun sank. Why had her sister been given such a beautiful gift, while she had been dished out that embarrassment, that monstrosity? She had been forced to watch its ugly spectacle day after day as it ripped into flesh. It wasn't fair. Nothing from that moment had been fair. But Grizelda had decided to make a virtue of it. She'd embraced the hand she'd been dealt. If she couldn't have what her sister had, she'd destroy it, destroy Life, little by little, piece by piece. Who, then, would be the winner?

And yet, here she was, holding her sister's gift. It was hers now. She'd won. So why did it feel like a hollow victory? She'd longed for this day, plotted for it, sweated for it, bled for it, fought for it and killed for it, time and time again.

And yet, here it was...but she couldn't bring herself to wring the little bird's neck.

She looked at her sister's body, slumped in the centre of the hall, the point of the lance still pushing slowly through her chest. A circle of blood spread around her, staining the ALETHEAN floor red.

You are a Life bearer too. That's what her sister had said.

No. The old woman wouldn't believe it. She couldn't.

This day I choose to share my Life with you. It will not end, it will continue in you.

Grizelda cringed. Despite herself, she could still feel her sister's presence with her. Even in death she was messing with her head.

'Fight it!' the old woman muttered. 'You've won.'

But her words had no effect. Something had changed. The proof was right there in Grizelda's hand. She hadn't wrung the bird's neck. There it sat, ruffling its feathers, looking up at her as if nothing was wrong. Grizelda felt powerless, as though the choice was not really hers to make at all. Quietly, without fuss or fanfare, her sense of who she was, was crumbling.

Life was bigger than she'd realised.

She'd sensed it in the BLACK LAKE. She couldn't remember exactly what she'd seen there, but it had left her with an uneasy feeling. Even there, even in that place of darkness, Life had been present. It had shaken her. And now this?

If Life *was* bigger than she'd anticipated, all those years of bargaining and defending, scrapping and stealing, hording and scheming, they'd all been for nothing.

For nothing, the old woman repeated.

That was the folly. *That* was the waste.

Grizelda felt a sharp pain in her fingers. She looked down. There were flames in her hand.

'Argh!' she cried.

The flames leapt up, shooting past her face, singeing her hair. She hopped and jumped, screeching like a crow.

'What's happening?'

It was the little bird. It was blazing. Flames crackled from its feathers.

But although Grizelda could feel it, the fire wasn't burning her skin.

'I won't let go!' she cried. 'Not now, not after all I've been through.' The bird was *hers*. There was no way she was going to let it go. She clung to it, despite the pain that shot through her arm.

The fire blazed brighter, its heat spreading through her shoulders and down into her legs. It was inside her, burning, smarting. Her whole body was aflame. It was excruciating. But alongside the pain, Grizelda became aware of a different sensation too. A glowing nub boiled deep in her core. It was small, but it blazed brilliantly, a nucleus of molten energy. What was it? It was spreading outwards, growing.

Get it out of me!

She could feel the cloud writhing inside her. It was angry. She'd become used to its ash, bitter in her mouth. It had always protected her, yes, but it had never let her rest. Now, as the heat pulsated, she sensed it being burnt away. She planted her feet, stilling herself. 'I've had enough of you,' she growled. She squeezed her eyes shut and allowed the fire to spread. As it did, the cloud gradually receded. The fire was refining her like ore being smelted, its impurities burnt to reveal gold.

Suddenly, the old woman laughed. 'Of course!' she cried. 'The Guardian of Hidden Treasure!'

When they'd been given their gifts, her sister had been awarded that name, while Grizelda had been labelled Guardian of Grit, Base Materials, Fire, Stone and Ash. It was another reason to despise her sister.

But now she could see it. Here, in this moment, the two names were being melded.

Once again you will bear our shared name.

She *was* being smelted like ore in a furnace. There was fire, yes, there was ash, but under it all was…

'Treasure,' the old woman whispered.

She laughed again, and then cried out as a great pillar of fire shot up from the bird. It reached the ceiling of ALETHEA and spread out, plumes of flame glistening above her. Grizelda stared up. She'd seen this before, at the Great Wedding Banquet. Back then, though, she'd feared it. She'd fought it. But now here she was, holding it.

It was a Firebird. She gazed up as bright droplets rained down.

The clatter of weapons broke her gaze. The time enchantment had ended. The NIGHTMARE army lurched back into real time, boots thumping, armour clanking. They crashed into one another, turning away from the circle to look up, cowering away from the Firebird.

As the bright droplets rained down, the hall fell silent.

Then, slowly, everybody turned to look at Grizelda.

'What you lot gawpin' at?' Her voice echoed around the chamber. 'Well? It's rude to stare.'

But they couldn't stop staring. The sight of Grizelda, fire pouring from her hands, was captivating. The old woman had transformed. Blazing wings rose from her back, reaching high into the air. Her black cloak hung from them in strips, like molten lava tumbling down the gold and red feathers. Even more mesmerizing, was Grizelda's face. The old woman had always kept it hidden. Now, everyone could see. Grizelda's skin was wrinkled and worn. She looked so human, just an old lady.

Sparks looked at Wisdom. It was a heart-breaking sight. She lay in a pool of her own blood, perfectly still. She'd been their friend. They'd lost so much on this quest. Sparks wanted to blame Grizelda. But as she turned back to the old woman, she couldn't help but see her resemblance to her sister. Wisdom looked out from behind Grizelda's eyes. If Sparks nursed bitterness as Grizelda had done, it would be a betrayal of her friend.

Wisdom gave her sister a second chance, Sparks thought. *She loved her to the end.*

Grizelda had transformed. She'd been changed through Wisdom's sacrifice.

The old woman's voice cut through the silence. It was shaky, unsure. 'I dunno what yer want from me.'

'Should we kill 'em?' one of the Trolls called out.

'No!' replied Grizelda. Then, realising what she'd said, she repeated it, quietly. 'No.'

The NIGHTMARE army glanced at one another, muttering.

'Alright, alright,' Grizelda said. 'I dunno who I am to tell yer anythin' anymore, but I'll give it a go.' She looked down. 'I ain't gonna give yer a pretty speech about happy endin's and all that bobbins, that ain't my style. And I ain't gonna tell yer it's all gonna be okay. I'm not stupid. I ain't gonna tell yer the world is split into monsters and 'eroes, neither. It's not. So-called 'eroes can be monsters, and perhaps monsters can become 'eroes too. You lot'll have to prove that to me. But...' the old woman paused, '...I will say this. If I can be a bearer of Life, anyone can.' She waved her hand over the NIGHTMARE army. 'If I'm included, you all are. There's no escapin' it. And I mean *everyone*. No excuses. Life-bearers, the lot of yer. And don't yer *ever* go forgettin' it.'

Chapter 37

Becoming Flesh

Libby looked up. That was it, the end of her mum's story. The last thing she'd ever written.

If I'm included, you all are... Life-bearers, the lot of yer... And don't yer ever go forgettin' it.

Somehow, Libby felt her mum had written those words especially for her. It was a message from beyond an uncrossable boundary.

She looked at her dad. There were tears in his eyes. Closing the book, she crossed to him and put her arms around his chest. He clasped her hands. 'Yes,' he said. 'It's good.'

Libby squeezed his hand in reply.

Her dad wiped his eyes and reached into his coat pocket. He pulled out a thin box, a present, wrapped in brown paper, tied with a red ribbon. He handed it to Libby. 'Go on,' he said. 'Open it.'

Quietly, Libby undid the bow and gently peeled back the paper. The box was leathery black. She lifted the lid. Inside was a gold pen. It glinted.

'Merry Christmas, Libby,' her dad said. Standing, he walked across to one of the kitchen drawers, slid it open and rummaged inside. He produced a long, red candle.

'Do you remember what your mum used to do every Christmas Eve?' he asked, putting a saucer onto the kitchen surface.

'She used to light a candle.'

'Yes. I'm thinking it's a tradition we should keep.'

Libby nodded.

Her dad took a lighter from his pocket and, clicking a flame to life, heated the bottom of the candle. The wax dripped onto the saucer. He stuck the candle to the plate.

He looked at her. 'You know,' he said, 'I'm glad you came here. I think it's going to be a good place to spend Christmas Day.' Then, holding the lighter to the wick, he lit a flame, and the room was filled with golden light.

* * *

Fletcher looked up. He was still kneeling on the beach, his trousers soaked through from the snow. The pen was in his hand. Quietly, he laid it down and looked at Scoop. She knelt beside him, staring at the page beneath her. It was filled with writing.

'What just happened?' he whispered.

Scoop shook her head. 'I think we made something wonderful happen.'

The light had faded and the first evening stars shone in the sky. Behind them, the brass band was packing up, the last of the children having boarded the ferry with their families, ready to head back to the mainland.

Fletcher looked towards the shadow of the beach huts.

He paused for a moment. 'Shall we go and see?'

Scoop nodded.

Silently, they folded their stories and put them into their pockets. Then, together, they moved back through the maze of beach huts towards Libby's mum's.

Scoop stopped Fletcher a little way from the cabin. 'We shouldn't intrude,' she said.

'But—' Fletcher stopped himself. Scoop was right.

He could see a candle flickering in the beach hut. A light had been lit. It was time to let it burn. Libby's story wasn't theirs to interfere with anymore.

It was strange to have reached this end, so quiet and still. 'So, what now?' he asked.

Scoop shrugged. 'We head on. We're adventurers, aren't we?'

Fletcher nodded.

With one last look at the beach hut, the candlelight flickering through its shutters, they turned and walked away.

* * *

As they walked back towards the jetty, a man in a Santa costume was locking the café. He was standing on tiptoe, reaching up to bolt one of the double doors, his fake, bushy beard pulled down under his chin. 'Merry Christmas,' he said, as Fletcher and Scoop passed.

They stopped and stared at him.

'Merry Christmas,' Scoop replied, quietly.

'What's up with you two? You look like you've seen a ghost!'

Fletcher laughed, nervously. 'Something like that.'

'Well, have a good one, anyway,' the man said, as he disappeared inside and closed the second door.

The two adventurers stared at it.

'He saw us,' whispered Fletcher.

'Yes.'

There was a pause.

'And…can you feel it?'

'Yes.'

'We're no longer Mortale, are we?'

'No, we're not.'

'We're real.'

Just then, there was a voice behind them. 'Woo-hoo!'

Fletcher and Scoop turned to see Hilary approaching. 'Hello again,' she said. 'Are you waiting for the ferry?'

Scoop glanced at Fletcher. 'Yes…I suppose we are.'

'Well, I'm afraid you just missed the last one. But you're in luck. I have my own little boat – a luxury for my retirement.' She winked. 'Would you like a lift back to Christchurch?'

'Oh yes,' said Scoop. 'If you wouldn't mind.'

'Not at all. But you'll have to give me something in return.'

'Oh,' said Fletcher. 'The thing is, we don't have much. We don't have money or anything.'

Hilary laughed. 'Oh no, nothing like that. But if you have a story to tell, that would do nicely. It will brighten the journey.'

Fletcher smiled. 'Oh, I think we can do that.'

'We certainly can.' Scoop agreed.

* * *

Ten minutes later, Fletcher and Scoop were bobbing across the harbour, away from the spit that had been their home.

'So, where should we begin?' Fletcher asked.

Scoop grinned. 'How about, "The girl awoke with a start..."'

'Yes, that seems like a perfectly good beginning.'

And so, there on the little boat, as the Christmas stars shone above them, Scoop began to tell their story.

* * *

Rufina finished digging a little hole in the earth and knelt up. She took the peace plant beside her and placed it in the hole. Covering its roots with soil, she patted it down. Beside her, the Mysterious Mountains rose, their peaks still covered with snow, despite the warm summer sun. She stood up and brushed down her trousers.

She'd been meaning to do this for months. But after the events at ALETHEA, she hadn't been able to. In fact, she hadn't been able to do anything. To say that the weeks following the breach of the NIGHTMARE army had been difficult, was an understatement. Rufina had never been through anything like it before. She hadn't wanted to leave her house. She hadn't wanted to see anyone. She'd felt such shame. She'd failed her friends: the Yarnbard, Alfa and Sparks. Most of all, she'd failed Nib. How could she plant a memorial to him when she had failed him so thoroughly?

But over the weeks and months, her pain had eased. The Yarnbard had kept reminding her that she'd acted out of love. If she'd not played her part, he said, things would never have resolved the way they had. And they had resolved. After Grizelda's speech, the NIGHTMARE army had disbanded. The old woman seemed to be truly altered. And then, in the freshness of the morning, they'd woken from DREAM to find themselves back on Fullstop Island. The Gigan Ticks retreated below ground again, and everywhere, villagers emerged from their cocoons. On the face of it, the island had returned to its natural rhythm. But nobody could deny that something fundamental had changed.

As she looked at the plant, its white flowers reaching towards the light, its roots burrowing into the darkness, it began to rain. It was a cool summer rain that sparkled in the light. It had been raining a lot recently, and the River Word was almost back to its normal level.

Rufina lifted her chin and allowed the cool drops to settle on her skin. She listened.

In the patter, she could hear voices. They were gentle but familiar.

She pictured her friends: the girl with back hair like a scribble, her features rounded like a question mark, and the boy with eyes as sharp as an exclamation. She could hear them in the rain. She could feel them in the breeze too. Somehow, they were weaved into the fabric of her world. They had crossed an uncrossable boundary, but they were still there, still with her.

As the rain soothed her, Rufina knew that although she was alone, she wasn't on her own. And that was enough.

Other Books in the Firebird Chronicles Series

Rise of the Shadow Stealers
(2013, ISBN: 978-1-78099-694-3)

Fletcher and Scoop are Apprentice Adventurers from the ancient establishment of Blotting's Academy, where all Story Characters are trained. The trouble is, they can't remember how they got there.

It's the first day of term, but the two apprentices soon realise something is wrong. Things are going missing, including their own memories, and Scoop has the unsettling feeling that something is creeping in the shadows.

As the children search for answers, they become entangled with the life of the Storyteller, the island's creator and king. They journey to his wedding banquet and find themselves uncovering a hidden past. What is their connection to this mysterious man? And is there more to him than meets the eye?

The Nemesis Charm
(2016, ISBN: 978-1-78535-285-0)

They say only the dead can cross a Threshold, the dead and those who have faced a Nemesis Charm.

When Apprentice Adventurers, Fletcher and Scoop, discover their mother has fallen under the curse of a strange sickness, they prepare to sail for its source, a Threshold, a doorway to the world beyond the Uncrossable Boundary.

But they are not the only ones seeking to cross the Threshold. Their old enemy, Grizelda, has heard that beyond the Boundary lives a woman with the same power as the Storyteller. With the help of a monster made with an undead heart, she plans to cross the Boundary and steal that power for herself. If she succeeds, the Academy, the island and everything in Fletcher and Scoop's world will be hers.

From the Author

Thank you for purchasing *Through the Uncrossable Boundary*. I hope you enjoyed reading it as much as I enjoyed creating it.

If you have a few moments, please feel free to add your review of the book at your favourite online site for feedback (Amazon, Apple iTunes Store, Goodreads, etc.)

Also, if you would like to find out more about my other books or catch me at an event, please visit my website for news www.danielingrambrown.co.uk or connect with me on social media. I look forward to hearing from you!

Thanks!

Daniel Ingram-Brown

www.danielingrambrown.co.uk
www.firebirdchronicles.com
Twitter: @daningrambrown
Facebook: www.facebook.com/danielingrambrown
Instagram: danielwriter

OUR STREET
BOOKS

Our Street Books

JUVENILE FICTION, NON-FICTION, PARENTING

Our Street Books are for children of all ages, delivering a potent mix of fantastic, rip-roaring adventure and fantasy stories to excite the imagination; spiritual fiction to help the mind and the heart; humorous stories to make the funny bone grow; historical tales to evolve interest; and all manner of subjects that stretch imagination, grab attention, inform, inspire and keep the pages turning. Our subjects include Non-fiction and Fiction, Fantasy and Science Fiction, Religious, Spiritual, Historical, Adventure, Social Issues, Humour, Folk Tales and more.
If you have enjoyed this book, why not tell other readers by posting a review on your preferred book site.

Recent bestsellers from Our Street Books are:

Relax Kids: Aladdin's Magic Carpet
Marneta Viegas
Let Snow White, the Wizard of Oz and other fairytale characters show you and your child how to meditate and relax. Meditations for young children aged 5 and up.
Paperback: 978-1-78279-869-9 Hardcover: 978-1-90381-666-0

Wonderful Earth
An interactive book for hours of fun learning
Mick Inkpen, Nick Butterworth
An interactive Creation story: Lift the flap, turn the wheel, look in the mirror, and more.
Hardcover: 978-1-84694-314-0

Boring Bible: Super Son Series 1
Andy Robb
Find out about angels, sin and the Super Son of God.
Paperback: 978-1-84694-386-7

Jonah and the Last Great Dragon
Legend of the Heart Eaters
M.E. Holley
When legendary creatures invade our world, only dragon-fire can destroy them; and Jonah alone can control the Great Dragon.
Paperback: 978-1-78099-541-0 ebook: 978-1-78099-542-7

Little Prayers Series: Classic Children's Prayers
Alan and Linda Parry
Traditional prayers told by your child's favourite creatures.
Hardcover: 978-1-84694-449-9

Magnificent Me, Magnificent You The Grand Canyon
Dawattie Basdeo, Angela Cutler
A treasure filled story of discovery with a range of inspiring fun exercises, activities, songs and games for children aged 6 to 11.
Paperback: 978-1-78279-819-4

Q is for Question
An ABC of Philosophy
Tiffany Poirier
An illustrated non-fiction philosophy book to help children aged

8 to 11 discover, debate and articulate thought-provoking, open-ended questions about existence, free will and happiness.
Hardcover: 978-1-84694-183-2

Relax Kids: How to be Happy
52 positive activities for children
Marneta Viegas
Fun activities to bring the family together.
Paperback: 978-1-78279-162-1

Rise of the Shadow Stealers
The Firebird Chronicles
Daniel Ingram-Brown
Memories are going missing. Can Fletcher and Scoop unearth their own lost history and save the Storyteller's treasure from the shadows?
Paperback: 978-1-78099-694-3 ebook: 978-1-78099-693-6

Readers of ebooks can buy or view any of these bestsellers by clicking on the live link in the title. Most titles are published in paperback and as an ebook. Paperbacks are available in traditional bookshops. Both print and ebook formats are available online.

Find more titles and sign up to our readers' newsletter at
http://www.johnhuntpublishing.com/children-and-young-adult
Follow us on Facebook at https://www.facebook.com/JHPChildren
and Twitter at https://twitter.com/JHPChildren